UNDER A CLOUD OF RAIN

UNDER A CLOUD OF RAIN

A NICK NOELLE MYSTERY

A. R. BAUMANN

INKSHARES

Published by Inkshares, Inc., San Francisco, California
www.inkshares.com

Edited and designed by Girl Friday Productions
www.girlfridayproductions.com

Cover design by Jason Ramirez

ISBN-13: 978-1-9417583-4-2
e-ISBN: 978-1-9417583-5-9
Library of Congress Control Number: 2015939058

First edition

Printed in the United States of America
16   2 3 4 5 6 7 8 9

To Peter Baumann, the love of my life, who inspired our best creations: our children, Willa, Ahmet, Max, and Ema, and our grandchildren, Atay and Ayla.

THE FIRST VICTIM

He slogged through the brown waters of the bayou, the glittering lights of Houston in the background. His muscles were taut as he carried the young beauty in his arms. Unlike the heavy trees that supplicated themselves overhead, she was as weightless as a feather, even in her futile struggles to free herself. He wore a mask. When he placed her in a canoe, her bright blue eyes accused him. He stuffed a dirty rag soaked with chloroform into her mouth and then fastened her wrists and feet together with heavy rope. He winced at the memory of her laughter while looking down her nose at him. This princess sneered and killed with words and dimples. Now her breath was slow and deep. The drug had worked, for the moment.

He fought mosquitoes and the itch beneath his mask as he rowed the canoe farther and farther through the bayou. When he reached the gardener's shack, he laid her gently, like a lover, onto a slime-covered log. He reached into his backpack, pulling out a chain saw. She was still beautiful to him. He stared at her breasts, plump with bold nipples beneath the peasant blouse. He desired nothing more than to kiss and touch her, but a distant memory

of her plagued him. What had happened to that sweet, innocent
child?

For a fleeting moment he thought of using his knife to cut the
electrical tape to free her, but he knew she'd only run back to the
wretched life she had created. With his index finger he touched the
soft swell of her left breast, just above her heart.

Suddenly she awoke from the chloroform and her eyes flew
open. The expression there changed; the bright blue that had once
sparkled stared at him, pleading, only to shift to loathing. Her
unspoken words screeched, *Do it! Do it, like you did when I was too
young to say no.* She had to be punished. He fired up the chain saw,
and as he cut into her, he was surprised that it took no effort at all.

He lifted her dismembered parts, carefully dropping each
one into a large black trash bag. He placed the bag under the gray
spiderwebs that hung from the shack. He would never forget the
whole, beautiful woman she had been during that brief time they
had once shared. Now, he was rid of her. He laughed, drowning
out the sound of mosquitoes in his ears. Once the job was done, he
pulled off his mask, sat on a log, and took out a Havana cigar. The
smoke tasted nasty in his dry mouth. He dropped it and pounded
it into the mud.

Silence filled his brain. He heard only the mockingbirds, tree
frogs, and mosquitoes of the bayou. It was over.

CHAPTER 1

That summer of 1970, Houston baked in the sun like mama's biscuits in the oven. Detective Nick Noelle felt as miserable as the weather. It had been only four months since his wife, Sally, had kicked him out of the cottage he'd bought for them, the home he'd thought would bring them peace. Sally used to call their little home "the love shack." That was then. Now he only saw her when she showed up at his crummy boardinghouse flat looking whipped as a dog and needing nothing from him but money. She was hooking again, but it wasn't going well for her. Between that and the goddamn heat, he was going crazy. That morning he called in to his precinct and told them he'd be in late.

He decided to take a fifty-mile drive to Galveston to clear out the voices in his head. Before Noelle knew it, he was staring out over muddy waters at the Sixty-First Street Pier in Galveston, but the trash talk kept babbling on. The beach town was dead and the once peaceful view over the gulf was now one of dark clouds and an ill wind. A foreboding storm was brewing and the sky was growing darker. He observed the still water gently lapping at the pier's supports and contemplated how those steady, gentle waves over time were eating away at the pier's foundation. He preferred to think about that instead of Sally or his urge to play poker at Sam's House of Cards. One cloud overhead started leaking small drops of rain. He lifted his face so the water would hit him square on.

There was not a big enough downpour to wash away his crazy thinking about Sally. He'd been nutty to fall in love with her, even more of a lunatic to marry her—a cop who thought he could rescue a hooker. What a chump!

He had to stop believing that maybe she'd loved him. He was nothing but a crusty Cajun cop, old and worn out like the pier beneath him. A veteran of the Korean War whose medal for courage had never wiped out the memory of him barely eighteen and the boy, a few years younger, he'd shot during one of the bloodiest battles of his service. Switching back to thoughts of Sally, he knew he had to stop giving her money; it only fueled his delusions.

The sky swelled with black clouds while whole barrels of rain began to pour over him. He let it soak his clothes as he stared into the muddy, churning bay. He could end it all, right here, right now. He could climb over the railing and just disappear. That was what his old man had done. His father, a big bruiser who talked with his fists, had abandoned him and his mom. His old man was a drunk and a coward who took a final dunk in the Mississippi. Like father, like son.

Fuck no, no way! Why now, after spending his whole lifetime fighting to make it right?

It took Noelle more than an hour to drive back to Houston with the windshield wipers fighting the rain. At the station he saw that nothing much was going on. For days it had been too damned hot for even criminals to work. He imagined all the thieves, rapists, and murderers in Houston holed up next to air conditioners or open refrigerator doors, too sluggish to move. The light in the squad room was dim, and gray filing cabinets, scratched metal desks, and black plastic telephones added more gloom. The fluorescent lights buzzed off and on while half a dozen detectives sat at their desks pretending to be busy. Beyond the squad room, their supervisor, Lieutenant Donnelly, a pudgy, bald lieutenant in a cheap suit, was in his office eating a Hershey bar.

Opposite his desk, Noelle's new partner, Juan Lopez, sat reading a Bible. Noelle did his best to stifle his snort of disgust. Lopez was a rookie with little experience, but at least this kid was fresh, and a looker. Noelle gave him credit for that, thinking it might give them an edge when interrogating female witnesses. Lopez had deep brown eyes and a full head of jet-black hair, unlike the thin gray strands that framed Noelle's still handsome, yet worn, rugged features. Lopez resembled a modern-day Aztec god, the kind you'd see on those colorful calendars at most Mexican restaurants in Texas—the classic Latin image depicting an Aztec warrior carrying a beautiful goddess toward the volcano.

Noelle still couldn't figure how Lopez had made detective. He hated the way he followed every single rule, even the ones that contradicted each other. He thought Donnelly was playing some kind of practical joke—assigning him a guy who would never smoke, drink, or sleep with hookers. Or maybe Donnelly was trying to save Noelle's soul by partnering him with a religious fanatic?

"Boss," Lopez called. "Where were you? I've been here waiting since nine this morning."

"Well, at least you put the time to good use," Noelle said sarcastically, nodding at the Bible. His humor was lost on Lopez.

"I was just taking a break, looking something up for my daughter. I worry about her, you know, being a teenager these days, with all the craziness loose in the world."

"Yeah, sure." Noelle wasn't really listening. Lopez wasn't a kid; they were actually closer in age than they looked. Unlike him, Lopez had a normal life, a house, a wife, and a daughter. Even Noelle had to admit there was something sincere about Lopez, something refreshing. Of course, Lopez smiled a lot. Those clean white teeth made Noelle self-conscious about his being chipped and yellowed with nicotine. It was probably a good thing, Noelle thought, that he wasn't a yes-man like Lopez; no one could have stomached a smiling Noelle.

He sat down at his own desk and flipped through his messages; nothing important, only a call from Sally. The air conditioners hummed loudly. It was only a little cooler now, with the rain. The phone on Noelle's desk rang. He picked it up. "Yeah? Who is this?"

"I'm Miss Davis. I live next door to the Ima Hogg house, Bayou Bend. When the winds picked up yesterday I noticed a terrible odor. I've reported it to the head gardener over there, but he never did a damn thing about it. Could you come out and have a look-see down there?"

Noelle replied, "Miss Davis, you have reached the wrong department. We are the homicide division; let me put you back to the front desk." After Noelle hung up the phone he grabbed the keys to the precinct's unmarked Plymouth and spoke to his partner. "Lopez, let's take a ride down to the Bayou Bend mansion to check out this old biddy's complaint. We got nothing better to do but sit on our hands here. Afterward we can grab some lunch."

CHAPTER 2

The traffic was light as rainfall flowed along the roads and highways, forming mini rivers, swelling gutters, and washing leaves and bits of trash into drains. They reached the Ima Hogg mansion just as the skies began to clear again. It was like that in Houston during the summer months: heavy rain and winds, sometimes for hours or a day, until the scorching sun came out again.

The place was surrounded with sprawling lawns and gardens; behind the gardens lay thick pinewoods, and beyond them, the bayou. Noelle had been to the Ima Hogg gardens a few times when he was younger, usually when a girl he was dating wanted to do something "romantic."

At the gate Noelle flashed his badge and asked to speak to the gardener. The guard told them that the head gardener's name was Angel Perez, and that they should pull over while he called him. Within a few minutes the gardener, obviously middle-aged but with the body of a prizefighter, walked toward the gate like he owned the place.

Noelle got out of the car. Perez gave his name and asked how he could help them. He said, "I have worked in the most cherished gardens in Houston for decades. I can answer any questions you might have about these grounds."

Noelle replied, "We just want to know why you haven't responded to the complaint by your neighbor about the smell coming off your grounds."

Perez tightened. "Officer, it's most likely the bayou stinking because of all this rain. I don't have time to go down there. My work keeps me too busy. I told that pesky neighbor Miss Davis the same thing. She has nothing better to do than complain about everything, even the traffic that the mansion brings to the neighborhood. But you are welcome to go down and look around yourselves." Perez pointed to the asphalt road. "There's the pathway."

The bayou steamed in the heat. Beneath the stench of swamp and rotting plants Noelle picked up another scent, a recognizable smell that always twisted his gut—decomposing body. Every murder case he ever worked started out this way: a feeling like he was about to face something he didn't want to see, like something horrible inside himself, and an even bigger feeling he preferred not to look at. In the underbelly of most of his thoughts, whether about work or love, lurked the question: *Was he worthy?* His greatest fear was that he could never live up to the responsibility life required of him.

Noelle held very still and listened before following his nose to the shed with rotting cabinets and empty Lone Star crates. He listened again, and this time he heard Lopez murmuring a prayer as they both saw a puddle of blood oozing from a large trash bag. He yanked and pulled the bag out from under the shack.

"Boss, shouldn't we call it in first?"

"Just whip your skinny ass over here and help me."

"But the book says . . ."

"This isn't about the book. This is about a human being."

He didn't give a rat's ass about the mud and crap falling on his suit. Even though he hoped he could rescue the victim beneath those crates, in his heart he knew it was too late. The stench of the very dead rose up to choke him, but he kept at it. He put his gloves on and opened the trash bag, finding only parts of what was once a female body now swarming with maggots. When he reached in, Lopez saw the face of the victim. He staggered away and retched. "Oh, Jesus! Oh, *Madre Maria!*"

Large rusted nails had been driven through her feet, and just above her left foot a diamond anklet glinted in the sun. Noelle leaned in closer to inspect the tiny pendant and saw a gold heart with a ruby cross inside it. He could barely make out the engraved initials *J. B.*

Noelle's spastic colon was on fire as he shouted to Lopez, "Call backup, now!"

It seemed like hours before the coroner's wagon got there to haul the body parts away. Cops swarmed all over the shed and a log nearby, where they found splattered bits and pieces of dried blood. They dusted for fingerprints, searched for more blood and strands of hair or fiber. There wasn't much of anything, thanks to the rain. He trudged the path leading into the woods and spotted a half-smoked cigar on the ground. Had the executioner purposely killed as the storm approached, knowing the rain would wash away evidence? Or was that just dumb luck?

He couldn't keep the frustration and anguish out of his voice. "Why?"

Lopez had no answers. Noelle didn't expect any.

———

Twenty-four hours later Noelle was back at his desk, studying the crime scene photos, hoping something would leap out at him. He knew an autopsy was useless. All they had to rely on was the cigar and the anklet. While chewing half a roll of Tums, he heated milk in the break room to soothe his stomach. Noelle had seen a lot:

rotting bodies in war, crimes of passion, drunks frying like eggs on the sidewalk, even an abandoned dead baby in the trash—the worst of the worst. But this killing—the cutting, hacking, the demented frenzy and strength it took to do something like this—was a new page in his book of horrors.

On the way home Noelle turned on the radio full blast and hoped that Hank Williams could drown out his crazy thinking. For a few moments the crime took a backseat to Williams singing his old classic, "I'm So Lonesome I Could Cry." Suddenly Noelle felt hungry for the first time that day. He stopped off at JJ's Barbecue for a greasy rib sandwich and a cup of rancid dishwater coffee to go. The coffee was still steaming hot when he pulled up in front of the old Victorian in Washington Heights, where he'd been renting a single room since the day Sally kicked him out of their love shack.

He climbed several rickety stairs to his front door. Inside, the place was nothing but a room with a nook for a kitchen, a cracked ceramic stove he never used, and a small icebox holding nothing but a Budweiser six-pack. On his card table in the dining area sat a full quart of Jack Daniel's. He had one shabby overstuffed armchair, upholstered in an old lady's pattern of red roses, tea-stained and ugly but comfortable. In the corner, a queen-size brass bed took up most of the space. It was the bed he had bought for Sally when they got married. When Sally kicked him out, she insisted he take it with him. Noelle knew how much she had loved that bed, and she knew how much it would remind him of all the times they'd made sweet love while her favorite Dylan song, "Lay Lady Lay," played in the background. It was the final slap in his face.

He sat for a while in the worn armchair, munching barbecue and washing it down with big gulps of beer, trying not to think of Sally, but now those fucking Dylan lyrics were stuck in his brain. He always missed her most when he was alone, hungry, and feeling sorry for himself. He managed to turn off the channel playing in his head, switching to his other favorite obsession: poker. Suddenly he was itching to gamble and to drink some good Irish whiskey at Sam's. Noelle took pride in how good he was at searching for reads in the faces of the opposing players as he fanned out his hand of cards. He'd mostly done all right, and he'd squirreled away good money for when he would finally retire one day and move to Vegas. For him the rush was not just winning, but being on the edge of something big coming his way.

During that short-lived honeymoon with Sally he'd just had a run of bad luck, that's all. No reason for Sally to get up in his face about it, after all he'd done for her. No reason to push him out after he'd given her what she needed. He even went to Gamblers Anonymous for her, three meetings full of suckers and losers with spooky eyes under the church basement's fluorescent light. He felt like an outsider there; he really didn't have a problem. He couldn't share with these wretched losers his real life, his job, the murders, the rapes, the brutality and the grind of the system: the very things that made him want to gamble.

There were two places he fit in; one was his old chair, and the other was at Sam's House of Cards. He tossed the ends of the wet chewy white bread into the trash. He drained the last swallow of Bud, snatched up his car keys, and headed to that place where he'd soon be holding aces.

It was only a little after seven, and the place was half-empty. The carpet was thick, the wood paneling dark, the bar long and polished. A couple of the poker tables were occupied, and a few guys sat at the blackjack tables. Cocktail waitresses sashayed between the tables. Noelle noticed one of Houston's cops entering Sam's. Everyone knew Sam kept the cops sweet and the city's rich and powerful even sweeter.

Noelle sat down at the bar and ordered a double Irish whiskey. The first swallow shot heat straight down his gut. He hadn't gambled in two weeks—he was owed, especially after the day he'd had. The second big swallow of whiskey sent a gentle wave into his muscles and joints, relaxing him even more. After the third shot, his hands itched and his eyes sharpened as he slipped into his groove. He was at the right speed to play a game of cards.

He picked up his whiskey and sat down at one of the poker tables between a tall, slim cowboy and a fat-assed, big-haired old gal wearing enormous gold hoop earrings. Starting small, he bought twenty bucks of chips and anted up a buck for the first hand. The first round he folded with two sevens and not much else. On his second hand he folded with a pair of threes and a pair of nines because he noticed that Ms. Big Hair's flowery perfume got stronger when she looked at her cards. He was right; she took the pot with a royal flush.

Just as he picked up his cards on the fourth hand, out of the corner of his eye he spotted Sam, the owner, leading two men with two knockout blondes on their arms toward the back room with the private tables. Noelle envied the lucky bastards who could afford those high-roller tables and wished he could for just one night learn how the other half lived. Sam and the two couples passed closer. When Noelle got a good look at one of the blondes, he focused on the dame who had the most intense blue eyes he had ever seen, lined with thick black eyelashes. She was all curves and she kept flipping her long, shiny platinum hair back and smiling like she knew she was being noticed. When she smiled, he saw she had a cute overbite that made her look a little country. She seemed more approachable than the other blonde, who had a haughty air about her.

Noelle recognized George Brunswick, a man of old Texas money who had his big arm wrapped around the cute, petite blonde he liked. Brunswick was obviously old enough to be her father. Noelle took in the other couple, a smaller, slightly younger man than Brunswick, but still much older than his built blonde beauty. Envy ran sharp through his gut, and he soothed that ugly feeling with another shot of that good old Irish whiskey.

The dealer looked over to the couples and smirked at Noelle. "Are you just here to enjoy the scenery, or are you going to play?" Noelle snapped to attention, looked down at his hand, and saw that he was holding a full house. He immediately thought that maybe the little blonde with the overbite had brought some luck his way. He steadied himself, kept his face empty of any expression, and played his hand.

———

While Noelle was gambling at Sam's, the River Oaks Country Club was all dolled up for a huge antebellum affair as great as the state of Texas itself. It was George's older brother James Brunswick Sr.'s fifty-ninth birthday. A string quartet played music for his guests, the who's who of Houston. The men wore tuxedo jackets, their hair gleaming in shades of silver or gray. The women wore silk or chiffon and sparkling jewelry, their hair big as Texas and highlighted in multiple shades of blond in bouffant styles; the youngest among them all resembled the Bond girls of the late sixties. Waiters glided through the ballroom with trays of cocktails and champagne. One after another, the guests rustled up to James Brunswick Sr. to congratulate him on his major achievement of staying alive for fifty-nine years.

The whole deal and all the fussiness made Brunswick impatient. James Brunswick had surpassed his own father's wealth. He ran one of the country's biggest oil companies and had married the beauty Cornelia and raised two kids. Tonight he'd been drinking bourbon and was more than a little ripped as he reminisced with his cronies. "What I'd really like is to go back to the good ol' days," he said. "Back when I was young and we'd dig a well and say every prayer the preacher taught us. Then that big ol' derrick would gush and it'd be like Christmas, your birthday, and the last day of school all rolled into one."

He had started to tell the men clustered around him about an argument between his father and a well digger when he was interrupted by a tiny tap on his shoulder. Irritated, he turned. "What?"

His wife, Cornelia, with too much rouge on her once flawless cheeks, looked worried, and it was obvious that she'd had too much champagne. She pulled on his shoulder and whispered in his ear. "That brother of yours, Mr. George Brunswick, didn't even show up for your birthday! After all you've tried to do for him. Charlene didn't come either. The poor dear, she must have figured it'd be too humiliating to come alone, considering George's reputation with other women."

James wasn't in the mood for her gossip and was dying to get back to his story. "Quit worrying about George; all he's got is Charlene's money, and Lord knows, one of these days she's going to cut that right off."

Cornelia made a face. "Old George will be lucky if that's all she cuts off, if you ask me."

George laughed at her tasteless joke. "Good riddance to bad rubbish."

Cornelia wasn't done. She stood there, tapping her heel on the floor, hesitating, and James finally said, "Okay, what?"

"It's Julia; she's not here either, and you know she'd never miss your birthday."

James looked around for a waiter. He needed another drink. The guests still stood there like dumb beasts, waiting for his story to continue.

"Will you stop worrying so much?" He hated it when Cornelia worried, and that was about all she did lately. She was a mother, after all, and he guessed fretting came with the territory. He patted her shoulder to calm her. "If there's one gal who can take care of herself, it's our Julia."

"But James"—Cornelia lowered her voice so he had to lean close to hear—"what if she's gotten into that trouble again, like last time?"

"Our girl's got more sense than you ever give her credit for."

James turned his back to his wife and started in again with his guests. The men around him started howling even before he got to the punch line.

CHAPTER 3

The next day, Noelle and Lopez drove back to the Ima Hogg mansion to question the staff. When they approached the gate, they asked for Perez; he was the first on their list. The guard instructed them to drive farther on toward the house where the azalea bushes grew.

They spotted Perez pulling weeds. When Perez looked up to wipe the sweat off his brow, he noticed the detectives. Noelle saw that Perez had two cigars in his work shirt pocket.

Now Noelle knew that Perez not only had access to the bayou and could have easily managed the crime, but on top of it, he was packing cigars.

"So tell me, what have you noticed that was different around here, other than the smell coming up off the bayou?"

"The curator told me that one of our tour groups coming through the gardens saw two water moccasins by the path down there by the woods when he mentioned the bad smell. He told me to make sure there wasn't a nest. So I poked around down there a little, but I didn't find any nest."

"And you never smelled anything down there?"

Perez answered, "I did smell something bad, very bad. I thought maybe it was a sewage leak somewhere. I don't like going near that bayou."

"You never go down there in good weather to get away? I notice you have some nice cigars in your pocket," Noelle said.

Perez had a fast answer. "You mean these? One of the tourists gave me a couple as a gift. He said he'd never seen such beautiful landscaping in all his travels. I think he said these came from Cuba."

Noelle asked, "Are all tourists so generous?"

"No, but he asked if I was from Mexico and I told him I was Cuban, and that's when he gave them to me. I've been saving them, hoping for a nice long break to enjoy one, but all hell broke loose when you found what you did down there—"

Noelle cut Perez off and said, "Let's move down that way."

"Why? I know nothing else. I didn't see anything and I didn't hear anything."

Noelle noticed that Perez's hands were trembling. "You never know, something may come back to you."

Perez let out a deep sigh and followed Noelle and Lopez down the muddy path through the brush. They pushed away the Spanish moss hanging from the trees in front of them as they trekked down to the bayou. The air got hotter and wetter and mosquitoes hummed, and Noelle noticed sweat beading up on Perez's forehead.

"I guess if I maybe looked harder, I would have found her, huh," Perez said. "But that sewage stink got right into my head and I had to go lie down for a while."

"Yeah," Lopez said. "Made us sick too."

They came through the woods to the crime scene, where the yellow tape still marked off the area. Noelle looked at Perez, wiping his forehead with a folded handkerchief. His shoulders were bunched together and he watched as Perez's face turned red with anger. "Did you touch anything or take anything away when you were down here looking for the snakes?"

Perez's rage was full on. "I told you, I didn't see a nest! There wasn't anything to take!"

Noelle put his hand on Perez's shoulder. "Buddy, calm down, nobody's accusing you."

Lopez hesitantly asked, "Did you notice anyone over the past month moving around down here or anything strange, anyone hanging around at all?"

Perez shook his head. "No, Señor, I'm always working so hard dealing with the mildew on the roses, the willows and weeds that would take over the whole place if I let them. And there are the tourists that want to talk, with a hundred questions about the plants and flowers."

Noelle searched the path through the woods with his eyes. The curator had told him the gates to the house and gardens were always closed up tight when the day was over. The iron fence that guarded the grounds was too high to climb, especially while carrying a body.

He turned back to look out over the bayou. "What about the water?"

Perez frowned and rubbed his chin. "Well, you know, the bayou floods from time to time, especially with the downpours we've been getting. A small canoe could get through if the killer was strong enough to fight the sludge in that murky water."

Noelle didn't know why, but his gut didn't like Perez. There was something primitive, like an angry rattler, about him.

"You know, we found a Havana cigar half-smoked near where we found the body. Is it possible you took one of those Cubans down here?"

"I'm a Cuban, and we all smoke cigars, but half the men in Texas do too. I swear I only got these yesterday, after you found that body. I never buy cigars; they are too expensive."

Lopez took pity on the guy as he watched him squirm and said, "Is it possible we can track down that tourist who gave you the cigars to corroborate your story?

Perez was dripping wet and said, "I never got the man's name, and I think he was just passing through Houston. Perhaps the tour bus company might have a passenger list, but I don't know.

"Thanks for your help," Noelle said. "We'll get in touch again if we need you. You're not planning on leaving town?"

"No, Señor, I'm here six days a week."

———

The traffic was one hot, sticky mess as Noelle and Lopez drove back to the precinct with the air-conditioning on full blast. They had spent all damn day in the neighborhood at Bayou Bend, questioning Perez's team of gardeners, the curator, the tour guide, and the kitchen staff, but no one had seen or heard anything. They even checked in with the tour bus service and learned that they didn't get names of passengers, since they just paid cash when they hopped on the city tour buses.

Back at the precinct, Noelle asked Lopez to check to see if anyone had reported a missing girl yet while he sat at his desk inspecting the diamond anklet. He'd seen the victim's mutilated body parts, even her guts, but he didn't know her name. He heaved a sigh as he looked at this anklet, the only thing he had to go on.

He and Lopez were going to have to hit all the jewelry stores and hope to God the girl, or whoever had bought it, had bought it in Houston; maybe the killer himself gave it to her.

Lopez was at his desk on the phone with Missing Persons, and when he hung up, he shook his head. "Nada."

"Alrighty then, how'd you like some overtime?" Noelle said. "I'm calling it a day, but you can hit some of Houston's fine jewelry stores as you make your way back home. Maybe they will recognize this ankle bracelet and tell us who bought it."

Lopez smiled and took the anklet from Noelle. "Leave it to me; you get some rest. You earned it."

After Sam's the night before and the long hours in the heat of the woods that day, Noelle was exhausted. He drove back home, bleary-eyed. He fumbled his way up the stairs to his rented room and headed straight for the Jack Daniel's. So what if he drank too much? What else was he supposed to do? Two whole days and nothing. He just felt in his bones that this killer might kill again. He didn't know why he had that feeling, but he chalked it up to the recent crime spree in LA, the multiple Manson murders.

Before he left the station he had searched through old crime files of serial-style murders and pulled up the records of the worst murder cases from Texas and across the United States. At home he put the files in his lap and poured a stiff drink. Knocking it back, he opened the folder that contained the details of the infamous Manson murders. It was last August, almost a year ago, when crazy Charlie Manson commanded a small group of his followers to brutally murder five people in a posh house in Benedict Canyon, the house of Roman Polanski. The victims in that case were beautiful, wealthy, and famous, especially Polanski's wife, the actress Sharon Tate. What made this crime most heinous to Noelle was the fact that Sharon Tate had been pregnant when her killer hacked her to death. All heartless, senseless murders. Maybe if he could get into the mind of Manson he could learn something about his killer or killers. Perhaps like those killings, LSD and cultism might be connected to his victim too.

Noelle knew that Lieutenant Donnelly, the other guys in the squad room, the press, and everyone was placing the whole case on his shoulders. None of them had seen the body, not the way he had. He swallowed another mouthful of Jack, then fell back into his ugly old armchair, still holding the bottle, not ready to climb into Sally's brass bed just yet.

His obsessive thoughts of Sally and that bed must have conjured her up, because there she was, knocking at his door again. He knew it was Sally because no one else ever knocked at his door. It was just past suppertime, when hookers usually started work. Maybe Sally had called in sick. Probably she just wanted money for supper. He'd never be done with her. Never.

She kept knocking, quick raps that hammered into his skull. She didn't have anywhere else to go, and he couldn't bear thinking that she could be hungry. "Okay, okay," he called out. He had to work to stand up on his legs. His head was swimming.

Her Alabama accent carried through the door. "Nick? I'm sorry, but . . ."

He pulled the door open, and she fell against him. Her hair brushed his cheek and he smelled her strawberry shampoo. She was a bottle blonde, but still, her hair was so soft and she was very pretty—he thought she was, anyway. She might have been truly beautiful if her mean old polecat of a dad hadn't broken her nose when she was a kid. She had the eyes of a cat, green and tilted up at the corners, so sometimes she could look sly. "Hey, Nick," she said, her voice gravelly from cigarettes. "You been drinkin'? Got any to share?"

"Come on in." When Nick didn't offer, she found his coffee mug, rinsed it out, and poured herself a slug anyway. This was the fourth time she'd shown up in the last two months, always needing money. She looked so pitiful that he almost went to her, but he knew if he did, she'd cling to him. *She's a whore,* he told himself over and over, flashing back to the night they met, when he had been walking back from investigating a suicide at a cheap motel. Sally had slipped and fallen on her face. She was too stoned to get up. Instead of turning her over to the police, he lifted her up and carried her to his truck. He cleaned off her face and found a very pretty girl under all that makeup. That was the fatal night he offered to take her home and give her a place to clean up.

"You must be broke again; slow night for street hookin', I guess?" he smirked.

She flinched like he'd slapped her. "Nick, you never used to be so mean."

He sighed and found his wallet, coming up with a twenty-dollar bill.

She left without saying anything. He sank back down into his armchair and heard her sobbing behind the closed door.

Noelle turned up the radio and caught the last verse of Hank Williams's "Your Cheatin' Heart" and cranked it even louder to drown Sally out.

———

As Noelle drenched his sorrows, across town Lopez was visiting his tenth jewelry store of the night.

Lopez knew he should be irritated that he got stuck doing all the legwork, but secretly he was pleased that Noelle trusted him to go out alone. He had the evidence bag with the anklet in his suit pocket, along with two fresh pens and his notebook. Just before he left the squad room, he'd fingered the gold crucifix he wore around his neck and said a silent prayer for the dead girl and also for Noelle and for whatever caused him so much misery.

On his way out, he'd overheard Detective Brennan talking to Lieutenant Donnelly about him. Donnelly asked, "Do you think Lopez can handle a monster case like this?"

"Lopez, that Mexican Dudley Do-Right? I doubt it." Brennan laughed.

Lopez knew Brennan was pissed that he had been passed up for the promotion. It didn't make sense to Lopez either; Brennan, a big red-headed Irish cop from a long line of Irish cops, was a shoo-in for Noelle's partner, so it made Lopez curious too: why him? He stood past the doorway, unseen, and kept listening.

Donnelly told Brennan, "I need a man to keep Noelle grounded. You know how he gets crazy, bending the rules when he feels like it. Lopez will be good for him, trust me."

Lopez assumed that Noelle had been raised in the Church because he had Cajun roots. He believed Noelle would be less miserable if he could return to his faith. Being a good churchgoer, Lopez was up for this challenge.

As he approached Becker's jewelry store, Lopez's stomach growled, and he checked his watch. It was just past seven and he knew that his wife, Maria, was keeping his dinner warm. As he stepped inside Becker's, his feet sank into the plush carpeting, making him feel shorter than he was. Becker's was the cathedral of jewels and luxury for those who worshipped diamonds, sapphires, and emeralds, gold and silver. Lopez was not self-righteous, but he took pride in knowing that he was storing up his jewels in heaven, and his faith made his lack of power and prestige on earth tolerable. He had to remember who was in charge here, God or man, as he put his hand on his gun in his holster.

Only two customers were perusing the display cases, a woman with blue-tinted hair and another twenty years younger at her side. Lopez squared his shoulders and remembered that he was an officer of the law with the power of God and the entire Houston police department behind him. He cleared his throat, and the salesman in an expensive gray suit and a fat paisley tie looked up and noticed the gun peeking out of Lopez's belt. He stepped away from the two customers. "Officer, what can I do for you?"

Lopez was pleased to hear the respect in the man's voice. He held up the evidence bag. "Can you tell me if this anklet came from here?"

The salesman peered closely at the pendant hanging from the anklet. His face twisted with anguish. "Where did you find this?"

"I'm sorry, I can't say."

"I'm sorry, too, but our customers count on our discretion."

"Even if they're dead?" Lopez answered.

The salesman paled. "Dead? Jimmy Brunswick's sister? He bought that piece for her twenty-first birthday."

Behind the salesman, the two women each clutched their hands to their chests, looking at Lopez with horror. He spoke to the salesman and the customers with iron authority in his voice.

"No one can know anything about this, not yet. Do you hear me? If this is true, we need to tell the family first. It's important you don't tell a soul. Do you understand me?"

All three nodded and bowed to his authority.

Lopez was in shock as he hurried out the door. This monster case, he realized, was about to blow up. Cornelia and James Brunswick of Brunswick Oil and the entire city of Houston would be up in arms. As he took those last steps to his car, he nearly staggered under the immense weight of it all. He had to get this information to Noelle and Donnelly right away.

———

Noelle left his lonely room and headed back to Sam's right after Sally left. He had just taken his seat at a table when the bartender told him he had a call waiting in Sam's office. When Noelle picked up his call, Lieutenant Donnelly barked into the phone, "The anklet belongs to Julia Brunswick, James Brunswick's daughter. You and Lopez need to get over to the Brunswicks' as quick as you can before someone leaks this to the press." Noelle, two sheets to the wind and his pulse racing, drove as fast as he could to pick up Lopez.

Noelle gave the wheel over to Lopez once they met up, explaining that he'd had too much to drink and was whipped. Lopez took over and drove through the streets of River Oaks to the Brunswick home on Inverness. It was a plantation-style home complete with Greek columns, sprawling lawns, a long, wide driveway, and dozens of windows, all of them dark. Lopez had never seen a murder victim's house that looked so creepy. "Well, here we go," Noelle muttered, and stumbled to the front door. He rang the bell and the moment the door opened, Noelle straightened up. A black servant, a throwback to the old South, greeted them. Noelle glanced around at the polished foyer, the oil paintings, the vases full of flowers. He wished he had had time to clean up and felt self-conscious of his wrinkled suit. From somewhere in the house, Noelle heard a high, keening cry, and he realized his shabby condition was the least of the Brunswicks' concerns at the moment.

"The library is this way, if you'll follow me," Thomas said.

Down a broad hallway, a pair of tall carved doors opened onto a room lined with books. Noelle took in the dimly lit chandelier and a low table covered with bottles of bourbon and wine and overflowing crystal ashtrays.

James Brunswick stood beside the sofa, where his wife sat doubled over, making that terrible sound they had heard down the hall. She sounded like she was dying. This was the part of the job he hated most, the agony of loss. Nothing was ever going to make it better for Julia Brunswick's mother. James Brunswick, puffy faced, stooped, hollowed and trembling, showed his pain in his red-rimmed eyes; he had been crying too. On the other side of Cornelia Brunswick, Cullen, the chief of police, sat in his dress uniform, holding her hand. Noelle knew Cullen was the kind of chief who loved the high-society part of his job.

"Detectives," James Brunswick said. "Do you have anything new for us?"

Chief Cullen jutted his chin at Noelle, a curt signal that meant *go ahead.*

"No, sir. No, ma'am. We came to pay our respects and to tell you we're going to do everything we can to find the person who killed your daughter."

Cornelia stared up at him with vacant eyes. She stood and stretched out a lean, bony arm; her hand clawed Noelle's suit coat. "You find him and then you make him pay." Her voice was a hiss until she shrieked again, "For what he did to our daughter—the electric chair is nothing. You make him pay!"

James touched her shoulder and whispered, "Corry," as he pried her hand from Noelle's coat. "They'll find him. It's what they do."

She nearly spit at her husband. "Don't you 'Corry' me. You're the one who said our baby was an adult. You let her get away with anything, and this is where it led her."

James turned away, flushed, and his wife fell back, sobbing.

Noelle saw the shame on Brunswick's face. "I know these are hollow words at this time, but I am truly sorry for your loss," he said. "Later, after you've had some time to grieve, we might have some questions." Cullen flashed Noelle an agitated look. "We'll get back to work now."

Thomas was already waiting in the foyer to usher them out, and he and Lopez hurried back to the Plymouth. Noelle asked Lopez, "Did you hear her say he let Julia get away with anything? I think we should find out what 'anything' means, to this crowd."

CHAPTER 4

The night before all hell broke loose over Julia Brunswick's murder, Richard Lowden was in El Paso on Brunswick company business. He was there to check on a Mexican employee who had been causing trouble at the rigs, creating an uproar with other Mexicans who earned half of what they paid the white workers for the same jobs.

Lowden was happy for this assignment and grateful to be out of Houston and in this pricy hotel suite, all on Brunswick's dime. He lay in bed caressing his young, beautiful mistress, Marianna de Pucci. As he ran his fingers through her thick, curly blond hair, she sipped the best champagne he'd ordered from room service. He felt he deserved the perks of his new position as assistant VP, better known around the office as flunky to George Brunswick. He knew Marianna wasn't with him for his looks or his prowess as a lover, though he did pay attention to her every need. She was a rich, spoiled girl with an Italian baron for a stepfather and a mother with all kinds of dough. Although she was in line to inherit it all eventually, her parents kept Marianna on a tight leash. Richard knew that Marianna was greedy and happy for whatever she could milk from him until the day she'd have her own millions.

He didn't care. He was loony over her. All he wanted was her, all the time, everywhere, and any way he could have her. He loved how she looked at him with her big, beautiful brown eyes, her thick, curly hair spilling over his chest and belly, that faint scent of orange blossoms with spice that filled the aura around her luscious body. He lived to taste her sweet salty skin and desired nothing more than to kiss those plump cherry-red lips.

He knew his boss, George Brunswick, wanted her too, but she was taboo to him since their families were too close, both personally and financially. It would be like incest, and the de Puccis wouldn't stand for it.

The phone rang, and from the insistent ring he knew the call was coming from the one glitch in his perfect movie, his nagging wife, Priscilla. She was calling for the hundredth time that day, wondering why he wasn't at home with her. He put a finger to his lips to hush Marianna. He picked up the receiver and said, "Yes?"

Priscilla's voice squealed through the phone, so loud the guest in the adjoining hotel room could probably hear her. "Why haven't you called? I've waited all day. My Fairlane has engine problems again, and I can't go anywhere."

Richard pictured her at the kitchen table making that face she used to make when her girlish pout was once charming to him, a time when she was younger and slimmer. Now she was just horrible—nearly obese, with a stiff black dye job and a face covered with too much makeup and mascara on those false eyelashes of hers. Marianna could hear her loud screeching through the phone. Richard, embarrassed, made an apologetic face. He spoke back to his wife patiently, like he was talking to a spoiled child. "Take the car to Ike's, that's the garage we use. They'll get it all fixed. You can find their number and address in the phone book in my study."

Marianna rolled her eyes and slipped out of bed. Her naked body glided across the room to the table, where she poured herself a foamy glass of Moët. Richard couldn't take his eyes off her as she seductively licked the bubbly spill on the side of her glass. With a girl like that, who needed porn? He studied her long legs right up to where they met that soft, silky triangle of hair. She giggled, and he had to struggle to keep his focus on Priscilla's babbling.

"I can't find anything in here. You have a secretary. You should send her out here to organize this mess."

"Sure, sure, you're right. I'll take care of that." Richard didn't even know what he was saying. All he wanted was to get Marianna back into bed. Now she was lighting a joint. He wished she wouldn't do drugs like all her generation did.

"When are you coming home?" Priscilla asked.

"How many times do I have to tell you? I'm coming home tomorrow."

"Once you're home, honey bear, I'll expect my wake-up kisses. You know I need those to start my day."

He felt sick to his stomach at the thought of his wife's kisses, with Marianna laughing at him. That made him angry.

———

The next day Priscilla Lowden was wolfing down a cinnamon roll while watching the news. The talking head shouted the horrid news that Julia Brunswick had been murdered and chopped to bits. Shocked, she called Richard's hotel room, but he didn't answer. She phoned her friend Nancy Love, a second cousin to the society Loves. Nancy didn't know anything more and told Priscilla that the family wasn't talking to the press or taking any calls.

Priscilla preened in front of the mirror and said, "I am sure Richard and I will be invited to the wake. After all, he did just get a promotion; everyone who was anyone in Houston will be there. I don't have a thing to wear. We'll have to go shopping together. Bye-bye, hon."

As Priscilla hung up she focused on her reflection in the mirror. If only what she saw in it were as pretty as the room she had decorated. She focused on her eyes, her one good feature. They were large, green, and almond-shaped. Richard used to tell her she looked a lot like Liz Taylor. Ever since that day, she had worn her hair teased up in a short black bouffant, just like Liz wore hers in *Cat on a Hot Tin Roof*. Priscilla's once lovely cheekbones now were lost in her fat face. Ever since she had passed the dreaded mark of forty, she could not deny that she had to struggle into a girdle to fit into her clothes. The evidence of her overindulgence was right there on her dressing table: a half-empty box of Texas pralines. She started to dump them in the trash can but grabbed one last candy and stuck it in her mouth and then hurled the box at her mirror.

The phone rang again; anticipating Richard, she picked it up quickly. She heard a breathy, sexy voice from the other end. "Is Richard there?"

A last bit of praline stuck in Priscilla's throat. She was shocked, and her voice squeaked with outrage. "Who is this?" The voice on the other end laughed. There was a click, then silence.

Panicky, Priscilla dropped down onto her rose chintz chaise. Could Richard have a mistress? He was working a lot, late into the night, and had seemed distant lately. He'd just gotten that promotion to assistant vice president. Their ambition had brought them together in the first place. That was what made them a good team as they rose, inch by inch, into the cream of Houston society.

Energized, she got up off the chaise. She'd get Ike's mechanic to come get her Fairlane and leave her a loaner so she could go shopping. She had to get an outfit for Julia Brunswick's funeral, the most perfect black suit at Sakowitz's. Already she could see herself sipping wine, murmuring quiet condolences to Julia's parents, exchanging a little gossip with the other guests.

It was late afternoon, after her successful shopping trip, when Priscilla decided to touch up her roots. She applied Clairol's Jet

Black #1 dye, and just as she was putting the shower cap on her head, she heard Richard's voice calling her from downstairs. "Priss, come down here, right now!"

She went to the landing and called over the rail, "I'm in the middle of something, darlin'."

"Now!" he shouted. "Right now."

Damn him! She had to keep this dye on her head for another fifteen minutes, and she really didn't like him seeing her like this, in her old dye-stained robe and a shower cap.

He was in the living room, pacing back and forth across her treasured indigo-blue Persian rug. She was all set to give him what for when she saw how pale he looked. She forgot all her annoyance and her hair dye and rushed right to him. "What's wrong? What's happened?"

He didn't answer. He went to the bar and poured two glasses of bourbon, handing her one. She drank a hefty swallow to fortify herself.

"Get this," he said. "We're not invited to the funeral reception."

Priscilla felt slapped in the face. "What? How can that be?"

Richard mumbled, "I hope to God you didn't run out and spend a ton of money on a dress."

She bit her lip. It didn't make any sense to tell him what he didn't need to know, not until she understood more of what was going on. He drank his bourbon down in a couple of big gulps and poured himself a second. Priscilla noticed his face was ruddy with anger and his jaw was getting soft. She secretly hoped he would become one of those men who got a wattle. Maybe then he would have to lighten up about her weight. How could they not be invited to the Brunswick wake, when Richard was such a good friend to George, Julia's uncle?

"There must be some kind of mistake! Stop that drinking and tell me what's going on. For heaven's sake, you work under the vice president of Brunswick Oil! Of course they'd invite you to pay your respects to the family."

He laughed, oozing sharp sarcasm. "Yeah, right, assistant VP in charge of shit, that's what I am. You have no idea about what I do for that man."

"You really think I'm stupid, don't you?"

He grinned, his canine teeth yellowed and prominent. "Look at yourself." He grabbed her tight by the shoulders, forcing her to look into the gilt-framed mirror over the sofa. "You're wearing a stained bathrobe and a shower cap on your head!" He laughed, long and hard.

Furious, she ripped the shower cap from her head. One drip of dye splashed down on her blue Persian rug. "Forget all your notions; to these people, we'll always be the chumps from nowhere." He waved his hand around at her beautiful living room, the antique bar inlaid with burled walnut and all the fixings. "What a waste. What a goddamn waste this whole thing is!"

Tears rolled down her cheeks as she watched the man sagging on her lovely cream damask sofa. Maybe he'd lost his pride and dignity, but that wasn't who she was, no sir. "Then we'll just go to the funeral. We'll send a big flower arrangement. White flowers only—lilies, roses, gardenias, and even some white lilacs. That'll be sure to be noticed by your boss. We'll be on their thank-you list."

"Oh, God, stop it." He got up from the sofa to pour himself another stiff drink, then snorted and pointed to the black dye that was dripping down Priscilla's neck and forehead. "What about black flowers? Don't you think black flowers would get even more attention?"

Priscilla picked up her shower cap and ran up the stairs. She felt bruised and beaten and looked exactly like the kind of trash she'd risen from.

CHAPTER 5

Julia Brunswick's murder was all anyone was talking about around town, that and the weather. The sun beat down on Houston, making the tar on the roads almost melt beneath a heavy sky, yellowed with clouds that flat-out refused to burst. At Neiman's the summer sale was on, and everyone came to the Galleria for a chance at a bargain and a few hours' relief from the heat.

Pamela O'Leary busied herself behind the makeup counter, the one department where nothing was ever on clearance. Even if she had no customers, Pamela loved makeup. She liked to emphasize her eyes and let her lips recede. She knew her lips were not her best feature, too thin and pale. Just for fun, she took a moment to try a shimmering rose lipstick. She thought the color would be something George Brunswick would love on her. She hadn't seen him since the night he took her and her friend Marianna and her boyfriend, Richard, to Sam's high-roller room.

Over by accessories she overheard a mother and her teenage daughter arguing about sunglasses. From her counter she also had an overview of the fine jewelry department, where she observed a high-society matron asking the clerk repeatedly, "Are you sure these are real pearls? I don't wear anything that isn't genuine."

These were her customers. As far as she was concerned they had way too much: money, education, friends, husbands, homes, and looks they paid for through the nose, especially if it hadn't come naturally. On days like these Pamela could work up a big old pity party thinking about everything she did not have. Her looks were nothing compared to those of the gorgeous rich girls she liked to call her friends. She believed she was attractive enough, and certainly had style, but she knew she wasn't beautiful, not like them. All she had was her crummy job and the dump called home where she lived with her mother. Just then, the very friends she had been thinking about rushed up to her counter. Jennifer Colby and Lauren Love were giddy from the heat, the sale, and their friend Julia's murder, in that order. "Can you believe this place?" Jennifer said. "Who are all these people? You'd think folks would like to stay home behind locked doors with a lunatic on the loose." Jennifer was holding a red silk sheath that looked fabulous with her dark hair and eyes.

Lauren shook her fall of auburn hair and in her affected upper-crust way said, "It's the sale. It brings out the rabble. These folks can only dream of shopping here once a year. Besides, they don't have to worry, I hear the killer is only stalking beautiful women."

Jennifer added her two cents. "Oh Lord, what are we doing out, then? Well, at least it's cool and quiet in your department. How do you survive it, Pamela?"

Behind her smile, Pamela thought, *Yeah, the rabble, people like me*. She waved a hand airily. "Most of them won't be stopping by my counter since we have nothing marked down. I don't mind; it's nice to have some peace." She knew her friends could never know what it was like working on commission.

Jennifer looked at herself in the oval mirror atop the glass counter. "I need a change, maybe more color. Can you make me look a little older? I'm sick of dating schoolboys."

"Oh, stop," Lauren said.

Pamela changed the subject. "Isn't it terrible about Julia Brunswick? I can't even imagine how bad the family must be feeling, especially her brother."

Jennifer cried, "Poor Jimmy. I know he put her above any woman he ever dated, even me."

Pamela's throat tightened as she thought about her own feelings for Jimmy Brunswick.

Jennifer and Lauren went from silly to solemn, looking down at their hands as if they were praying. "It's just awful how Julia got in with that bad crowd," Jennifer said, shaking her head.

Lauren said, "I saw Jimmy earlier with his father at Marianna's chateau. They were all just devastated."

Pamela knew how easy it was to distract her friends and changed the subject again with trinkets. She hadn't made a sale all day and needed these gals to buy something. "Enough tragedy. My mama always says, 'Don't buy trouble; buy makeup!' Who's first?"

"We're going out tonight," Lauren said. "Make me look sexy. I don't care if it's over the top. I want a certain someone to notice me."

Pamela laughed and hoped that certain someone wasn't a Brunswick, particularly the one she had her hooks into. "Where are you going?" she asked, dabbing concealer under Lauren's eyes.

"Jennifer's parents and my parents are taking us to the Houston Club downtown."

Pamela found a deep gold eye shadow that would look dramatic at night as she casually said, "Sounds wonderful."

"Oh, Pamela," Jennifer said. "We'd invite you too if we could, but, you know, it's kind of a family thing, especially right now with everyone all a wreck over poor Julia's horrible end. Most likely it will be a dreary night."

"That's all right." Pamela smiled and shook back her hair. "I already have a date. Maybe we can get together some other time."

"Oh, sure," Lauren said. She closed her eyes so Pamela could apply the eyeliner. "On one of your days off, let's all have lunch at the country club."

"I'd love that." Pamela kept her voice and face neutral as she rang up the sale, knowing her commission might be enough to pay for a glass of iced tea at the country club. "Now you know, girls," she said, "always come to me. I know exactly what looks best on y'all."

As her friends left to see what more damage they could do with Mommy's credit card, Pamela was holding the pen Lauren had just signed the charge slip with. She held it so tightly that the plastic barrel snapped, and ink sprayed all over her fingers.

——

With the Brunswick family tragedy, Pamela knew that her lover, George Brunswick, could not get away, so that afternoon she accepted a date with a college boy, Howard Wolvensky, whom she had known since high school. She needed distraction after her long, horrible workday. He invited her to drive over to Austin and watch their pal Tim Henderson at practice with the Longhorns. There was no way she could bear a night at home with her insane mother. She knew Howard had been romantically obsessed with her ever since high school, and she used it to her advantage.

Pamela had overdressed for Howard, in a pale blue mini-dress and heels, but she wanted her mother to think that she was seeing George Brunswick and not just an ordinary college boy. It was her mother's dream for Pamela to snag a Brunswick. Maggie had once had some of Pamela's good features and was jealous of her own daughter's attractiveness to men but still expected her to use her looks as a meal ticket to get them out of poverty. If she suspected that Pamela was wavering from her plan by dating poor boys, there'd be hell to pay. By the time Pamela left work early, Maggie had already hit the bottle. Maggie never needed an excuse to start drinking early or to criticize her daughter.

Despite the fact that Howard was shorter than Pamela and wore thick horn-rimmed glasses, Pamela enjoyed the attention she got from him. She had dated some of the players from the Longhorns; as a matter of fact, Pamela was well known among the boys at UT. She particularly favored Howard because she knew she could ask him for anything and he would do her bidding. She intended to enjoy the long ride to Austin and Howard's attention. She was also secretly longing to see Jimmy Brunswick on the field but knew that was unlikely because of his sister's murder.

She and Howard arrived just as the day's practice ended. Tim Henderson jogged up the bleachers to where she and Howard sat. He gave Pamela a friendly grin as he high-fived Howard. Pamela sat up straight, delighted to see Tim's eyes drop down to her breasts. It was obvious that she did like buff, tall, handsome men like Tim. Two years ago she'd had a crush on him, but not anymore. When Tim's eyes finally came back to her face, she shook back her hair and raised one eyebrow to let him know she'd seen him looking. She reached out to touch him on the arm. "You did good out there, a one-man fighting machine. I saw you intercept that pass practically out of the quarterback's hands."

Howard changed the subject. "I made a reservation at Sully's for six. We should get going." They started down the bleachers, and Pamela's high heel caught on a nail. Howard and Tim each grabbed an arm to steady her.

She had to take a minute to catch her breath—it would have been a nasty fall.

Tim stared down at her feet and groaned. "Pammy, what the hell are you doing wearing shoes like that? We're only going to Sully's."

Inside, she cringed and fumbled for an excuse. "I had to stop by Marianna's place before I came here. Her stepdad, the baron, gets very fussy when women aren't all dressed up and expects her friends to do the same."

Tim laughed. "That's hard to believe. Marianna could wear a paper bag and men would still drool! I mean, c'mon, I know he's European, but you really believe that?"

Pamela flushed, trying to hide her embarrassment and shame behind a fake smile.

Howard shoved his glasses up his nose with one finger. He still held Pamela's arm. "She's got nothing on you, Pamela. You're smart and way more fun to be with than Ms. Snooty, Marianna Stuck-up."

Tim trotted down the bleachers while Pamela stepped down cautiously, one riser at a time, Howard hovering close in case she started to fall again.

Tim called back over his shoulder, "I'll shower and change and meet y'all at Sully's. Hey, order a pitcher, okay?"

"Sure," Howard called down.

As they walked to his car, Howard gave her another one of his starry-eyed looks. "It's so great to be out with you, Pamela." She gave him a generous smile, and, taking his hand, she lied. "The feeling is mutual, Howard."

———

Two days later, on the morning of Julia Brunswick's funeral, Pamela awoke in a suite at the Warwick Hotel, with Jimmy Brunswick sleeping beside her. She was glad he was still asleep so she could enjoy looking at him. His hair was golden, falling below his ears, and tousled after sex and sleep. He looked like a Greek god with his smooth, broad forehead, his perfect nose and full sensuous lips. She pulled the sheet back so she could see more of his long, muscular neck. Pamela loved to kiss it right where it met his shoulder. His chest was perfectly muscled and his belly taut, without an inch of fat. Pamela could not help but compare Jimmy's athletic body and his uncle George's hairy potbelly and lack of sexual subtleties. She touched Jimmy's right hand, where he wore a gold ring with the head of a lion, a gift from his father. The things Jimmy could do with his hands! That was another thing he had on his uncle George. Not only was she grateful for the rare night with Jimmy, she was also glad it was at the Warwick, with its plush carpet and thick walls, because Jimmy had made her cry out over and over again. With George, she might cry too. George was rough. She thought it came with the territory, a small price to pay for financial freedom to fulfill her mother's plans. However, she knew Jimmy Brunswick was the only man she would ever love.

She would be horrified if Jimmy learned she'd been sleeping with his uncle. Jimmy was the family's pride; he was smart, majoring in business and playing quarterback for the Longhorns. He was also funny and charming, and one day he'd inherit a very great fortune, one of the biggest in Texas.

Pamela rolled onto her back and stared at the ceiling. She knew that Jimmy was only using her. Jimmy had known how Pamela felt about him since he dumped her in high school. He just came back to her whenever he needed a quick fix. He could be himself around her, and that was why they were so good together. He had taken a year off to run around Europe; now he was back at UT, a senior at twenty-three. At school he dated those sorority and country club girls, the ones Pamela knew could never love him the way she did.

He shifted his legs, making a small noise. She could tell he was about to wake up. Quickly covering him, she sank into her pillow and pretended to be asleep. A few minutes later, she felt him watching her. She had gotten up at the crack of dawn to brush her teeth and put on some makeup. She knew she had a fabulous body that looked damn good in clothes and even better out of them.

He began tickling her and she rolled over, giggling, hoping he'd want her again.

Instead he got impatient. "Pamela! Wake up! I've gotta go soon. You know today's the funeral. Order us some breakfast, would you?"

Disappointed, she slid out of bed stark naked, went to the phone, and ordered his favorite breakfast. She ordered a boiled egg and half a grapefruit for herself. She was starving, but she thought Jimmy would never like a girl who ate too much.

He headed into the shower.

Julia's funeral was two hours away, followed by a reception at Brunswick's home. She did feel bad for Jimmy, with his younger sister murdered and all, but she truly felt worse for herself. She had packed her black dress and black heels, knowing ahead that Jimmy might invite her to ride to the funeral with him, but after that, he'd be with his family, and she'd be on her own except for her so-called girlfriends, who she knew would be there too.

The food was delivered just moments before Jimmy came out of the shower wrapped in a towel and sat at the table.

"You gonna eat, Pammy? You know I hate eating alone," he said.

She glided gracefully into her seat and tapped at the shell of her measly hard-boiled egg.

CHAPTER 6

A fierce noonday sun burned down like the fires of hell on the grand Palmer Episcopal Church in Houston. Steam rose off the sidewalks as the black funeral cars arrived one by one and parked in front of one of the oldest churches where the rich and famous congregated.

Noelle stood in a corner, near the altar, trying not to look out of place. He was there to observe the mourners, just in case the killer was the type to show up at his victim's funeral.

Julia's closed casket was covered with a blanket of white roses and lilies. At the rear of the church, James Brunswick stood, accepting condolences from the society mourners streaming in. Brunswick's silver hair gleamed as he stood up straight in a dark three-piece suit, but in his rheumy eyes and gnarled hands Noelle saw the rage he was fighting back. Cornelia Brunswick had aged a hundred years since Noelle saw her only a few days earlier. Cornelia wore a simple black dress that probably cost more than Noelle's rent, and her strawberry-blonde hair was pulled up into a French twist. The net veil could not cover her puffy red eyes, and she leaned into her husband as if she were drunk.

Yesterday at the station, Noelle had examined newspaper photos and clippings of the Brunswick family, so now he recognized Julia's brother, Jimmy, standing on the other side of the doors, shaking hands. Noelle's inner crime detector went off; there was something wrong about Jimmy. He moved woodenly, like his joints couldn't bend much. Between the handshaking and the condolences, he kept looking over at Julia's casket and his face would lose all expression, like there was nothing but empty space in his heart. Noelle suspected that Jimmy was on something. Noelle already knew that alcohol flowed freely in the Brunswick family, but he made a mental note to discreetly find out about drug use too.

James's brother, George Brunswick, was also in the reception line. Seeing his wife next to him, Noelle could understand why George had a reputation of tomcatting around. George's wife, Charlene, was from a fine New Orleans banking family that was rich as Croesus. No one in their social circle could ever understand why his wife never used some of that family money to improve her looks. She unfortunately had been born with a short forehead, a long nose, a receding chin, and a sour face with lips so thin they were nearly invisible. She kept a tight clasp on the hands of her two children—a girl about eighteen and a son around twenty. Both offspring had been lucky enough to inherit the Brunswick genes for good looks.

Mourners in designer black flowed into their seats for the service. Not one of them looked like someone who could murder a friend's daughter, much less attack the body in such a grotesque way.

Noelle spotted the guy he had seen with George Brunswick and the two blondes that night at Sam's. He definitely recognized this guy's ruddy face, with the soft slack in his cheeks and neck. The woman he was with bore no resemblance to the woman he had been with at Sam's that night. Noelle assumed the chubby broad clutching his arm had to be his wife. Noelle watched her plump breasts jiggle as she preened like a peacock, leading her husband up the aisle, waving and smiling at the society families until she found seats toward the front. Her husband was the picture of agony. Noelle made another mental note. This poor sucker looked like he could easily have had a motive to kill, although more likely his wife than Julia.

The guy turned his face back toward the doors of the church, and suddenly his anguished look on a scale from one to ten jumped to a ten. Noelle strained to see what he was looking at and recognized the two drop-dead gorgeous blondes in the church doorway. Noelle especially remembered the blonde with the sexy overbite and smile that had caught his eye at Sam's.

The two beauties glided up the aisle and took seats directly behind the plump-breasted peacock and her husband, who got even twitchier. Noelle could easily guess why.

The priest approached the altar as Noelle slipped down the side aisle to an available end seat about two-thirds of the way back. Noelle was just about to kneel when he noticed two latecomers rush in—two men: one tall and built like a truck, and the other small with big, thick glasses. Both wore suits that didn't fit right, and they hurried up the side aisle, taking seats just behind Noelle. Noelle silently made his way to the rear of the church so he could keep an eye on them.

Several chords rang out from the organ, and the mourners began to sing a hymn. Noelle kept silent. He pulled out his notebook, jotting down more notes: drugs, the Brunswicks, George and Jimmy Brunswick, the ruddy-faced guy and his peacock wife, the two lovely young blondes and the two young latecomers, big and small, whom he assumed were Jimmy's or Julia's college friends.

Just as the service ended, Noelle ducked outside so he could watch people leaving. It was so damn hot, he wished he could yank off the tie and get out of his monkey suit. There was still more to come: the reception. Noelle perked up when he thought about being served a good whiskey over ice at the wake.

———

Shortly after the service at the gates of the Brunswick mansion, half a dozen red-coated valets parked a long line of shimmering Mercedes-Benzes, Bentleys, and Rolls-Royces along River Oaks Boulevard. Noelle stood beside the gate, sweating in his suit and watching the guests arrive. A slick red Ferrari with a large dent in the driver's-side door pulled up to the gates. Jimmy Brunswick got out of the passenger side.

On the very first day of the investigation, Lopez had checked with motor vehicles and found a red Ferrari registered in Julia Brunswick's name. Since then, patrol officers had been looking for that car. The driver jumped out of the car in a rush to catch up with Jimmy Brunswick. Shocked, Noelle saw she was the same hot blonde who had caught his eye at Sam's and again at the church. From that distance it appeared that she and Jimmy Brunswick were laughing, and it pissed him off.

Noelle straightened his tie and smoothed down his suit coat. In the morning when he'd put on his suit, he'd thought it looked sharp, but as he stepped into the Brunswick megamansion, he realized it looked cheap. His shoes were so worn he nearly skidded on the slick white marble floor in the front hall. The shame he'd had to push down all his life flared up. He felt clumsy, like he might stumble into a rare antique and shatter it to bits, and then everyone would turn and stare and see who he really was.

Noelle peered out the picture windows at the dense vegetation of elephant ear palms and azaleas in the gardens. He had seen this garden before, when the River Oaks Garden Club had led a tour the spring before he married Sally. He had taken her there to see all the flowers so she could get ideas for the beds she hoped to plant around their cottage.

He felt a pang of longing for that sweet, short time in his life with her, but then sloughed off his bitter and sentimental feelings; he had to get to work. The room was breathtaking, filled with crystal candelabras and pristine white silk damask sofas and chairs. But as large and grand as the room was, Noelle felt suffocated as he observed the crowd of many mourners holding cocktails and nibbling fancy finger foods.

Cornelia Brunswick sat on one of the sofas, flanked by a burly redhead with bunches of jewels around her neck and a thin, elegant woman wearing a string of pearls. Mrs. Brunswick barely moved. Noelle knew from the portrait that hung above the fireplace that she had been a beauty. Now she looked hollowed out, a shell of a woman, sitting there on the sofa. Her daughter had been brutally murdered by a killer who was still out there, and most of these mourners were acting like they were at a Hollywood red-carpet affair. Noelle wondered why death required such a party.

Jimmy staggered into the room without his suit coat, his tie hanging crookedly. His cheeks were flushed and he was rip-roaring drunk. He fell against the two young men Noelle had seen at the church. Jimmy thanked them in slurred words for being his sister Julia's good friends. "Best ever," he said as he looped an arm around the smaller man. "Anything at all for you guys. You just ask."

He squinted down on the short guy with the glasses and said, "You loved her too, right?" He opened his arms to all the guests in the room. "Everyone loved Julia, right? So who the fuck . . ." His own tears choked and cut off his words. He snatched a glass of wine from a passing waiter and drank the whole glass in one gulp. He took a second glass while he stepped up onto an ottoman. "Please, everyone, a toast to Julia!"

Noelle thought it would be great if he could ask Jimmy some questions while his defenses were down. He'd just have to find a moment when Jimmy was away from the crowd. The word had come down from Chief Cullen that the Brunswicks had agreed to let Noelle observe, but observe only.

Everybody raised their glasses to Julia. Jimmy stepped down off the ottoman, and sat down heavily in a chair, closing his eyes. He didn't look like he'd be moving anytime soon.

Noelle took a glass of wine from one of the waiters, planning to carry it in order to fit in, but then he took one sip and another, finishing that glass in a few seconds. Noelle rolled his shoulders back and casually approached Jimmy's two friends, knowing he was going to do what he wasn't supposed to.

"Jimmy looks like he's had a few," Noelle said.

"Yeah, but who can blame him. Jimmy can usually hold his liquor pretty well," said the large guy with the big, powerful hands. He looked to be about the same age as Jimmy. He was good-looking, with a square chin, but he had age lines radiating out from the corners of his eyes that made Noelle think he must have been a ballplayer who spent a lot of time squinting into the Texas sun.

"I know," Noelle said. "It's unbelievable. She was such a beautiful girl, and fun, I hear."

The smaller guy made a face Noelle couldn't decipher. He was so pale; he looked like he hardly ever stepped outdoors. He had a strong nose and intelligent eyes behind those horn-rimmed glasses. "*Fun's* one word for it," he said.

Noelle acted casual. "Oh? What word would you use?"

"I don't know. Wild, maybe."

"Trouble," the bigger man said.

"Oh, I'm sure you're exaggerating." Noelle said.

"Are you kidding?" the small man answered, his Adam's apple bobbing frantically. "Once she got into drugs, she really changed."

"Drugs? Hard to believe, coming from such a good home . . ."

At that moment, Jimmy stumbled up and clamped one hand on Noelle's shoulder. "Detective, why are you questioning my friends?"

The two men both flinched. "You didn't tell us you were a cop."

"No, I didn't," Noelle said. "But since I heard Jimmy say that you'd both been such good friends to Julia, I figured you wouldn't mind helping me catch her killer."

"How can they help?" Jimmy raised his voice and slurred his words. "They're just guys who knew Julia and me at school. Don't you get it, Detective? Unlike you, we're all friends and family here. Her killer's out there somewhere! That's where you should be looking, not here."

"Fine," Noelle said. "But just for the record, can I get your names?" He pulled his notebook out of his pocket; the big guy said his name was Tim Henderson, and his smaller buddy was Howard Wolvensky. Noelle didn't want to antagonize Jimmy Brunswick— or worse, his parents—so he took his glass of wine to a quiet place and resumed observing.

At the double doors, a small ruckus was heard, and suddenly the preening peacock he'd seen at the church burst through and made a beeline for Cornelia Brunswick, with her husband on her tail. He looked like he was holding her purse at the mall as he carried two glasses of wine and lagged behind her.

"Oh, Mrs. Brunswick!"—She clutched her two hands together at her bosom—"Richard and I—you know, Richard Lowden, my husband, is assistant vice president at your husband's company— well, we have been just horrified at all you two are going through. I'm Priscilla, Priscilla Lowden, by the way. If there's any way we can help, please let us know."

Noelle made a mental note of their names: Richard and Priscilla Lowden. Now Noelle understood Lowden's connection to George Brunswick.

Cornelia Brunswick didn't respond. Priscilla took a glass of wine from her husband, drank a hefty slug, and, scanning the room, went on, "Did you receive the white rose wreath we sent? I didn't notice it at the church. I asked the florist to make it all white because I read how you like white and also because white is the color of innocence and purity, and poor Julia was such an innocent victim. I asked the florist to make the wreath especially big, because Richard and I just feel so much for your loss. Richard especially, because he works so hard for your husband's company and admires him so. Really, sometimes Richard tells me that your husband is practically a father to him, or maybe a grandfather who looks out for him."

Richard Lowden, blotchy and embarrassed, yanked her elbow. "Priscilla!"

"Richard, please! I'm talking with Mrs. Brunswick."

"Not now." His hand gripped her upper arm. "Please excuse my wife, Mrs. Brunswick," he said in a low voice. "And please accept our condolences."

He tugged Priscilla over to the table laden with food. Noelle could just imagine the fight they'd have at home later and made a note in his book about Lowden's repressed rage.

The other mourners ignored the Lowdens. Noelle knew the wealthy were very good at acting like anyone or anything they found disagreeable did not exist. He also noticed his favorite cute blonde on the other side of the room, standing alone, observing everyone. She was watching Cornelia Brunswick closely. Noelle tried to read the expression on the blonde's finely sculpted face as she looked admiringly toward Cornelia. A trio of young, beautiful women wearing black designer suits and sparkling jewelry joined her: a redhead, a brunette, and the same snooty blonde she had been with at Sam's. He assumed this one was Richard Lowden's mistress.

He smiled at the thought of these four young women going on his list to interview as soon as possible. After all, it was his job and they might know something about Julia's alleged drug use or a boyfriend or two. No one could fault his eagerness to maneuver his way through the crowd to introduce himself. As soon as he did, Lowden's mistress gave her name. "I'm Marianna de Pucci. I knew Julia at school. We all knew her there, at Kinkaid, although I was much closer to her brother, Jimmy."

"What can you tell me about Julia?" Noelle asked.

The redhead gave her name too. "I'm Lauren Love, and I hate to say it, but the poor thing had been falling apart for the whole past year or so."

"What do you mean, falling apart?" Noelle asked.

Lauren Love blushed and looked at her brunette friend, who frowned and didn't say anything. Noelle asked her name, and she reluctantly answered, "Jennifer Colby, but I can't tell you anything about Julia that could help your investigation."

Marianna snorted. "I'll tell you what *falling apart* means, Detective. She'd gotten into drugs—cocaine at first, just snorting it, but then, who knows how or where, she met some real garbage who introduced her to heroin. You should be looking at those hippies down at Hermann Park. They're exactly the sort to commit all kinds of murder."

Noelle couldn't get over the air of superiority this Marianna spoke with. He wrote all the girls' names in his notebook, and next to Marianna's, in parentheses, he wrote, *Queen of Sheba*. The vanilla-cream blonde dream girl he liked looked up at him from underneath her dark eyebrows. Her alluring look made him hungry for a black-and-white sundae. "I'm Pamela, and I remember something that might help you. There was a guy at Kinkaid, a senior on scholarship. His name was Taylor Brock. There were rumors about him, that he might have been the guy who got Julia hooked on drugs."

Marianna said, "That's right. Julia's father had the dean kick Taylor Brock out of school. We never saw him again after that."

Jennifer Colby finally spoke. "People tried to help Julia. Even Jimmy tried, but there wasn't anything anyone could do." As Noelle made notes in his book, the four young women started talking among themselves about setting up a lunch date for later in the week. Noelle was a little shocked at the way they were treating their friend's wake like just one more social event on their calendars.

"Wait," Noelle said to the blonde he fancied as they began to walk away. He looked directly into her amazing blue eyes and said, "I didn't get your last name."

She smiled flirtatiously and said, "O'Leary, Pamela O'Leary."

A burst of laughter erupted from beyond the front hall. Pamela frowned, biting her lip and revealing that charming overbite. She caught Noelle watching her as she followed her three friends out of the room. Noelle decided to find out where that inappropriate laughter was coming from. He moved through the front hall, down a corridor, and into a music room.

Inside the room, George Brunswick was leaning against a mahogany grand piano, munching on a large cigar between his lips. Based on all the gossip about George, the family's black sheep, Noelle guessed that George may have been the one doing the laughing. He had a big, loud mouth and his black eyes looked like stones. His wife sat on a green damask sofa drinking, with a crooked smile plastered on her thin, plain face. Their children sat in armchairs next to her. The scene looked very somber and Noelle wondered what George could have laughed at. Noelle turned on his heels and continued along the corridor to see what else he might notice.

The walls were lined with framed photos of the Brunswick family from happier days. He noticed one photo of Julia playing tennis for Kinkaid. She was clutching a silver trophy and grinning happily, all of her shining. Noelle pondered how in the hell a girl with all that beauty and privilege could end up in a garbage bag. Was the answer as simple as drugs? He came to another living room, this one cozier. Jimmy sat slouched over a sofa, his head hanging between his knees. Noelle heard muffled sobs.

James Sr. sat beside his son with one hand on Jimmy's shoulder, one hand wrapped tightly around a glass of Scotch. "It's okay. Just let it all out." He noticed Noelle in the doorway and said, "Have you found out anything that might help?"

Noelle shook his head. "I wish I could offer you more news, but it is likely we are looking for a crazed junkie."

Jimmy lifted his head, showing his tears and sweat. "Then just get him, would you? Get him, and get out of here!"

"We're doing everything we can," Noelle said. "I'll be going now, Mr. Brunswick. Thank you for allowing me into your home on this sad and tragic day. I'll do my best, I promise."

On his way out, Noelle realized he had to take a leak and opened one door and then another, looking for a bathroom. On the third try, he saw Pamela leaning over a fancy table. She screeched and tried to close the door, but it was too late; Noelle had already seen the white powder around the rim of her nose. He shoved his way inside. He picked up the baggie of cocaine and said, "Is this yours?"

Her bright blue eyes looked terrified. "I found it here, I swear. It's not mine."

"I could arrest you right now for this." Noelle stuck the baggie into his coat pocket. "You're taking a ride with me, young lady! You're going to tell me everything you know, like what you're doing driving Julia's Ferrari, for starters."

CHAPTER 7

Noelle drove Pamela over to the G&B Icehouse. Cops liked the good barbecue. They often went there to blow off some steam. It was already four o'clock and the day hadn't cooled down one bit. Noelle was looking forward to a nice cold beer and a heated chat with Pamela. He led her into the dim place that always smelled of smoked meat and dirty ashtrays. The joint was almost empty, with only two guys at the end of the bar. He asked Pamela what she was drinking. "Beer's fine."

Sitting across the scarred wooden table from her was some kind of a dream. Her blond hair draped the sides of her face like silky curtains, and her eyes were the brightest blue he'd ever seen. His gaze dropped down to her breasts, which were large for her slender frame. Up close, she looked fragile. The beers came and she sucked hers up like she'd been drinking Lone Stars since the day she'd been weaned off her mama's milk. The beer left a wisp of foam on her lip that made him smile when she licked it away. For a brief moment he let her charm make him forget why he was there, until he snapped back to business. "What's the deal with you and Jimmy? Are you his girlfriend?"

"Not anymore. He only calls me sometimes when he's in town. We dated back in high school, but he's a UT man now and he can get any sorority girl he wants."

Noelle heard the bitterness in her voice. She knocked back more beer and then, like she was just laying out the facts of life for him, she said, "Jimmy's family has plans for him that would never include a girl like me."

"And what kind of girl is that?"

"A girl who works the makeup counter at Neiman's," Pamela said.

"Are you trying to tell me that on your salary you couldn't afford that cocaine I caught you with? If that's so, then it must be Jimmy's. You came to the reception with him."

"Please, don't arrest him!"

Noelle wasn't going to promise anything one way or the other. The cocaine might explain why Jimmy had been laughing when he was getting out of the Ferrari. "What was he laughing about when you pulled up at the reception?"

Pamela frowned. "He wasn't laughing. He was hysterical and crying, berating himself for not watching out for his little sister better than he did."

"Why was it his job to watch out for her?"

"My God, she'd been a mess for years." Pamela finished her beer. "Will you buy me another? I'm really thirsty."

"Sure." Noelle signaled the bartender for two more. He spoke as casually as he could, bringing the conversation around to what he really needed to know. "So how'd you come to be driving Jimmy in Julia's car in the first place?"

"He asked me to."

Noelle kept his poker face. "Really? Did you know we've been looking for her car since we found the body? Where's it been all this time?"

"At the Brunswick place, where else?"

That didn't make any sense, Noelle thought. Why wouldn't Julia have been driving it? Where had she been on the night of her murder? Maybe she had been driving it, and whoever killed her brought it back to the Brunswicks'? If the killer parked it at her parents' home, that meant he was familiar with the Brunswick grounds and house: a servant, a tradesman, a relative, maybe?

Lieutenant Donnelly and Chief Cullen were just going to have to let him question the family. Why hadn't the Brunswicks told him that Julia's car was at their house all along?

"Why was Jimmy driving it? Doesn't he have his own?"

"For all I know, he has more than one," Pamela said, "but he wasn't driving today, because he asked me to. He'd taken some Valiums from his mother's stash. He's careful never to drink, drug, and drive."

"Good to hear. If he's so careful, though, how'd the driver's-side door get dented?"

"I doubt Jimmy had anything to do with that. Julia probably did it," Pamela said as she sipped her beer.

"Let's get back to the cocaine," Noelle said. "Where'd Jimmy get it?"

Her face turned scarlet. "I wouldn't know," she mumbled.

"This is not a narcotics case, but it could turn into one. So tell me everything you know about Julia, drugs, and what she was like."

Pamela sat silent, and Noelle got impatient.

"Look." He pointed a finger at her. "This is about a murder, a really nasty murder! Do I need to show you details of what this sick fuck killer did to her?"

Pamela paled and tears slid down her face. In a whisper she said, "Please don't. I don't want to know!"

Noelle felt a grim determination. No girl, no matter how cute she was, was going to hold back information from him, so he tried to push her to breaking. "A vicious animal is still out there and if my hunch is right, girls like you are his target. He drugged Julia with chloroform and dragged her to the bayou, where he cut up her pretty body with a chain saw. If there is anyone in your circle of friends you ever had the smallest fear of, now's the time to talk about it."

"I don't know anyone like that. I hardly knew Julia or who she hung out with in the last three years. After Kinkaid, she left for college in Colorado, and shortly afterward, I heard she dropped out and came back home. Next I heard, she was in with a bad crowd. Just like Marianna told you, Julia did drugs, but not the way Jimmy and I do occasionally. She was a serious addict from what I heard."

"Well, if you're being honest, then thanks." He paid the bar tab and offered to drop her at the mall, where she told him her car was parked. He was saving the next questions about her date with George Brunswick at Sam's for another chance to be with her again. He couldn't trust his face not to reveal the feelings for her that were building up inside. Jealousy was one emotion he had trouble hiding. Noelle knew that if his vices of booze and gambling didn't get him, his desire for helpless young women would be the death of him for sure.

When she got out of his car, he gave her his card and told her to call him if she thought of or heard anything important. He drove off frustrated, full of lust, with a strong urge to play some cards. He had put in another long, hard day on the job. The night was still young, so he headed over to Sam's.

———

The following day, Noelle and Lopez parked the Plymouth in front of the Brunswick house. Only ten in the morning, and Noelle felt that damn burning in his gut again. He grunted getting out of the car.

Lopez asked, "Boss? You okay?"

Noelle felt bad that he hadn't told Lopez what he had been up to with Pamela, and his superiors didn't know about the little visit they were about to make at the Brunswicks' again.

The butler, Thomas, greeted them at the door. He led them down through the marble-tiled foyer and the corridor to the library. Against a backdrop of shelves that held hundreds of books, Mr. and Mrs. Brunswick sat on a black leather sofa. Noelle wondered if the Brunswicks had actually read any of these rare and expensive books.

James Brunswick shook Noelle's hand and just ignored Lopez, as if he were one of a dozen workers on his house staff. Brunswick's breath reeked of alcohol, but his appearance was neat and crisp in a white button-down shirt and tie, silver cuff links, and black shoes that were as polished as the marble floor in the foyer. Mrs. Brunswick remained seated and held a snifter of cognac in her trembling hand. She was the one he really wanted to question. Noelle assumed that mothers always knew more about their daughters' secrets than fathers did.

"Thank you for seeing us," Noelle said. Lopez, as instructed, kept his mouth shut.

"Please sit, detectives," Brunswick said as he sat down beside his wife on the couch, while Noelle and Lopez took the oversize armchairs beside the fireplace. Brunswick instructed their butler to bring Noelle and his assistant something to drink, asking them what they'd like.

"A cup of black coffee, thanks," Noelle said.

Brunswick objected. "No, I insist. You and your assistant must have a real drink with us." He looked over at Lopez for the first time and said, "You'll never taste whiskey any finer in this town. Thomas, pour them some."

Noelle didn't usually drink at ten in the morning, but he wasn't surprised the Brunswicks were drinking. They probably hadn't stopped since they'd first learned of Julia's murder, or perhaps it was the family's favorite pastime.

Thomas brought them each a crystal glass filled with an inch of whiskey. Noelle took a sip, even though it made his gut burn hotter. Brunswick began shooting questions at him, like he was the one in charge of the case. "Tell me, Detective, what you have found out so far. My wife and I have been waiting patiently; I want answers. Do you have any suspects yet?"

"Sir, I wish we had more solid news."

"How many psychos can be out there, anyway?" He waved a hand toward the window. Noelle knew he didn't mean River Oaks. He meant the city beyond, with its dirty streets and crumbling blocks and sidewalks full of hookers and junkies.

Mrs. Brunswick didn't speak. She only sipped quietly from her snifter, that one hand trembling, the rest of her cool and still as stone.

"Mr. Brunswick," Noelle said. "We have to ask a couple of questions. Did you or your wife know Julia's car was parked here?"

Brunswick frowned. "What's that got to do with anything?"

"We've had patrolmen looking for that car. It would have helped to know it was here."

"Well, Detective, I didn't see it. At my age, I don't drive anymore; the chauffeur brings the car around for me. He might have seen it in the garage but didn't think anything of it. I still don't understand why that's an issue."

"We're trying to figure out where she was, who she was with in the days before her murder. Did she drive her car here and leave it? Information like that can perhaps lead us to her killer."

Mrs. Brunswick cleared her throat. "Yes, Detective, she did, over a week before she . . . died. She got into a little accident— nothing serious, but it scared her. She had problems, I know, but she didn't want to hurt anybody. She told me she didn't need the car where she was living. She asked me to call her a cab and I did. I gave her money for the fare."

Noelle leaned forward, eager. "Where was she living?"

"She wouldn't say."

Noelle and Lopez were going to have to make a trek out to Hermann Park, question the hippies there, and hope to God they'd get some info that made even one lick of sense.

Cornelia Brunswick blurted out, "It was that Taylor Brock! It was all his fault! Question him! He was on a scholarship at Kinkaid School when my baby met him, and that's when Julia started doing those drugs. Of course, my husband made sure the school expelled him. We didn't need that *kind* at our alma mater."

"All right. We'll check him out, but the next thing I have to ask for is a list of the people who work for you, especially laborers who do small jobs, going back at least six months or a year or so."

"Now you're talking, Detective. We'll get you that right away. Though I'm damn certain none of our regular people could have done anything like this. They all loved Julia. She was the sweetest and always most polite to the help. If I had some lunatic working in my house I'd know it, but the others, I couldn't swear to. Most of them I never interact with. Thomas took care of all that. Ask him."

"Thank you." Out of the corner of his eye, Noelle saw Lopez put his glass to his mouth and pretend to take a sip. Noelle could see he was learning on the job.

"Now then," Noelle said. "What about the people who were close to her?"

Brunswick flashed an irritated look at his wife. "How would we know anything about those people?"

"No, sir, I wasn't clear. I don't mean people she was with after she left your home; I mean the people around here and the family she was close to."

Brunswick's face went red. He slammed down his glass. "You must be joking! Someone from our circle? Impossible!"

Noelle had to step carefully. "I agree with you, but we have to check every box we can."

Brunswick got up and paced the room. "I don't need any damn boxes checked; I want you to find the madman who took away our little girl!" He threw up his hands. "This whole visit has been a waste of my time."

Mrs. Brunswick suddenly spoke, sharply. "James, sit down. Detective, do you have more questions?"

"Yes, thank you. I want to get back to the question about where she was living. She didn't tell you when she dropped the car off, but I'm guessing that you were sending her money."

"What was I supposed to do, let her starve? I can give you the post office where I sent the money. We don't know where she was living for the past five months. She moved and didn't tell us where, and that was the last we heard."

James spoke up again. "Cornelia, when she dropped her car here, why didn't you at least get Thomas to follow that cab, or call that investigator so he could talk to the cabdriver?"

"James, don't you dare blame me!" Cornelia's hand trembled even harder. "You're the one who let her get away with everything!" She burst into sobs.

Noelle's ears perked right up when he mentioned an investigator. He should have known that rich people like the Brunswicks didn't just let a daughter get in trouble and then disappear. They would have been keeping tabs on her all along.

"Hold the phone; y'all had a private investigator on Julia?"

"Yes, Jerry Jones; we hired him to give us regular reports when Julia was living with some hippie over by Hermann Park. He lost track of her when she left with the hippie. Since then no one knew her whereabouts until you found her."

Lopez finally spoke. "I'm so sorry, Mrs. Brunswick."

Something in Lopez's words, or maybe his sad and liquid eyes, must have pulled at Cornelia Brunswick. She turned to Lopez, her eyes blazing. "I could kill that hippie bastard! Taking her away from us, giving her drugs that she paid for with our money! God, we loved her so much!" She plucked down at her husband's arm. "James, please. Give them the reports from the investigator. Maybe there's something in there that will help."

Brunswick went over to one of the wooden filing cabinets and brought back an inch-thick folder. "Here, Detective, take it." He looked pointedly at Noelle, then Lopez. "When you find this maniac, there'll be money in it for you."

Noelle was so pissed he couldn't speak. He just wanted to get out of there. Who did Brunswick think he was to insult him with a bribe to do his job? He took the file folder from Brunswick. Cornelia tried to stand up, but her legs gave out and she fell back to the sofa. What he'd taken for regal posture and cool politeness was just her way of trying to hide that she was drunk as a skunk.

The butler was suddenly there to escort them out. How would he know it was time? As Noelle followed Thomas down the corridor, he heard James shouting at Cornelia.

A blast-furnace heat hit him full on as soon as he stepped outside. He got out of his suit coat as quickly as he could and threw it into the backseat. Lopez followed. Noelle started the car, irritated to see Lopez with wet eyes whispering a prayer and crossing himself. Noelle hated teary emotion, especially in men. He believed it got in the way of seeing the big picture, and prayer was just a waste of time. "Can it!" he said to Lopez. "We have work to do."

He started to head back to the squad room. "I'll drop you off at the precinct. I'm going to take this file home and read through it there. How about we meet at one thirty? We'll get something to eat and figure out what to do with the PI's reports."

"Boss, we have to take that file to Donnelly."

"Sure, that's the way it should work in most cases, I'd agree, but he's gonna get all balled up if there's something in here that makes the Brunswicks or their circle look bad. We don't have time for that. Once we figure out our next move, I'll tell Donnelly about the file."

Lopez heaved a sigh. He wasn't happy.

CHAPTER 8

Noelle took the afternoon to swing by the PI Jerry Jones's rundown office off the Fifth Ward of West Gray. They shot the shit for a while before Noelle learned that there wasn't much to learn. Jones told him that Julia Brunswick had lived in a scummy railroad flat with a hippie named Chris Porter. Chris and Julia smoked weed and shot heroin all day and night unless they were out scoring from dealers. What Noelle didn't get was why, after Julia's father learned this, he didn't take his daughter out of that nightmare and throw her into some kind of psychiatric hospital for addicts.

Jerry read his mind and said, "Mr. Brunswick thought his daughter was made of tough stuff, so he was the crazy one. After two weeks of me spying on his kid and the deadbeat druggie, they up and disappeared like that." The PI snapped his fingers.

Noelle groaned. "I thought you were watching them."

Jones squinted at Noelle through his heavy glasses. "Detective, I gotta eat sometimes."

Noelle shook his head. "Did you know they were gone?"

The PI took off his glasses and rubbed them on his holey polo shirt. "Nah, not at first; I could hear a Jimi Hendrix record playing over and over. I wouldn't have guessed they gave me the slip until the record kept skipping and didn't stop. That's when I went to their door. I thought they might have OD'd, but that's when I realized they were gone. I found their door open and nothing left inside but a threadbare mattress. After that, I questioned their dealers and such but couldn't find Julia or Chris. It made me sick to hear how she was killed. I should have called you myself when I read the papers, but the Brunswicks—well, you know how it is. They'd have strung me up if I broke my confidentiality agreement."

Yeah, Noelle knew how it was.

———

The next day, at the precinct, Noelle gave Lopez their agenda for the day. "I want to head out early to interview Taylor Brock, the kid the Brunswicks got kicked out of school. I found his family's residence from the Kinkaid records. I put Brennan on the job of running Chris Porter's name through the system. A deadbeat junkie like that must have a record somewhere. If Brennan comes up empty, we might have to go slumming over at Hermann Park to see if we can find Julia's lover boy."

Lopez made a face. "Those kids, what is wrong with them, ruining the bodies and brains the good Lord gave them?"

"You got me," Noelle said. "This generation has taken feeling good to a whole other level. All I ever need is a cold beer and a couple shots of Jack. It does me just fine."

Lopez made another face. Noelle knew he thought a beer and a couple shots of Jack were almost as bad as marijuana and heroin, but Lopez would have to admit at least it was legal.

"One thing, Lopez. We can't go over to Hermann Park looking like cops. There's a gal down in Vice who'll help us dress for the part. Give your wife a heads-up so she's not shocked when you come home looking like a dirty hippie. But first things first—Taylor Brock's folks' house."

The Brocks lived over in Montrose, an area humming with gays, young people, and hippies. Noelle found their house, a small red bungalow with concrete steps leading up to a brown wooden door. It was still damn hot out, but a couple of drops started sprinkling down on their heads. "Maybe these pregnant clouds will finally burst open and we'll get some cooling off again," Noelle said.

Noelle pounded a brass knocker on the door three times before he heard someone cry out, "Coming!"

A middle-aged woman with salt-and-pepper hair cracked open the door, leaving the inside latch still hinged. "Yes?"

Noelle flashed his badge and introduced himself and Lopez. "Are you Mrs. Brock?"

"That's right. Emma Brock."

"We need to ask you a few questions about your son Taylor. May we come in?"

Mrs. Brock unlocked the inside lock. "To talk about Taylor? Yes, you may," she said, opening the door wide.

She was an attractive woman, with good bones and pretty green-gray eyes, but there was a great sadness in her face. She led them to a bare-bones living room furnished with a tiny love seat, a scratched wooden coffee table, and two straight, unwelcoming chairs. There was only one picture on the wall, a portrait of a handsome young man in an army uniform with the stripe of a private first class on his sleeve.

Noelle was taken aback when Mrs. Brock started to cry. She plopped down onto the tiny sofa and waved her hand to the picture on the wall. "My son, detectives, what is it you want to ask about him?"

"It's about Julia Brunswick. We learned that the Brunswicks were responsible for getting your son kicked out of school."

"If you think my Taylor had something to do with it, you are out of luck. Four months ago, my boy was killed in Vietnam. Two chaplains came to my door, gave me a salute, and told me he stepped on a land mine. They shipped his body back in a cheap wooden casket. That's the outcome of the Brunswicks' dirty work—getting my boy kicked out of Kinkaid. Good riddance to Julia Brunswick and her kind, I'm sorry to say."

Lopez was taken aback by her coldness and asked her, "Are you blaming the murder victim for your son's death?"

"My boy had worked so hard for that scholarship. He was only eighteen, and the minute he got kicked out of school he got drafted. If you're looking for suspects, look at the Brunswicks; they're the real criminals."

Lopez surprised Noelle by reaching across the coffee table to take Mrs. Brock's hand. "Ma'am, I'm sorry for your loss. I have a daughter, and I guess I might feel just like you do if anyone harmed her. Can you tell us anything else that might help?"

Her tears dried up, and she said, "It was all one big lie. Taylor didn't start Julia on drugs. He took her out on one date. He worked weekends at the hardware store to save up his money to take her to a nice place. He had such a crush on her. Once they got there, she ditched him to go off with two hippies, leaving my boy to drive back home on his own. Taylor wasn't even mad at her like he should have been, but he was so concerned for her safety that he stopped off at the Brunswicks' to tell them about Julia going off with such bad company. Later that night she came home all crazed up, and the Brunswicks called the police. To protect her bad friends, Julia told her parents it was Taylor who had given her those drugs. My son never did any drugs! They never found any drugs on him or in his truck, not even any alcohol on his breath. The police arrested him anyway and made him spend a night in jail before they dropped the charges. The school kicked him out as a 'bad influence.' Taylor was just too sweet for his own good."

Noelle was steamed. He found it easy to believe Mrs. Brock's side of things, but the Brocks weren't completely off the hook yet. "Mrs. Brock, what about your husband? Where is he, and does he share your opinion of the Brunswicks?"

"He died of cancer five years ago, Detective. It was just Taylor and me. Most days I wonder why the good Lord didn't take me too."

"Those hippies Julia went off with that night. Did Taylor say anything about them? Did he know who they were?"

"Not only did Julia walk out on my son, but she was cruel and told Taylor he wasn't cool enough to go to Hermann Park and smoke grass with her friends. He said she acted all smug, like she was proud of it, and made no apologies for dumping him on their date. I warned my son about those rich girls."

"Did he say what the hippies looked like?"

"He described them to the police that arrested him. The report of Taylor's arrest must be in the police file somewhere. I'm sure you can look it up."

Noelle guessed that the boy's arrest had probably been unofficial and not recorded anywhere, just a favor to the Brunswicks. Noelle stood. "Thank you, ma'am, this has all been a big help."

Mrs. Brock stood up to show them to the door. "I suppose I should be glad, if I've helped you to catch her killer. I wouldn't want to see anyone else's children suffering under the hands of this maniac."

On the way out, Noelle stopped to look at the picture of Taylor on the wall. "They gave him a Purple Heart," Mrs. Brock told him. Noelle flashed back to memories of mortar fire from his time in the Korean War. Taylor Brock had been a handsome, skinny kid, like he once was. Noelle could easily imagine the hard time the kid must have had in Vietnam. He did not look like a boy cut out for war.

Noelle turned. "Your kid was a good soldier and a hero."

She wiped at her eyes. "Thank you, Detective."

After they finished with Mrs. Brock, Noelle and Lopez got back to the station and learned that Brennan had found nothing in the system on Chris Porter, so they headed over to the gal in Vice for their undercover hippie makeovers. When she got through with them, they looked at each other and fell into a spell of laughter. They had on styled wigs down to their shoulders, and both wore Nehru shirts and tattered jeans.

Still cracking up, Noelle said, "You need to grow some whiskers, Lopez, 'cause without them, you make a real cute girl."

Lopez retorted, "At least I don't look like an old refugee from a biker gang."

Noelle said, "You be good cop, and I'll be bad cop—I mean, good hippie, bad hippie."

On their way out, Detective Brennan saw them leaving and wolf whistled at Lopez. Lopez turned and flipped his wig and his finger at Brennan. Noelle was happy to see that Lopez could have a sense of humor for a change.

Outside the precinct, Noelle and Lopez got into a late-sixties VW van. Even though it pissed Donnelly off, he'd arranged to borrow it from Narcotics. The inside of the van had Indian tie-dyed curtains and trash and ashtrays filled with cigarette butts and pot roaches. Lopez got a kick out of how real it looked.

"Here we go," Noelle said. "On our way to Hippie Hill, I mean, Hell; home of LSD and psycho killers."

Lopez said, "What if this Chris Porter is another Charlie Manson, like out in California, land of all the fruits and nuts? That was some devil worship going on there."

Noelle grunted. "Yeah, it could be something like. We gotta find Porter. It's very likely that he could be our killer."

When they reached the park, young people were everywhere, acting like little kids or escapees from a mental ward. "How are we going to find one crazy hippie among all the rest?" Lopez asked.

The air was thick and sticky as molasses and reeked of marijuana. Noelle noticed a stench wafting over from four young men in a cluster sitting under a patch of trees.

"I'll do the talking," he told Lopez.

As they approached, one of them hid a pipe behind his back.

"What's happening?" Noelle asked.

All four guys shrugged.

"We just got into town. We've been following the Dead around since we left Frisco last year."

"They ain't here," the guy who'd hidden the pipe said.

"Yeah, we'll be going to Austin in a couple days, but we heard there was a good scene here in Houston too."

"It's cool, but nothing like Frisco," one of the other guys said.

In his best hippie lingo, Noelle said, "Frisco is so cool, man. Best pot in the country—no hassles. They grow it up north in Humboldt and Mendocino. Sweet country. You can buy it as easy as a pack of Marlboros."

One of the other hippies said, "Oh, man, you make me wanna go west right now, but I'm a little too high to drive."

His buddy agreed. "Yeah, and besides, you don't got anything to drive!" He fell on his back, laughing up at the trees.

"Hitch with us," Noelle said. "We got a van and need someone to pitch in for gas. By the end of the Dead tour, sooner or later, we'll be heading back."

The guy sat up. "Hell, you mean it? Y'all got room for us?"

Lopez smiled. "The more the merrier."

"All right!" As the four hippies high-fived one another, the pipe fell onto the grass.

Noelle nodded. "Good stuff?"

"Not bad."

"Cool."

"You want some?"

Noelle shrugged. "I'd love a hit, but we've got dough and need to buy some for the road. You know who's selling?"

The redhead pointed toward a guy with a banjo. Noelle saw that he had long blond hair. If this was their guy, they might break the case and then all this dress-up would have been worth it.

Noelle asked, "You buy from him before? I hear the pigs are tight in these parts. He's not going to trust two dudes he never met."

"I'll introduce you," said the guy who'd been holding the pipe. Noelle gave him their fake names, "I'm Hunter, and my strong and silent buddy here is Mario."

"Nice to meet you, I'm Sammy."

When they reached the blond hippie with the banjo, Sammy said, "Hey, Chris. These are my friends, Hunter and Mario; they're looking to score."

Chris looked up at them through tiny round glasses. "Who says I'm holding?"

"No problem." Noelle held up his hands. "Just looking for a lid; stash is getting low."

"They're from Frisco," Sammy said. "Following the Dead. We might be headed over to Austin with them."

Chris, on the nod, looked up and commented, "Houston ain't Austin—the Dead, huh? What's your favorite song?"

Noelle didn't hesitate. "Gotta be 'Dark Star.' Saw them recording it live at the Fillmore." Noelle had done his homework.

Chris perked up. "No shit?"

"Helluva night, too."

"A lid, huh?" Chris said. "I guess I could do you that."

"Got anything stronger?" Noelle asked.

"Not cheap, man."

Noelle pulled out his wallet and flashed some big bills.

"That'll work. I got some fine brown shit from Mexico."

Noelle said, "How much, and can I get a taste?"

"Sure, man, but not here. Where's your ride?"

Noelle and Lopez led Chris toward the van. On the way up Noelle asked, "Man, you ever been to Frisco?"

"Sure."

"You know a chick named Starfire?"

"No, man, but with a name like that, sounds like she's hot."

"Yeah, man," Noelle said. "She's something. I just wondered because she always talked about some guy she was gone over in Houston who had long blond hair like you. Thought if you were her guy, I'd let you know that she's missing you."

"That's groovy; some chick I don't know from Frisco is missing me."

"She had a tattoo with her name and yours in a heart just above her navel: 'Starfire and Chris.' There must be lots of guys named Chris. I think she said his last name was Jones. It would be weird if you were Chris Jones."

Chris replied, "No, I'm Porter, Chris Porter."

As they reached the van, Chris looked straight at Noelle and shifted the conversation to business. "So what y'all want?"

"Ten dime bags," Noelle said as they climbed into the van.

"Okay, good." As Chris pulled some plastic baggies out of his boot, Noelle and Lopez flashed their badges and said, "You're under arrest. You have the right to remain silent . . ."

———

A few hours later, back at the precinct, Chris Porter was one unhappy customer in a holding tank after being booked for illegal possession with intent to sell. His long blond hair was dirty and tangled; next to his feet was a puddle of vomit on the floor. Noelle had let him stew in his juices without a fix until they brought him inside the claustrophobic grill room. Donnelly and Lopez stood outside, watching through the two-way mirror. A while later Noelle entered and sat across the table from Chris.

Chris stared at Noelle, then looked away, like a cowering dog. He sniffled and wiped his nose on the sleeve of his Jim Morrison T-shirt.

Noelle still didn't say anything; he just waited until Chris began to cry. "Man, why'd you throw me in here? I didn't do nothing."

"You really don't know? You can shoot yourself up higher than the moon for all I care, because that stuff will kill you sooner or later. The way I see it, you're already doing time, but that doesn't give you the right to kill a girl."

Chris's eyes got big. "Julia? You think I did that?"

"You're the last one who saw her alive. So yeah, stands to reason you're the one who killed her."

Chris was shaking his head. "No way, man, no way! I loved that chick. She was my Sunshine; it was true love with us. I could never hurt her."

"Right, you could never hurt her—only shoot her full of heroin till the sunshine was snuffed out of her."

"You got it all wrong. I helped her out. I made sure she would never OD. I'm telling you, she was my sunshine princess, but when she wanted a fix sometimes she wanted to get more than mellow. Sometimes she wanted to be . . . gone, just gone. I was trying to keep her alive. When she walked out on me, I was scared for her, you know what I'm saying?"

Chris put his head down, clutched at his stomach, and moaned. "Shit, you gotta get me some smack."

"Keep talking and we'll see. So she walked out on you? Didn't that piss you off? And where was she going?"

Tears poured down Chris's face. "She said she was going home."

Noelle couldn't hide the surprise in his voice. "You mean, to the Brunswick place in River Oaks?"

Chris was moaning again. "All she told me was she was going home."

Noelle reached across and grabbed Chris's chin in his hand, forcing him to look him in the eye. "When, goddammit? Tell me when. What day did she leave you?"

"I don't know." Chris was whimpering, but Noelle didn't show an ounce of pity.

"I don't even know what day it is today. I can't think straight without a fix, man."

"You tell me what I need to know and we'll talk about what you need later."

Chris screamed, "*I need it now!*"

"When I'm finished, if you tell the truth," Noelle said.

Chris's whole body shook in spasms, and it was clear the kid was useless in his condition.

"All right, asshole, I'll see what I can do."

Noelle left Chris shaking like a leaf and called down to Narcotics. Donnelly was all over him. "What the fuck are you doing?"

"I have to get Porter some medication if I'm going to get anything out of him that makes sense."

"Okay. But if things go south, it's all on you—I didn't know anything, you got that?"

Noelle nodded. He thought Donnelly was getting his panties in a bunch for nothing. If things went south, who was going to care about a dead junkie?

Ten minutes later, with Donnelly and Lopez watching through the two-way mirror, Noelle sat down with a glass of water in one hand and showed Chris the two pills in his other hand. Shaking and moaning, Chris tried to lunge for the pills, but the shackle at his handcuffs jerked him back.

"You'll get these if you finish your story about Julia going home. How was she planning to get there?"

Chris blubbered. "She called somebody, I don't know who. I said, 'Sunshine, who are you calling?' She told me a friend. I didn't know she was planning to leave me for good yet. She just . . . went away."

Noelle was getting steamed as Chris wept and wept. He reached across the table and slapped his face. "Get it together. What day did she leave?"

"I don't know! I don't live by clocks or calendars. All I remember was Sunshine shaking and I was on the nod and couldn't get her more smack right then. I was going to get her some, but man, she said she didn't want it. She was going to take Valiums. She said she wanted out of our life, that she was going back home to her rich daddy and didn't want me anymore."

"That could make a man want to kill," Noelle said, but in his heart he knew Porter was telling the truth. It was clear that Porter could not be the killer. His arms were thin as string beans and his hands shook like he had palsy. He could barely move out of his apartment, let alone carry a body through the bayou and handle a chain saw to mutilate a body.

He gave Chris the pills, and with his hands shackled he had to bend his head to the table to drink from the glass. He managed to gulp down the pills as though he had cancer and they were the cure.

Noelle stood and waited a while, watching Chris's shakes slow down. "Okay, now, one more time, when did Julia leave you?"

Chris just laid his head back against his chair.

Noelle almost slapped him and yelled, "Damn it, how many days ago?"

Chris breathed deeply. "I think two weeks, maybe? I was so sad; I was dead without her. Yeah, I think it was two weeks ago."

"Did she call her parents?"

Chris's breathing became more relaxed. "I don't think so. All I remember is she told me she was going to reveal a secret to her whole family. When she talked about it, the cold bitch in her came out. The sunshine went right out of her. I'd seen it before, but not like this."

"What secret?" Noelle asked.

Chris was crying again. "Her family never treated her right. They were the ones who turned her into that cold bitch. With me, she was always Sunshine, you get it?"

Something was rotten in the Brunswick family, Noelle knew for sure. He'd smelled it that first night he went there to talk about Julia's death and again when he learned about her car being in their garage all that time. He knew his hands were tied when it came to turning over that rock to see what would crawl out.

He left Chris in the grill room. When Noelle came out he saw Donnelly and Lopez both shake their heads. "What now?" Donnelly said.

"We've still got him on drug charges," Noelle said. "Let Narcotics deal with him. I need to interview Jimmy Brunswick. Come on, Lieutenant, you know I'm right. Jimmy knew all of his sister's friends. He might know who she called that night."

"Absolutely not. Leave the Brunswicks to their grief, for God's sake!"

Noelle sulked. "Okay, but if I can't get information from them, who can I interview? Is all of River Oaks off-limits too?"

"Watch it, Noelle. I'm still your boss. You can interview her girlfriends. Just keep it casual like and don't do anything to rattle them. It might even be a little thrill for them. You know how bored those society dames are."

Noelle's spirits lifted a little when he imagined a casual lunch at the country club with those hot chicks he'd met at Julia's funeral.

CHAPTER 9

The following day, Noelle planned a visit to the River Oaks Country Club to interview Julia's friends. It was 102 degrees, with the humidity at ninety percent. Noelle was thinking if it didn't rain soon, he might turn into a killer himself. He had lived in the stinking swamps of Louisiana as a boy and in Houston for thirty-five years, but he was never going to get used to the heat. Everyone in the city was grouchy: husbands and wives, parents and children, men in bars, and women in supermarkets all showed signs of exploding temper.

Chris Porter hadn't panned out, leaving Noelle with no real suspects or evidence. They'd interviewed everyone in the vicinity of Porter and Julia's apartment; they'd checked asylums to see if any nut jobs had been released; they'd interviewed the staff at the Brunswicks' and the Ima Hogg house. They were checking on Angel Perez's alibi for his whereabouts on the night of Julia's murder. So far it all amounted to a big fat nothing.

———

At the River Oaks Country Club, Lauren Love and Jennifer Colby sipped gin and tonics. From their table at the window they could see a bright summer sky, a luxurious fountain, and the broad expanse of the golf course off in the distance. Between the huge Greek columns Pamela sauntered in, looking like she belonged. As the hostess sat her at their table, she said, "Please have the waiter send over whatever my friends are having." When she took a seat, Lauren and Jennifer flashed each other conspiratorial smiles. Pamela knew from their look that one of them had important news.

Jennifer closed her menu and mentioned the latest newspaper reports about Julia Brunswick's murder. "Do they have any clues at all?"

"It doesn't seem like it," Pamela said. She'd didn't bother to mention to her friends that she had already been grilled by the lead detective on the day of Julia's wake.

"I don't want to talk about it," Lauren said. "There's nothing we can do now, and it's too nice a day to think about tragedy."

Pamela's drink arrived. She took a long, cool sip, letting the gin relax her. "So what else is in the news?"

Lauren held out her right hand. "Look."

On her third finger sat a gold ring with a brilliant-cut sapphire encircled by tiny rubies, glimmering in the sunlight. "Jimmy gave it to her," Jennifer said, grinning broadly.

Pamela forced a smile. "That's wonderful. I'm so happy for you, Lauren." This news caught her off guard, since she assumed that Jimmy had gone back to Austin right after the funeral.

"He took me to Tony's last night," Lauren said.

"He was so different from his usually cocky self. I swear this mess with Julia has changed him. He actually said he was done playing around and wanted only me, from here on out."

Pamela hid her shock and sorrow while thinking how Jimmy had never given her anything but a good screwing. She'd been just a cheap, easy lay to him. She took consolation in seeing that Lauren was wearing the ring on her right hand, so she knew it wasn't an engagement ring.

"Do you expect we'll be reading about your engagement on the society page of that dreary newspaper any day soon?" Pamela asked.

Jennifer frowned. "Well, that's the big question, isn't it?"

"I know, I know," Lauren said. "We'll see. I'm not stupid. I know he hurt you, Jen . . ."

Jennifer waved a hand. "Old news."

A couple of years back, Jimmy had seduced Jennifer and convinced her she was the love of his life, until he dumped her at a party in front of all their friends when some other girl caught his eye. Jennifer had been humiliated, but three months later she bounced back and did a one-eighty with her life. She stopped depending on men and enrolled in medical school. She was planning her future as a doctor.

As the waiter served their lunch, Lauren said, "I tell you what, if he goes back to his old ways and cheats on me, I'm not giving this ring back."

"Good," Jennifer said. Suddenly Pamela's stomach was in knots over her feelings about Jimmy. Sometimes she wasn't even sure she wanted him or loved him, but she knew she could never trust him, or any man for that matter. She didn't think it was fair that Jimmy should give Lauren a ring like that when she already had so much!

"Have you told Marianna yet?" Jennifer asked.

Lauren shook her head. "I couldn't get her on the phone. If I do end up marrying Jimmy, you know, Jen, that you and she will be my bridesmaids."

Pamela bit the inside of her mouth to hold back her emotions. Lauren cried out, "And of course, you too, Pamela!" Pamela knew she'd never be Lauren's bridesmaid, even as Lauren reached her hands out to clasp both hers and Jennifer's. "I'm so lucky to have you two as friends." She changed the subject when the waiter approached to take their order. "I wonder when that detective is going to get here. Maybe we should just order for all of us."

As Lauren squeezed Pamela's hand, Pamela smiled and recognized that her own strength was her ability to hide whatever she was feeling. She swallowed a big swig of her drink and checked her watch. "I'm so sorry, but I have to go. I forgot that I promised to cover the late shift today. You'll have to make my apologies to that detective."

"Okay," Jennifer said. "But you haven't had any lunch yet. Let's at least hang out one Saturday night at the Lone Star together before Marianna leaves for Europe."

"I like that idea," Pamela said as she ran off.

As Pamela waited for the valet to bring her car around, she saw Noelle pull up in front of the valet station. He walked up to her and said, "Leaving already? I have a date with your girlfriends. They told me you were joining us."

"Detective, I have to work for a living. Enjoy," she smirked.

"I'm sorry—I was hoping to see you sooner rather than later. We have unfinished business," Noelle said with a smile.

"I hope you mean friendly business." Pamela winked just as her car pulled up. The valet opened the door, and she sauntered in and peeled off without another word.

Noelle, now hot under the collar but grateful for the perfect temperature-controlled country club, walked through the large dining room. The cool atmosphere sure topped the cooling system in his dinky room, where he used a small fan and an open refrigerator door to cool down. The host led him to the corner table where Lauren and Jennifer were giggling, already tipsy from their drinks. Noelle asked the maître d' to send the waiter over with a beer, whatever was on tap.

Noelle sat down and thanked the girls for their invitation to conduct the interview over lunch.

"Of course we want to help any way we can," Lauren said. "I hope you don't mind, but we ordered without you. The newspapers said that you hail from Louisiana, so I ordered you the gumbo. It's the best ever here. I'm just starving 'cause I haven't eaten anything in days."

"Is it because of your grief over Julia's murder?" Noelle asked.

"Quite the opposite; it's because of Jimmy Brunswick," Jennifer said in a dry voice.

"Julia's older brother?" Noelle asked.

"It's not important, Detective, just stupid boy-girl stuff."

"Jimmy Brunswick is quite the man about town, you know." Jennifer said, looking like the cat that ate the canary. "I just discovered that he gave Lauren a special ring. Show him, honey."

Lauren flashed her ruby. Noelle looked confused. "Did he propose before or after he buried his sister?"

Jennifer still looked smug. "Jimmy has always been a fast worker. But it's not an official proposal, just a pre-proposal. Jimmy has trouble with commitment."

Noelle said, "Like most men, I guess."

"Jimmy Brunswick has had all our names in his little black book at one time or another. He even screwed Pamela back in high school."

Lauren interjected, "Yes, but I'm the only one to ever get a pre-proposal ring."

Jennifer jumped back into the truth-telling. "Pamela moved on from Jimmy long ago, and now she's graduated to a senior Brunswick, Jimmy's uncle George."

Noelle was happy to see that the booze had loosened the lips of these two chicks since his first encounter with them. He noticed that Jennifer still had a real smart mouth on her.

Lauren must have been thinking the same thing, because she tried to change the subject. "You're not interested in all this gossip, Detective."

The waiter brought his beer, and another waiter appeared with a heavy tray. Noelle's stomach growled when he saw the biscuits and honey placed in the middle of the table, but he got down to business. "When was the last time either of you saw Julia?"

Lauren jumped in to answer before Jennifer could.

"I saw her about a week before she died. She was at Neiman's, at the makeup counter where Pamela works. She had on a hippie maxi-dress, cut too low in front and with a slit all the way up her thigh. She looked really trashy and she wanted Pamela to make up her face, but she was so stoned she could barely sit up straight in the chair."

"Did you talk to her?"

"I tried to, but she could hardly put a sentence together."

"Was she with someone?"

"I was there, too," Jennifer said. "She got mad at Pamela and told her she was making her look old. After she left, Pamela told me that Julia already looked like an old woman, with no flesh on her bones, and that all the erase in the world could not cover up those dark circles under her hollowed eyes. It was just awful the way she let herself go downhill."

Jennifer chimed in. "I think it was easier for Julia to talk to Pamela because of Pamela's iffy background." She went on to gossip about Pamela's mother, Pamela's scholarship at Kinkaid, and how she didn't get enough money from UT to go there so she had to work at Neiman's.

"Pamela likes the finer things she can't afford on a sales clerk's salary," Jennifer quipped, like it was a fate worse than death.

Smug little bitch, Noelle thought. He wanted to slap her. What did she know about girls like Pamela—or Sally—and what they had to do to get by? Instead he took a mighty gulp of his beer.

He couldn't figure out why Julia had thrown her rich, privileged life away to live the life that Sally had tried so hard to escape from. At least Pamela had an honest job and wasn't turning cheap tricks in the street like poor Sally.

"Do you know," he asked, "before she got into the drugs, did Julia ever hurt herself?"

Lauren's eyes got big. "You mean, like suicide?"

Jennifer added, "When I was dating Jimmy he told me that when Julia was fifteen she swallowed a whole bottle of aspirin. Her mother got the chauffeur to rush her to the hospital. Obviously she lived."

Noelle asked, "Did they make her see a shrink then?"

"Oh no," Jennifer said. "The Brunswicks are not into that sort of thing."

Noelle finished his beer and ordered another as a waiter passed by. He knew he would have to find out what made fifteen-year-old Julia swallow a bottle of aspirin. Perhaps it had something to do with the secret she had planned to reveal to her family when she left Chris Porter. He knew for sure now that he was going to question Jimmy Brunswick.

CHAPTER 10

After Noelle's informative lunch at the country club, he was back at his desk to update his notes and game plan. A little before sundown he took a break and looked outside. He saw that the clouds had finally burst and a much-needed rain had begun to pour down onto Houston.

Some people were so thrilled they stood out on the sidewalks and let the rain soak their clothes right through. Wives and husbands kissed and made up. Parents and children set up board games and had fun together. Men in bars played liar's dice and laughed, and women in supermarkets joked with the cashiers.

Later that same night, Sally huddled under an awning, hoping some man with a lot of cash would pick her up and take her someplace dry. Her platform boots hurt her feet and the rain was smearing her mascara, making her look pitiful. There were lots of other girls out on the street, and most of them were younger. In the dark deluge, cars slowed to survey the merchandise, but no one was giving Sally the eye. She began to feel too damn old for her occupation, but the truth was that all she had left was the twenty that Nick had given her the last time she hit him up. Once it became clear that she wasn't going to make any money, she headed to the diner, where she could get a hot cup of coffee and sit for a spell to rest her aching feet and figure out what to do next.

Sally sat in the booth closest to the door. It was a habit from all the times she had to make a quick getaway. A waitress wearing a brown nylon dress and fuzzy slippers took her order. Sally imagined that at the rate she was feeling her age, she might have to start wearing her bedroom slippers while turning tricks. The waitress brought her coffee, and Sally avoided her eyes; she couldn't bear seeing the sour disappointment in her waitress's face. What did she herself want from her life? She'd had all sorts of stupid dreams when she was a kid. She'd wanted to be a ballerina or a princess, or live in a palace and sleep in a big brass bed.

Nick was the only man who ever even came close to trying to make some of her dreams come true. It wasn't a palace, but a cozy cottage set back from the road where they moved after he married her. She never forgot how he swept her up in his arms and carried her over the threshold into the bedroom, where he laid her down on that brand-new brass bed.

Now, sipping her coffee slowly, making it last so the waitress wouldn't kick her back out into the rain, Sally couldn't figure out why she'd blown it with him. She'd tried so hard to make it work. She'd cooked up new recipes, planted a garden, kept the cottage clean, and dolled herself up for Nick before he came home every night. But their little love shack was miles from anywhere, and she didn't have a car. Nick gave her money for groceries and odds and ends. He would buy her little gifts, but she never had money of her own, and she didn't have any friends.

Sally had too much time to dwell on her horrible childhood and her battered mother and her rotten father, who broke her nose and threw her out in the streets at fifteen when he found out she was pregnant. She could never blot out the pain of the days that followed: she was raped by a truck driver and almost bled to death from the miscarriage she'd had in a gas station restroom while hitchhiking to Houston. Before long the normal routine of her safe marriage just wasn't enough, and she started thinking about the rush of the needle in her arm and the dive into that happy place where there was no pain or memories.

She zipped open her boot and rummaged out the twenty to pay for her coffee, then sat waiting for the change. The front page of a newspaper left in the next booth caught her eye. It was like she'd conjured Nick up just by thinking about him—the headline was about the murder case he was working on. She couldn't help feeling proud of him. The waitress returned with her change. Sally carefully counted all the bills and coins before she zipped them back into her boot, grabbing the paper as she went out the door.

Back on the street, that wad of ones and fives in her boot made her foot ache worse than before. The rain fell down hard on her face, spattering down on her head before she could duck back under an awning. She watched as cars stopped for the younger girls, but no one stopped for her. She was all alone: no man, no friends, no pimp. All she had was nineteen crumpled dollars and some loose change in her trashy hooker boots.

She took a deep breath, and a voice in her head, an angel's voice, maybe her mother's, or Nick's, spoke softly: *You don't have to do this anymore. You can have a better life.* Right then and there she decided to take that newspaper with the story of Nick's case on the front page and go back to her rented room; there she would read the want ads for an honest job.

She remembered how Nick had stopped gambling for her. Now she would stop turning tricks again for him. Maybe she was crazy and only hearing voices, or maybe she was finally getting sane. Either way, she had mixed feelings of fear and excitement. She nearly ran down the street to her room at the sleazy motel.

Inside her room, she unzipped her boots, throwing them down on the ratty shag carpet; she piled the bills on the little nightstand.

She would start from the bottom up. She washed all the makeup off her face and looked at herself in the discolored mirror. Without the heavy makeup she looked young, and she remembered how beautiful she'd been as a girl before her father broke her nose. She had thrown herself away because she believed she deserved nothing, but if she could be pretty again and prove to herself that she too could work and stay away from hooking and junk, she could win Nick back.

She realized a man like Nick was all she ever wanted. She went to her bedside and for the first time since she was a little girl, she fell on her knees and prayed.

CHAPTER 11

Rain fell all day, and Noelle and Lopez wasted their time following up on leads that went nowhere. They had been over Angel Perez's testimony, and Lopez learned that Perez's alibi was ironclad. He had been in Huntsville, Texas, welcoming his first grandchild when Julia Brunswick was left in the bayou. They found over ten witnesses who saw him there over that long weekend.

Noelle wasted more time arguing with Donnelly about bringing Jimmy Brunswick in for questioning. He didn't think Jimmy had killed his sister, but he did think he was keeping some cards very close to his vest. Jimmy's adamant way of protecting his family pissed Noelle off.

Donnelly stuck to his guns. "Keep the Brunswicks out of it and stay focused on the druggies and psychos."

"What about Pamela O'Leary?" Noelle asked, careful to hold his poker face. "The girls at the country club said Julia was close to Pamela."

"Yes, good. Get something out of her, for Christ's sake!"

That was just what Noelle was hoping to do. He was angry that Donnelly wouldn't let him talk to Jimmy but refused to let it stop him. One way or the other, he'd get to him.

It was nearly six o'clock and the rain had dried right up, but water steamed up from the streets, creating a hot fog over the city. The Galleria was a mob scene. At the ice rink, a competition was going on and people leaned over the rails, watching girls skate past in short dresses. Noelle stopped in at a men's store to buy a new blue tie, then drank a coffee waiting at the Bar & Coffee Hut, where he was to meet Pamela after her shift let out. Noelle kept checking his watch and ordering refills, and finally, a half hour later, Pamela strolled up to him, smiling that shy grin that made him forget how long he had waited.

"I'm sorry, Detective. Someone stole some expensive jewelry and security had to check our purses before we could leave." She shook back that shiny platinum blonde hair and complimented him on his new tie.

He felt his face getting red. She'd think him a fool if she knew how excited he was to be there with her. Pamela took off her pink suit jacket and folded it onto the empty chair beside her. He waited until he had her full attention again and asked, "Do you know a guy named Chris Porter?"

"I don't think so. Should I?"

"He was Julia's junkie boyfriend; he told us that just before we found her body, she had called a friend to come get her. Lauren and Jennifer told me she was closer to you than to either of them. According to Chris, Julia was leaving him to go back to her folks' place to reveal some secret to her family."

"You're thinking that friend was me?" Her blue eyes flashed with anger. "If I knew anything about Julia's whereabouts at that time, don't you think I would have told you?"

He could see that she was upset. He offered to buy her a beer and decided to have one too. He had had enough coffee to keep him up till a week of Sundays.

"Yes, a beer. Thanks."

From the bar, he turned to observe her. She was wiping her eyes with a tissue. He felt like a heel for trying to play bad cop. She was just a girl trying to get ahead in life. After everything Lauren Love and Jennifer Colby had said about her, he could understand why she needed an older man to take care of her. Unfortunately he also knew he'd have to win a lot more hands at poker to spend the kind of money on her she was accustomed to. He paid and carried the beers back to their table.

She sipped at hers and said, "I was thinking about who Julia might have called. Have you asked Marianna de Pucci? They were best friends at one time. Or Jimmy, she'd have called him before anyone else." She smiled with a timid turn of her lips.

"The top brass don't want me disturbing the Brunswicks in their grief."

He wanted to ask more and more questions, just to keep her there.

"Do you know if Jimmy and his uncle George are close?"

She blushed. "I suppose, but George is a lot older."

"You call him George?"

"Yes, Detective, he's my friend too."

"A friend like Jimmy?"

She laughed. "I told you, I dated Jimmy when we were kids. Now I'm all grown up, you see?" She opened her arms, displaying herself to him. "George is a different kind of special friend."

"Huh. What kind, exactly?" He wished she knew that he had seen her that night at Sam's with George Brunswick.

"George is a good friend and a great man. He gives more of his wealth away than any of his family, even Mr. James, who has much more. If you must know, Detective, we see each other socially sometimes."

The tables all around them were filling up with customers, and the loud girls in ice-skating skirts chattered all around them.

Noelle had to work hard to stay focused. "I heard George's wife is the one who doles out all their dough."

"Whoever said that must be jealous, that's all. I'm very fond of George. Does that surprise you?" she said.

"Why should it? Every man likes to feel young when he's getting too old to remember romance."

"Our relationship's a lot more than that, Detective. We have plans; he's going to divorce his wife."

Noelle didn't know whether to laugh or cry. Was she really that stupid? "Really? He might just be playing you. You know that song 'It's Cheaper to Keep Her,' don't you?" He knew his words were mean, but he didn't care.

She scowled at him and said, "He's shown me the divorce papers."

Jealousy fired hot in his gut, but he forced his voice to stay calm. "Well, Pamela, I'd be careful; most men would promise a whole hell of a lot to a woman as beautiful as you are."

She didn't like what he'd said about Brunswick, but she liked knowing he thought she was beautiful. The only boy who ever called her beautiful was poor nerdy, schmucky Howard. Not even George, who she knew worshipped her body, ever complimented her on her looks.

She shook her hair back again and smiled. "Thank you, Detective, you're a sweet man." She gave him the once-over with a flirtatious tilt of her head. "I can see you're smart enough and strong enough to catch this killer."

He wondered who was playing whom now. "Aren't you worried for your own safety?" he asked.

"I'm shocked and saddened about Julia, but I haven't been scared. Should I be?"

"I'm sorry. I forget not everyone sees what I see, being a cop. Let me walk you to your car."

"That's not necessary. George is picking me up and taking me to dinner. Do you have any other questions?"

Jealousy twisted his gut again. "Not right now, but I might later, so don't go anywhere."

She grinned innocently and while leaving said, "I'll be right here if you need me." He melted into a puddle of self-pity as he watched her saunter away on those long legs in that pink miniskirt to meet George Brunswick. Donnelly would go nuts if he suspected what Noelle was feeling about Pamela.

———

Pamela waited almost an hour for George, but he never showed up. Exhausted and furious, she drove home while her mother's voice berated her in her head. She cowered at the thought of what Maggie would say when she learned that George had stood her up. *Think you got it hard—at least you got a mother. All I had was a father who beat me, then kicked me out after I got too old for his liking. You got all the chances in the world. Just keep your mouth shut, or men will see that overbite.*

I will never be like my mother, she thought. *I wish the old hag would die.* By the time she got home her head was pounding, and no matter how rotten she felt, she couldn't let her mother see her weeping. She took a few deep breaths and quietly went inside. As she stepped through the door, she could hear her mother laughing in the kitchen. Her mother was keeping company with a deadbeat loser named Michael, and whenever he was over, Maggie got happy drunk until she noticed Michael giving her daughter the eye. Pamela tiptoed through the living room toward her bedroom, but just as she made it to the hallway, her mother yelled out in a happy singsong, "Is that my fancy daughter coming home so early?" Pamela steadied herself for what was to come.

Pamela could smell the whiskey from across the living room as Maggie waltzed out of the kitchen. She was dressed in a bright pink and orange polka-dot blouse and blue jeans, a size too small, that made her ass and thighs look even bigger than they were.

Michael came up behind her and slung his arm around her. "Maggie, that daughter of yours is a beaut, all right."

Maggie snarled and pushed him off her. Pamela could easily see they'd both had more than enough whiskey, and the night was still young. Michael couldn't take his eyes off Pamela. Maggie, slurring her words, said, "If she's such a beaut, it's because of me. I taught her how to please a man. The only thing her daddy ever gave her was that ugly overbite."

Michael winked at Pamela. "Who's looking at her teeth? It's that tight little ass that's got my attention."

Pamela's skin crawled.

"Michael, you are such an asshole," Maggie said as she pushed him back toward the kitchen. "Go get yourself another drink. I gotta hear about Pamela's night with Mr. Fancy Pants."

Pamela quickly slipped into her bedroom and locked the door. Her mother smacked the closed door with her fist while Pamela waited, listening, until she heard her mother stomp back toward the kitchen.

———

Later that night, a frustrated Lauren Love drove around looking for a parking space outside the Lone Star. She finally found a spot at the very edge of the parking lot, where the lights were burned out. For a passing moment she felt fear in the dark so far from the bar, but she was there to forget all about Jimmy Brunswick, who she'd just learned was cheating on her. She opened her car door and unfurled her umbrella. In her black boots Lauren tiptoed around the puddles. She noticed a short man at the side of the building smoking a cigarette, so she hurried toward the door where there was light.

Just before she got there, the man was behind her. He grabbed her neck and dropped a cloth over her nose and mouth. She bit his hand as hard as she could and tried to squirm out of his grip. She started to scream, but he pushed something into her mouth. "Relax, I'm not going to hurt you" was the last thing she heard as she sank into pitch-black nothingness.

CHAPTER 12

The day after his encounter with Pamela, Noelle was sitting in his worn armchair sorting through case notes, attempting to make sense out of the few clues he had. A cigar butt that may have been left by the killer or dropped there by any cigar-smoking man in Texas was useless, especially now that they knew Perez was off their possible suspect list.

His phone rang and he snatched it up. "Noelle here."

The voice on the other end was loud. It was Donnelly. "Chief Cullen just called me. We got another one, out at the bayou again. *Goddammit!* Get Lopez and get out there right now."

By the time Noelle and Lopez arrived, cops were swarming the bayou with flashlights. The body was near where Julia Brunswick's had been, draped over a fallen, rotted log. Her arms and legs were cut off, and the face was torn apart, but her driver's license was pinned between her breasts: the photo ID of Lauren Love.

Noelle gasped for air. It was just what he had been afraid of. He felt dizzy for the first time since he was a rookie. He'd just had lunch with the girl a couple of days ago! He'd eaten gumbo with her and now here she was, butchered like stew meat.

"Boss!" Lopez said as he took Noelle's arm. "It's the same thing!"

Noelle made himself breathe in and out until he was steady again. "What's the same?"

"The rain! It was pouring last night and rained all day today. There's not going to be anything; it's all washed away."

Noelle pulled himself together. He circled the body, searching wider and wider, until he came to a track on high ground that wasn't washed out because there were heavy tree branches above it. There he saw two sets of footprints, one large and one small, and something shiny. He picked it up and scraped the mud off the hard metal—it was a Girl Scout pin.

Back at the precinct, he sat at his desk drinking a glass of milk, hoping it would cool and calm his gut. Brennan was on duty and ribbing Lopez as usual. "Since y'all are such hot-shit detectives, why can't you find any clues?" Lopez wasn't taking his bait.

Donnelly came out of his office. "Can it, Brennan." He dropped a file folder on Noelle's desk and announced, "We got a report on the Girl Scout pin. It's from 1955, and it would have been given to a girl about nine or ten years old, the right age range for both victims. I personally called Mrs. Brunswick, and she told me that Julia never joined the Girl Scouts, so it might belong to Lauren Love. You'll have to ask her parents about that."

Lopez added, "With the footprints we might be looking at a team of killers."

Donnelly cried, "Hell, any Texas boy who ever played cowboys and Indians knows how to cover his footprints, so why would these killers leave 'em there? They could be footprints of some lovebirds caught out in the rain."

"Right, and just maybe our killer has an imaginary friend whose shoes he carries around so he doesn't feel all alone while he's out killing," Noelle said in disgust.

Lopez, missing the humor, said, "Or maybe to point us in a different direction?"

"I think the heat is frying both y'all's brain cells," Donnelly said, giving Noelle and Lopez a dirty look. "Cullen's coming down here any minute, so I need you both in my office now with everything you got."

Noelle sighed. "Lieutenant, we have to get over to the Loves' so they don't hear about this before we can tell them."

Donnelly held up his hands. "I know, but Cullen wants five minutes before y'all head out there."

A few minutes later, Donnelly was back at his desk, tucking half a chocolate bar into a drawer. Noelle and Lopez were in the two visitor chairs, and Cullen had one haunch perched on the corner of Donnelly's desk.

"Fortunately for us," Donnelly told Cullen, "this victim came with ID. The Loves, as you know, started Houston National Bank, and, like Julia, she was very beautiful. Besides being friends, she also took up with Jimmy Brunswick."

No matter what Donnelly said, Noelle decided, he was going to talk to Jimmy, even if he had to drive over to UT and tackle him right there on the fifty-yard line.

Right now, he was getting pissed off, watching the way Cullen kept the crime scene photos in front of him on Donnelly's desk. They'd all seen it, Lauren Love's naked body, missing arms and legs. Cullen should have had the decency to put the picture back in the file. Noelle hated the way Cullen acted like the parents' wealth made these victims more important than any other poor girl who met the same fate.

"You need to get out there and beat those bushes," Cullen said. "Find the scum who did this. Check out the flophouses and the winos and junkies, ask around about any men acting crazy and violent around girls, especially rich girls."

"You mean half the men in Texas?"

Donnelly flashed Noelle a dirty look.

"Chief, we've done that, and we'll do it again if you want," Noelle said, "but I think we should look closer to home. This is a tight circle and we can't be sure someone in one of these great Houston families isn't a killer."

Donnelly's ruddy face flushed bright red, and Cullen's look turned to stone while Lopez sat staring down at his own hands. Noelle's stomach dipped like a roller coaster. He wondered about his boss and if he was on the take.

"Well, for now, y'all got your work cut out for you with the junkies and the winos," Donnelly said. "You get that? Are we in the same camp?"

Lopez sat up straight. "Yes, sir."

"Okay, then," Noelle said. "But first we do have to notify the Loves."

On their way out to the Plymouth, Noelle couldn't help telling Lopez what was bothering him. "It's still not finished."

"What do you mean?"

"The killings. Whoever's doing this is going to do it again. I feel it in my gut. I'm still going to question Jimmy Brunswick. I don't care what Cullen says. I don't think he's a killer, but it might be someone who's close to him or after him."

Lopez shook his head.

———

It was late in the afternoon, and the same rain that had swept clean their crime scene had left only an empty sky burning like hell. Sweat ran down Noelle's back as he got into the Plymouth and started up the engine, letting the air conditioner get going before he pulled out into traffic, headed toward River Oaks. It ticked him off that Lopez wasn't seeing his side of things. He couldn't figure out if Lopez was stupid or just sucking up to Donnelly. Noelle found it hard to believe Lopez was just like everyone else: a star-ry-eyed acolyte to ambition and wealth who believed that rich people couldn't be sick criminals.

What he needed was a stiff drink before telling the Loves about their daughter, but there was no time now to get one. He calmed the heat burning in his gut with the image of cards fanned out in his hand, the chips in the pot, four aces, and maybe a chance to see Pamela at Sam's again.

Noelle and Lopez drove along River Oaks Boulevard and turned through the massive gates of a magnificent Tudor home with leaded windowpanes shimmering in the afternoon sun. Between the youth and beauty of the victims, the brutality of the killings, and the rich throwing their weight around, the case was getting to both Noelle and Lopez.

At the door they flashed their badges, and the Loves' butler, Lewis, led them into the library. Solid-looking, like his house, Mr. Love sat behind a broad mahogany desk with a sheaf of papers scattered across it. He had peppered hair and wore a well-tailored blue suit. "Lewis, see if the officers would like something refreshing to drink; I know it's a scorcher out there," he said.

Noelle for sure wanted something strong to drink, but he was so exhausted and so ragged that he knew a drink would put him to sleep right now. "Water's fine, or coffee if you have it made," he said. Lopez asked for a Tab.

Mr. Love scrawled something on one of the papers he was shuffling, stacked them all together, and said, "So, what can I do for you, officers? Aren't you the detective investigating Julia Brunswick's murder?"

"Mr. Love, I'm afraid I have some bad news. Another body was found today, and we have identified her. I'm so sorry to have to tell you that it is your daughter, Lauren."

Mr. Love's face paled as he rose from his desk, staggered to the cabinet, poured himself a whiskey, and drank it right down. "No, not my baby . . ."

Noelle stood up. "Yes, sir. I'm so sorry."

Love's glass slipped from his fingers and crashed on the polished oak floor. His shoulders slumped, and his jaw and hands began to tremble. The butler entered with the coffee and Tab, noticed the glass pieces, and said, "Sir, I'll clean that right up."

"Not now!" Love shouted. Lewis set the drinks down and left.

Noelle said, "Sir, why don't you come and sit on the couch here."

"I suppose we'll need to tell my wife, but let's leave her out of it for now. She'll never be able to take it," Love said as he covered his face and cried.

"Anything you can tell us will be helpful," Noelle said.

The door burst open and a woman in a summery yellow dress and matching heels rushed in. Noelle could see that she looked just like her daughter, with auburn hair and beautiful skin. "Honey, I just heard on the news there's been another murder. I heard a crash in here. Are you all right?"

Love held out his arms to her. "It's our baby," he said.

She backed away, her face drawn, her green eyes wide, and screamed, "My God!"

"Please, ma'am, sit down here beside your husband," Lopez said as he took her arm and tried to guide her.

"No! Tell me you're lying! It can't be, it just can't be."

Mr. Love choked out words. "Darling, you have to be brave. Our Lauren is the girl who's been murdered."

Mrs. Love turned on Noelle and Lopez. "I won't believe it. There must be some kind of mistake. Lauren is a good girl. She was nothing like that Julia! She has her whole life in front of her. She was practically engaged to Jimmy Brunswick."

Noelle caught Lopez's glance. He could read the look on his face, thinking that even in grief Mrs. Love could throw Julia to the wolves. Lopez said, "Mrs. Love, I am so sorry, but there is no doubt that the body we found this morning is Lauren. We have already received the findings that match her dental records, and the killer left her driver's license at the crime scene."

Mrs. Love sank back down on the couch beside her husband. "But that doesn't prove anything," Mrs. Love said as she began to sob. "Did she suffer?"

"No, ma'am," Noelle lied. At some point the Loves would find out their child had been hacked to bits, but for now he knew the truth was too cruel.

Mrs. Love looked up with a grim expression. "I want you to get him." She spoke evenly and coldly. "And when you do, I want him drawn and quartered . . ." She started to choke on her rage and tears and then went speechless.

Noelle said, "I'm sorry to have to ask this now, but do either of you know where Lauren went yesterday?"

Mrs. Love replied, her eyes bloodshot and teary, "We spoke briefly on the phone yesterday evening. She was meeting some friends at that Mexican place the kids like, the Lone Star. I told her not to go out in that terrible rain."

"Thank you," Noelle said, and handed her his card. "If you think of anything that might help, please call us, but now let us offer our sincere condolences. I'm so very sorry. Chief Cullen told me to let you know he offers his sympathy and will do anything he can to ease your grief."

When they left the Loves, Noelle and Lopez drove straight to the Lone Star. They found Lauren Love's car at the far edge of the parking lot, locked up and undisturbed. They found nothing else around it—no car keys, no footprints, no scarf she might have dropped, no blood. Inside, they questioned bartenders and wait-resses. There had been a lot of other pretty girls there, but no one saw Lauren coming in or going out. It had been just a regular night of Texas young folks drinking and flirting. No one had heard any quarrels or screams.

The morning after, Noelle woke up feeling sicker than a tortured puppy. He peered around his cramped boardinghouse room, attempting to focus, but his eyesight was still blurry. After the new murder and the interview with the Loves, he'd spent a long, empty, lonely night at Sam's staring into a hand of cards, wishing to be swept away by his fantasy girl. His stomach burned like he'd swallowed hot coals, and he had a splitting headache. As he rose from his bed, the case came into focus and he saw the pieces of poor Lauren Love's body in his mind's eye. "Oh, sweet Jesus!" he said out loud, and rushed to shower and get dressed.

CHAPTER 13

Chief Cullen marched into Donnelly's office, where Donnelly was caught off guard. His desk was covered in empty McDonald's bags and paper coffee cups. Cullen witnessed him in the act of finishing off the last bite. Donnelly looked up as he wiped the sauce dripping down his chin.

Cullen, in a stiff pressed suit and wearing a medal on his collar that the Texas legislature had given him, barked, "Jesus H. Christ, man, it's only nine thirty in the morning! Didn't Mrs. Donnelly feed you this morning?"

Donnelly snapped to attention and apologetically cleaned the wrappers off his desk, motioning to Cullen to take a seat.

"The old lady has got me on a diet. All I get is healthy food at home. You know a grown man can't live on that."

Cullen didn't mince words. "Donnelly, we've got a real problem with Noelle. I'm getting complaints from the Brunswicks and the Loves about how he's handling the operation. Obviously our good ol' boy has forgotten how things are done in Texas. Last night I was at Sam's at the private tables with George Brunswick, letting off a little steam. As we were leaving, we saw Noelle slumped over a bar stool. Sam told me that he had been there for hours bad-mouthing some of Sam's best high rollers and spoutin' all kinds of shit to one of his bartenders about the case and the Brunswicks."

Donnelly swallowed hard and spoke. "But sir, Noelle is a seasoned detective. It's hard to believe he'd act—"

Cullen tersely interrupted. "I don't give a rat's ass if that Cajun prick is more seasoned than his mama's gumbo; if he doesn't get with the program he'll be dog meat. And if this case isn't cracked soon, it's your ass too. You got it?"

Donnelly's face turned green as Cullen rose from his seat. Cullen picked up a half-eaten roll from Donnelly's desk and growled, "And for God's sake, man, get your shit together before I demote you to rookie on the street beat. The exercise would do you some good."

The minute Cullen left, Donnelly picked up the phone and rang Lopez's desk. "As soon as Noelle gets in I want the two of you in my office immediately."

———

When Noelle left his meeting with Donnelly, he was as jittery as a polecat, sitting at his desk waiting for his next interview. Donnelly had demanded that he bring Pamela in for more questioning. He was worried because he knew they would be watching his every move now, and he was afraid that Pamela would blow it and say something about the time they had spent after Julia's funeral, after he caught her with the cocaine. He wasn't sure how it would go down.

When Pamela arrived in a short, sexy, turquoise dress, Donnelly greeted her and showed her to the grill room and left her waiting for Noelle there. He and Lopez watched her outside the two-way mirror as she sat in one of the metal chairs and crossed her legs. Most people usually fidgeted while waiting, and often girls would cry, but Pamela just sat there like a mannequin in a shop window, with no expression on her face. Noelle nodded to Lopez and Donnelly and entered the grill room. He saw a different Pamela, nothing like the scared girl he'd first questioned on drug charges and again over drinks at the mall.

On the other side of the two-way mirror, Lopez said to Donnelly, "Man, she's cold."

Noelle felt empathy for Pamela. He wanted to protect her, but he had to look tough. He felt awful putting her through this, but he didn't waste a second and jumped right to the hard questions. "So, the Loves tell me you were the last person to see their daughter alive."

Pamela's big blue eyes filled up, and one lone tear rolled down her cheek. "She was my best friend. I begged her not to go see that drug pusher, but she wouldn't listen."

"What drug pusher?"

She covered her face with her hands and burst into sobs. "She and Jennifer always kept lots of secrets from me. They often left me out of their plans."

Noelle sat waiting, wishing he could touch her.

After a minute, her sobs quieted. As she wiped at her eyes and nose with the back of her hand, Noelle gave her his handkerchief. Pamela dabbed her eyes with it, and Noelle looked for motivation to get tough on her. He remembered how she had walked away from him at the Galleria to go be with Brunswick. That helped.

"Lauren and Jennifer told me that you used to date Jimmy Brunswick. Are you still seeing him?" Noelle said.

"No." She sat up, her face fierce and insistent. "Detective Noelle, I'm finished with him now. That night at the Lone Star with Jennifer and Marianna was terrible. We were all concerned about Lauren. In all that bad weather we were afraid she'd gotten into an accident or something."

"She was there. We found her car in the parking lot."

Pamela looked at Noelle with a childlike fright. "When I heard the news about her, I got so scared. Detective—what if I'm next?"

That was the thought that tortured Noelle too, how the two victims were connected to Jimmy. "Do you want police protection?" Silently, he begged her to say yes.

Pamela shook her head no; her voice got higher with tension. "I'd have to tell my mother why you were guarding me, and that would really upset her."

She clutched Noelle's handkerchief as he asked the next question. "I suppose you knew that Lauren was dating Jimmy when I last spoke to her and Jennifer at the country club."

Pamela's lips tightened as she answered. "The new rumor at the Lone Star that night was that Jimmy had been cheating on Lauren with Marianna. That's why she went looking for drugs. She was really upset when she asked us to meet her there. We were so worried. Marianna was one of her best friends. Are you asking Jennifer about this too?"

Noelle said, "Don't worry your pretty little head about my job. I plan to. Jennifer had told me that Marianna was dating some older man. Do you have any idea who that might be?"

Pamela began to weep. "They all dated older men just for kicks sometimes, but Jimmy was the real catch. Marianna had dated Richard Lowden a few times, but I don't know if it was serious. From what they told me, Lauren and Jennifer had socialized on occasion with Marianna and Richard, maybe even George Brunswick. They were all socially connected families, except for Richard."

Noelle was careful not to ask anything more about George Brunswick since he knew they were being watched.

"Well, Pamela, we might call you in again. See if you can remember any other names. It would be a big help to us."

Pamela's face knotted up with tension. She reached across the table and grabbed Noelle's hand. "Please, promise me you won't say anything if my mother's at home when you call."

Uncomfortable with the other cops seeing her hold on to him, Noelle eased his hand from her grip. "We'll do our best to keep your mother from worrying about you."

He escorted Pamela out of the room to the elevator. Noelle wiped his hand on his pant leg; her hands had been sweating. She was scared—some brutal killer was out there killing her friends— but Noelle wasn't sure whom she feared more, her mother or the killer.

"If you're afraid of something, you can call me anytime, Miss O'Leary," he said.

Her smile was bright and grateful. "Detective, I'd feel a whole lot better knowing you were looking out for me."

His mouth dried. "I'll do that."

She touched his arm lightly. "Good."

———

The following day, Noelle awoke from fitful sleep with his head pounding and his throat dry. He immediately recalled a night-mare he'd been having about Pamela and his ex-wife, Sally. In the dream, some monsterlike man wearing S&M leather duds and a hooded mask was directing a match between the two women in a mud-wrestling pit while they battled to the death. He woke up just as it got really bloody. He dismissed his hangover nightmare and went straight to obsessing about Pamela again. Every time he thought of her, he felt twenty years younger. She had this way of looking at him that made him think that was how she saw him too, like he was still good-looking and full of piss. He knew getting close to her could pay off, and he could protect her if she was in grave danger. He picked up his phone and dialed her number. He'd memorized it the first time he questioned her. "Pamela?"

Her voice was a soft purr. "Yes?"

"Do you know who this is?" She laughed, and he sat up straighter in bed, his headache suddenly gone. "Of course I do, Detective Noelle."

"I want to see you." As soon as the words left his lips he felt like he'd stepped into quicksand, but he didn't care.

In a husky voice, she said, "For another interview, Detective?"

"No. I want to take you out."

"Tonight?"

Noelle sucked in his breath. He couldn't believe his luck. "Yes, tonight. I can pick you up at Neiman's. We can go to dinner."

"Should I dress up, or are we going casual?"

He'd been on a good winning streak at Sam's, and he'd spend every cent of it on her, if that made her happy. "Dress up."

Her voice sounded breathy, excited, and he clutched the phone. "I'll try to look my best—for you, Nick." She hung up the phone.

He leaped out of bed and took stock of his naked body in the bathroom mirror: shoulders good, arms muscular and strong, face older but with character, chin a bit dragging, stomach loose and flabby. He worried about that, but she had said yes to dinner. That was a start. He sucked in his gut and lifted his chin, thinking he wasn't so bad for an older gambling man on a good-luck streak, so he'd play the hand. It was crazy, the whole thing was crazy, but he felt like a kid who'd just scored a home run.

That evening, after another hard day at work finding nothing to help break the case, Noelle drove out to the Galleria. He straightened his tie, even though it was already straight, and brushed lint off his jacket. He'd spent his afternoon washing the Plymouth inside and out, by hand. He was taking Pamela to Rudi's, a homey yet elegant Italian restaurant. A gardenia corsage sat wrapped in a plastic box on the front seat. Should he bring that into Neiman's or wait until she was in the car? Was it an old-fashioned idea?

By the time he made his way past all the shoppers to her counter, his throat was dry and his stomach jumpy. She saw him, smiled, and waved him over. When he reached her counter, she took hold of his shoulders and looked him up and down. "Well, what have we here? Detective Noelle, you sure look snazzy tonight."

He prided himself on his poker face, but he could feel his face flush. He knew nothing was going to change the fact that he was middle-aged and had more gut than he should, but when she touched him, he felt like a million bucks.

She was a knockout in a flowing dress. "You're looking pretty good yourself," he said, his voice huskier.

She turned to the other lady working the counter and said, "Thank you for closing for me. As you can see, I've got a date."

Noelle escorted Pamela out of the Galleria. He opened her door, but before she could get into the car, he plucked out the boxed corsage. "For you."

She opened the box and lifted out the flower. There was something lovely in her face. "I've never had one of these. Thanks, Nick, this makes me feel like I'm real special."

Noelle began to pin it to her dress. "It's hard to believe no one has ever given you a corsage before."

"Jimmy Brunswick was supposed to take me to the prom, but we broke up and he took Jennifer instead. She got the gardenia and I never went to the prom." She looked up and smiled a shy smile, that overbite prominent, her eyes glowing. Nick leaned in and tried to kiss her, but she put her hand up to stop him.

"Oh no, not yet, you bad boy." She laughed. "We might be headed in that direction, but I'm not that fast and easy."

Headed in that direction; he liked the way she put that. He could barely think of anything else. As soon as he stopped the car at Rudi's, Pamela went very still. "What's the matter, Pamela?"

In a quiet voice, she said, "George comes here all the time with his buddies from Sam's. If he finds out I'm with you, he would put an end to us. I mean, we are practically engaged."

He thought a minute, his thumbs tapping an impatient rhythm on the steering wheel. "Well, if a woman wants a man to marry her and he's moving too slow, a good way to stir the fire is to show that man he's got some competition."

Pamela burst into laughter. "You know, you're right, I never thought about that. So if you don't mind me using you like that, let's go stir the fire."

Noelle came around to open her door, sinking a little inside. So much for all his dreams about that direction they were headed in. She really did want to marry Brunswick.

Rudi's was a cozy, elegant Italian place. Inside, the dim lighting and dark gray leather booths made Noelle think he'd made a good choice. He'd be able to get closer to her here. The waiter led them to their banquette and pulled out the table for Pamela. Noelle slid in beside her. He was carefully keeping his face shielded from the other diners, but Pamela's gaze searched the room. If she saw Brunswick or one of his pals anywhere, she didn't say anything.

Noelle ordered a bottle of Moët & Chandon, and they each looked at the menus. This whole night was going to cost him a mint, but he didn't care. The waiter brought the champagne over and poured two glasses, and Noelle lifted his to toast Pamela. She took a hefty slug and he sipped from his. He didn't want to get bombed. He ordered soup and veal scaloppine, and she ordered salad and chicken marsala.

"So, how are you coming along, finding that killer?" She looked so interested in what he had to say, he felt all puffed up again.

"Well, I can't talk about the case in depth." He couldn't help reaching out to touch her hair, brushing a strand from her face. Her skin was so soft. "But I'll tell you this—we think there's going to be another killing."

Pamela's eyes glowed in the candlelight. "You do? How so?"

"Because it looks like the work of a serial killer, which means he will kill again." Pamela had already drained her second glass. Noelle refilled it, emptying the bottle. "Go easy now," he said. "Too much too fast and you'll feel sick."

She laughed. "There's no such thing as too much—I like it all. And I like it fast too." She poked a finger in Noelle's ribs. "So, this killer has to be a strong man, huh?"

Noelle frowned. That finger in the ribs hadn't felt too comfortable. He could see the champagne hitting her. Her eyes were getting bloodshot and glassy, and she was giggling too much. "You know, I'm dealing with this case all day and all night; can we change the subject? I want to know more about you."

Just then the waiter brought her salad and his soup. She picked up her fork and ate half the salad in the time it took him to finish his bowl of soup. He asked her questions about her life growing up, about her family, about places she'd been—and he felt like he was tugging conversation from her with a pair of pliers.

By the time the waiter brought their entrées, she'd finished that third glass of champagne and didn't seem drunk anymore. She was talking smoothly, asking him questions about himself. He ordered a second bottle of champagne. He watched her start in on a fourth glass, wondering what kind of girl she really was. Some part of her had a big *Do Not Enter!* sign on it. As the night wore down, they finished their meals, and she didn't want dessert. Nick was tempted to ask the waiter if he could take that second, half-full bottle with them, but he didn't. He worried she'd think he was cheap.

He drove her back to the Galleria parking lot to her car, a red Mustang convertible, which he guessed was a present from Brunswick. He leaned in to kiss her good night, but she jumped out of the Plymouth, waving a hand and calling back to him, "Bye, Nick! Call me!" He waited while she got into the Mustang and drove off without another wave or a glance back at him. He felt like a real chump; she hadn't even thanked him for the champagne and dinner.

————

Lopez was at his desk early, combing through the list of the Brunswicks' and Loves' household help and contractors. He noticed two employees they had in common, Carlos Martinez and Angel Perez. Even though Perez had done special gardening projects for both families, he was cleared of suspicion for Julia's murder.

The other worker, Carlos Martinez, was the go-to guy for woodwork, marble, and cleaning fine antique furniture. He was known for building exquisite pieces of burled walnut, teak, and mahogany for most of the prominent families in Houston.

Mrs. Love told Lopez that on some occasions, when they had guests with children, Carlos would invite their mothers to let the kids watch him work and give them a little lesson about wood-working. Mrs. Love hadn't thought much of it at the time, but now she thought it might be worth looking into.

Noelle finally made it in, worse for wear, the morning after his frustrating date with Pamela. He could still feel the ache of blue balls. Lopez, all chipper as usual, showed him what he'd found in the files, so they decided to take a trip to Martinez's home in Bellaire.

Lopez said, "Boss, you know, it makes me a little nuts to see these rich white folks always blaming things on us Mexicans."

It was the first time Noelle had ever heard Lopez protest anything.

"Good for you, Lopez. I've been waiting for you to speak your mind."

Lopez sighed. "Thanks, boss."

Carlos Martinez's house was a pretty red-brick two-story with a small netted porch, larger than the others on the block. Compared to his neighbors, Martinez did well.

The detectives dashed up the front path to Martinez's porch. Lopez rang the bell. "If anyone spreads a rumor that Martinez is a suspect in the murders, no Mexican, not even me, will be safe in Houston."

Noelle said, "I know all about discrimination in this town. Just being poor is enough to not let you drink from the same water fountain. I'm sure being Mexican makes it even worse."

Lopez replied, "My only salvation is that I trust in my God to bring justice in this life or the next."

Noelle shook his head. "I'll let you worry about an afterlife. This is hell enough, right here, right now—this life, this city, these killings. There's nowhere God could send us that's any worse than this."

"There can be heaven here too. Look at those flowers, the toys in the yard. This house looks happy."

"Maybe for Carlos Martinez," Noelle grunted. As they stepped onto the porch, Noelle sensed he wasn't any closer to catching the killer. Nothing about this place said *crazy*. A small, pretty Mexican woman with a trusting face opened the door. "Yes?"

Noelle and Lopez both showed her their badges while Noelle asked to talk to her husband. As she led them through a house filled with beautiful polished furniture to the garage where Carlos had his workshop, she said, "Please, you must know my Carlos is a good man and knows nothing about who killed Miss Julia and Miss Lauren."

"A few questions should clear it all up," Lopez said.

At the door to the garage, she knocked and in Spanish told Carlos the police were here. "It's okay, Gloria," Martinez said. "Come in, I will speak with them."

Martinez sat on an unfinished table, a bottle of beer in his hand. He gave Lopez a look that Lopez interpreted as judgment against him for going after one of his own kind. The case was getting to Lopez more than he even realized.

Noelle explained he wasn't a suspect; he and Lopez had to check out anyone who worked for both families. Martinez scratched his head and said, "You must have a very long list. Half the city works for those families."

Lopez added, "We just want to know anything you can tell us about the Brunswicks and the Loves, and their daughters."

Martinez looked him straight in the eye. "I am a good Catholic; you can ask the priests. I've seen you many times at our church. I could not even think of how anyone could do such things."

"What about the friends of Julia Brunswick or Lauren Love? Have you seen anything strange there while you were at work?"

"I never saw Miss Love, she was always at school, but Miss Julia, when she was a little girl, she was very sweet and kind. Her father always was working, and her mother sometimes sleeping too much or out for charity lunches. Her big brother, Jimmy, always gone too with so many friends; I think it made Miss Julia sad and lonely. Only the nannies I see her with and sometimes with her uncle George. He gave her lots of toys. She loved animals too, but Mrs. Brunswick don't like animals in the house, only horses at their ranch."

Noelle's ears perked right up when Martinez mentioned Julia's uncle George.

"Mr. Martinez," he asked, "do you remember how old she was when her uncle gave her these toys?"

"I don't know the years, only she was little. I have done work there on and off for a long time."

"Did you ever see her arguing with her uncle or her brother?"

Martinez shook his head. "No, sir. Mr. George was always nice to her. Once, he gave me one of his cigars."

Noelle and Lopez looked at one another, both wondering if there was any connection to the cigar stub they'd found.

Noelle said, "Do you remember the brand of cigar?"

"No, but I'm sure it was the best. I don't smoke too much."

"I have just one more question. What were you doing the nights of Julia's and Lauren's murders?"

"I am home at night with my wife and kids always, except on Wednesdays, we all go to volunteer at the mission downtown. We feed the hungry."

Noelle perused the workshop, noticing all his tools. He could see that Martinez, although small, had strong arms and legs all right, strong enough for the killings, but he was pretty sure that he didn't have the heart or stomach for such deeds.

Martinez's eyes lit up. "I remember now that night of the killing. There was lightning. The houses on this street all lost their power. I went to my neighbors with flashlights and candles to see if they needed help."

Lopez looked at Noelle and shook his head. "Thank you for your time, Mr. Martinez," Lopez said. Noelle assured him as he was leaving that he would tell the Brunswicks and the Loves that his name would be cleared from the possible suspect list as soon as they verified his alibi. Before they left the neighborhood they asked around, and everyone confirmed Martinez's story.

CHAPTER 14

It had been two weeks since Lauren Love had been put to rest. Very little progress toward finding a genuine suspect for her or Julia's murder had been made. Noelle had even gone back to the Loves' home to inquire about the Girl Scout pin found on their daughter's body. Mrs. Love told him that Lauren and most of the girls in her circle had been Girl Scouts together, and she did remember that Lauren had won a medal for her charity work with the poor. She also remembered that shortly afterward, the medal had disappeared. At first Lauren was upset about losing it, but she never mentioned it again.

The Houston summer heat only grew more unbearable as the July fourth holiday was approaching. Everyone was afraid that the next storm on the move toward Houston would hit town and ruin the fireworks show. Noelle knew that was the least of his worries.

———

While most folks were home and battening down the hatches, Jennifer Colby was going stir-crazy in her cool apartment in

Montrose. She lived in the young, hip section of Houston and she loved her apartment and her independence, but tonight she felt like she needed a friend.

A strong rain was beginning to fall and drops hit the sliding doors of her living room. The harder it rained, the more her suppressed grief came to the surface. She had been holding down those feelings since she'd learned about Lauren's murder.

Her eyes watered as her mind jumped from one dreadful thought to the next. For some reason she started thinking about what she once had with Jimmy Brunswick, before he dumped her. She hadn't let Jimmy occupy space in her head for a long time. Why now, on top of everything else, was that old wound coming back?

She knew Jimmy was in Austin taking summer classes and could be of no comfort to her now. Marianna was always busy with her men, no matter how bad the weather, and with no one else to turn to she decided to invite Pamela out for a drink. When she called the house, Pamela answered and was curt on the phone. Without any explanation, Pamela sounded rushed or almost downright rude. She had just said she had plans. Pamela's abruptness made her feel even worse.

She looked through her bookshelf to see if she could find a good trashy novel to escape into and noticed her medical textbooks that had not been cracked open since Julia's funeral. She had signed up for a few summer premed classes, but with everything happening she could not bring herself to show up for them, so she had dropped them with the intention to pick them back up in the fall.

Friends be damned! She decided to go out anyway. Jennifer hunted on the Formica kitchen counter and in the couch cushions and finally found her car keys. She put on a raincoat and headed out to the Lone Star. Perhaps some new friends, some music, and a cold beer could wash away the thoughts of Jimmy, Julia, Lauren, and that ungrateful Pamela. She didn't need any of them clouding up her brain.

As she headed out of the parking lot, the wiper blades strained to push away rivers flowing down her windshield. She could barely see the exit onto the dark street, so she rolled down her window and stuck her head out and eased slowly into the street. A sudden bang startled her. She pulled her head back inside the car and from out of nowhere she saw a person in a clown mask slapping a hand on her car hood. He poked his head through her window. "Let me help you!"

She tried to roll up her window, shrieking, "Get away! Leave me alone!"

He grabbed the wheel with one hand and pushed something in her face. She smelled a powerful chemical scent and fell back against the seat. A bright light flashed before she blacked out.

CHAPTER 15

It was the second night in a row of heavy rains pouring down on Houston. Richard Lowden knew his wife was suspicious of the nights he spent out on the town with George Brunswick, so he came home early for a change. Priscilla only tolerated his late nights with George because she knew it meant more power and prestige for them, but if she knew that Richard had fallen head over heels for Marianna, she'd kill him. He had to keep his wife ignorant and happy. He swallowed the rest of his Scotch with a hefty slug and looked over at his wife lounging on the couch, eating her favorite pralines in front of the television. The sight of her sickened him, and after the booze took effect, he realized he didn't give a rat's ass. If she started to nag him about his drinking, he'd pick a fight to end all fights. Sure enough, Richard hadn't even poured his third drink when Priscilla started her whining and pouting. "How many more of those are you going to have? You know I hate it when you fall asleep down here because you're too drunk to climb the stairs to our bed."

Richard retaliated with a wisecrack. "How about I match you shot for praline? It's not the liquor that keeps me out of the bedroom; it's that fat ass of yours."

Priscilla's face turned the color of a tomato, and she flew into a rage. She threw the box of pralines at him and rushed at him, hitting him with all her weight. They both tumbled over the damask couch that she claimed had so much class. She punched with her ridiculous chubby fists, tearing at his hair and cursing him. He shoved her off and scrambled onto his feet. She just sat there on the carpet with her dress pulled up. The sight of her panty hose straining around her thick thighs sickened him even more as she heaved and cried, looking at him like he'd attacked her.

She cried out, "You think I'm stupid, don't you? Well, let me tell you, I called your office last night, and you weren't working late. I even spoke to your boss, Mr. George Brunswick. He said you told him you were going home before the storm hit hard. I was up all night with that horrible thunder and lightning, scared out of my wits worrying about you. No one knew where the hell you were. So tell me, what piece of young ass were you with and where?"

Richard fixed her with a deadly stare and said, "You don't want to know that." He got up and poured himself another drink and added, "I can't stand this anymore. I'm going to sleep in the guest room! Don't even try to come in; I keep my gun in there. If you even think of getting near that room, I will shoot your fat little feet off. You hear me?"

He picked up his drink and went to the study for the .45 that he kept in the desk drawer. He had a momentary fantasy about her fighting him with that gun; they'd struggle for it, and then somehow it would go off accidentally, and she'd end up shot right through the heart. He chuckled at the thought.

———

The next morning, as soon as she heard Richard leave for work, Priscilla got out of bed and hurried to the guest room to find his gun. The bed was all unmade, the room dark, messy, and smelling of hooch. She realized he was the first person who'd ever slept in that bed. They never had guests. She didn't even know why they had a guest room, although she knew it was something you were supposed to have. She figured Richard would have slept with the gun under his pillow, but the gun wasn't there. She even checked between the mattress and the box spring. It wasn't there either. "Fuck!" she screamed aloud, and went to his study to check the desk, but all the drawers were locked. Either he'd locked the pistol back up or he'd taken it with him to work.

All the fight went out of her. She knew he wouldn't really shoot her, even in the feet. He loved her, she told herself. They were a team. He'd always said that she was his best teammate. She blamed herself for the fight. Once she got the weight off, he'd look at her and see that girl he'd fallen in love with at the Maid Stone Grill. If she could drop that extra weight, they'd look so gorgeous together, the way they used to. Richard would take her to one of those society parties his boss George threw and someone would take their picture and she'd end up in the newspaper: the beautiful Mrs. Richard Lowden. All she had to do was quit eating those damn sweets and their life could be perfect.

In the kitchen, she opened the pantry and pulled out the Mexican pralines, the Pepperidge Farm Milanos, and the peanut butter. She threw them in the trash and poured Joy liquid dish soap all over her goodies. It was going to be so hard to give up her sweet friends! Her stomach still growled at the sight of all that lush creaminess going to waste.

She started to bawl, but she squeezed her fingernails into her palms until her tears dried up. She just had to lose weight, for Richard. She had to do it fast, too, before one of those skinny rich bitches got their claws into him.

CHAPTER 16

The rain had tapered off, but trash still swirled along the overflowing gutters as Noelle drove to work. Frustrated over his job performance and his failed prospects with Pamela, he had been making matters worse by hitting the sauce harder than ever. By the time he made it to his desk, the sight of Lopez smiling those big pearly whites gave him a headache. Just as he plopped down at his desk, Donnelly rushed in. "Brace yourself, we just got a call. Another body was found at the fucking River Oaks Garden Club."

"Shit!" Noelle said, as he jumped up and motioned to Lopez. "Let's go."

Noelle and Lopez sped over to River Oaks, taking San Felipe past the railroad tracks to the garden club. When they got there, they saw a few cops milling around with umbrellas. Noelle hurried out of his car with Lopez on his tail.

Noelle said, "I'm beginning to think the killer might be the local weatherman. Julia at the bayou, Lauren Love killed on a night it was pouring, and now this last forty-eight-hour storm." He shoved his way through the garden club toward the sprawling grounds filled with roses and flowering bushes, rare succulents, and a variety of trees.

Men in blue rain slickers stood around. Beneath the dead azalea bushes lay a young woman with long dark hair. Her face was crushed, her arms were mangled, and her stomach had been sliced. Her legs had been cut off at the thigh and one was placed over the other in the shape of a cross. This was something new. It looked like the killer was trying to make a statement or send a message, but what?

Noelle shook his head when he noticed Lopez making the sign of the cross.

"Lopez, it looks like our killer is a fan of the cross too. What do you think of that?"

"I can't believe anyone who loves God can do such a thing." It was obvious that the victim hadn't been murdered there. This job had to take a bit of time and could not have happened in an open public space. Her body had been brought there and set up as a gruesome sculpture among the flowers. Noelle tried to wrap his head around the killer's creative sick mind. The good news was that the risk of this public display meant that the killer was getting more out of control.

Noelle suddenly felt queasy as acid shot up, burning his throat, and he wobbled.

Lopez put a hand on his shoulder. "Get a hold of yourself, boss."

Noelle turned to him, surprised. Lopez, who'd barely held it together at the first crime scene, was now taking the lead. Noelle pointed at the cops.

"Where's the goddamn photographer?" Noelle barked. "I want shots of everything."

After the coroner took away the pieces of the dead girl's body, and after the cops had left the scene, Noelle and Lopez went back to their precinct. As they sat in Donnelly's office watching him eat a Danish and stir his coffee with his pencil, Noelle's irritation was palpable.

"After three murders, the only physical evidence we have is a cigar stub and a Girl Scout pin from 1955."

Lopez said, "But we do know that Lauren Love was grabbed from the parking lot outside the Lone Star and killed in the bayou, like Julia. This new body was also moved, so there is some kind of pattern shaping up, maybe."

Donnelly added, "Yeah, and you found two sets of boot prints, one a man's size ten, and the other a man's size six. We also knew that Lauren had been planning to meet Jennifer Colby and Pamela O'Leary at the Lone Star the night she was snatched. Who else knew she was on her way there?"

"Pamela told me Lauren had been upset because she learned that Jimmy Brunswick had cheated on her with Marianna de Pucci."

Lopez offered his two cents again. "Now we have the third body hacked up like the others and moved like Lauren's; this is our clue connecting all the murders."

Noelle shouted, "Except that they all knew each other and Jimmy Brunswick too! There's a whole lot of *ifs* and *maybes*, but none of it seems random. If it were random, it might be Julia, Martha, or Nurse Janet from the medical center. Lieutenant, you know I'm right. If it's not random, then it means it's closer to home."

Noelle informed Donnelly that he had learned from Carlos Martinez that George Brunswick had been especially nice to Julia, but not to Jimmy particularly. "And we suspect that old Uncle George might have slept with these young gals."

Donnelly gave him a hard look. "Don't say it out loud! I know what you're thinking."

"It's a motive," Noelle said. "We sure as shit don't have anything else."

"If you even hint at that, and the Brunswicks get wind of it, Cullen will be all over me," Donnelly said.

Noelle felt breath steaming out of his nose. "Your career or the case; I see you've got your priorities out of order. If I can't follow the evidence and get near the suspects, how am I supposed to solve this case?"

Donnelly's face was beet red, and he was glad for the distraction of his phone ringing. He held up a finger to Noelle. "Wait." He answered the call, listened, and slammed the phone down. "Damn it! That's Missing Persons. Dr. Colby just called in a report that his daughter Jennifer didn't show up for a family function last night, and she is not answering any calls at her apartment. Well, we most likely know who the number three victim from the country club set is. The coroner's confirming dental records right now."

Noelle felt a sickening fear. Julia, Lauren, Jennifer. Would Marianna and Pamela be next? "Lieutenant, we've got to put a watch on the two girls who were the victims' close friends."

Donnelly rubbed his temples like he had the world's biggest migraine.

"The rain," Lopez said as he turned to Noelle. "Big old gully washers the nights Julia and Lauren were killed, and now the same with Jennifer. If the killers want to get Miss de Pucci or Miss O'Leary, it'll be when it's raining."

"For God's sake," Donnelly said. "This is Houston; it rains all the damn time."

Noelle said, "Okay, I get that you don't want me talking to George Brunswick; how about his flunky, Richard Lowden? Or better yet, what about Jimmy Brunswick? He's had a long enough time to grieve Julia's death by now. Rumor has it he's slept with all his sister's friends. Maybe he knows why the killer would pick them. If we can learn that much, at least we'll have some direction to go in. It beats waiting for the next big rain."

"He's still a Brunswick, and if Cullen gets wind of it—"

Lopez interrupted Donnelly. "But, Detective, everyone knows that Noelle likes some friendly wagering on the Longhorns. What harm would it do if we took a little drive to Austin to see what Coach Royal's doing with the team? Sometimes you just bump into people and talk, like Jimmy after practice, right?"

Noelle perked up and was so grateful that Lopez was on his toes. He knew they would go straight to Austin right after they broke the bad news about Jennifer to the Colbys.

———

By the time Noelle and Lopez got done with their sad deed at the Colby home, it was approaching high noon. The flood zones were drying up under the merciless heat. It was a three-hour trip by car to Austin, and on the drive over, Noelle's fatigue hit him hard. He let Lopez drive as he rested his eyes. He couldn't believe only a week had passed since he'd been drinking champagne with Pamela. It had only been a month since he first laid eyes on her that night at Sam's after Julia's murder. The four weeks between Memorial Day and now seemed like ages. So much had happened: three girls murdered and another he now felt compelled to save. At least he had stopped obsessing about Sally, but the more he thought about Pamela, the worse he felt. He still held on to a slim strand of hope. Since the sun was high in the sky and there was no report of more rain in the forecast, he didn't have to worry about Pamela, or any others, at least for time being.

When Noelle and Lopez got to the UT campus, the football team was just wrapping up practice on the field. They watched as Coach Royal led their last play and then sent the boys off to the showers.

It was the muggiest day Austin had seen all year. Noelle could feel the sweat running down his face as he and Lopez trudged up to the bleachers to wait for the guys to come out of the locker room. Noelle noticed Darrell Royal, the famous UT coach, coming their way.

"What the hell are you guys doing up here?" The coach blocked their view of the locker-room exit, his arms folded across his chest. Noelle started to pull out his badge, but Royal waved it away. "I know who you are, so I'm asking again: What the hell are y'all doing here?"

"We were hoping to see how well your boys are playing, and we are looking to have a few words with Jimmy Brunswick while we're here."

Lopez added, "He might have some info on the case."

Royal looked like he was about to explode. "You got to be kidding me! I keep these boys so busy and tuckered out they don't have time to get to Houston, let alone kill anybody over there."

"Look, Coach. There are no suspects here; we're just fishing for information from anyone who knew the victims."

Royal fumed a minute and then thought. "Well, Jimmy left practice early, but his buddy Tim Henderson's still here. Maybe he can spare a few minutes of his time."

Noelle smiled. "That would be great."

"Okay, but I don't want you upsetting the boy. I need him solid. We've got a lot of hard practice going on until the season starts."

Noelle grinned. "Yes sir, we know that. Don't worry. I want Henderson in tip-top shape for the season."

Royal shook his head. "Sure wish all this could wait till after the season's over."

Noelle wasn't surprised that he seriously meant football was more important than finding the killers, but he hid his disgust and said, "I understand what you mean—this is Texas." Noelle did know Texas was football, but he was still pissed. "We'll get out of your hair as quick as we can."

By the time Tim Henderson made it out of the locker room, Noelle's shirt was soaked but his temper had cooled. Henderson was no surprise; Noelle remembered him from Julia's funeral. Noelle figured he was nervous, the way he kept wiping his hands on the tails of his shirt.

Lopez was looking down at Henderson's feet, and Noelle cast a quick glance there too as they both had the same thought—his shoe size. Maybe his would fit the boot prints.

Noelle dove right in. "So, Tim, what were you doing the night of May thirty-first?"

Henderson's all-American face paled. "The night Julia was killed? I was with Jimmy. We were both fighting over some girl at a bar here in town."

Noelle didn't relent. "Got any witnesses who saw you there?"

"Yeah, Jimmy, of course."

"Were there any other witnesses besides Jimmy?"

Henderson wiped his forehead and twisted his hands in the tails of his shirt. "I'm trying to think. We didn't know anyone at that bar, but I'm sure the bartender would remember us. We were pretty loud."

Lopez said, quietly, "Why are your hands shaking?"

Henderson's eyes bulged. "It's ninety degrees out here and I've been running in this heat for three hours and you're treating me like I'm a murder suspect. Do I need a lawyer before this goes any further?"

Noelle stood up. "Tim, believe me, if you were a suspect, you'd know it. We're just asking a few simple questions. Once you have your lawyer, we'll arrange for you to come to the precinct and talk to us, if that's what you want. But we don't want you missing practice."

Noelle waited a few beats, observing Henderson's shoulders sag. He looked like nothing more than a tired kid, with the weight of the world on his shoulders.

"Okay, Detective, I have been thinking about this. I knew those girls and it hits me weird that I dated them, except for Julia. Jimmy did too." He made a face, and Noelle couldn't tell if he was proud of himself or ashamed when he said, "Jimmy and me, we left a path of broken hearts. Maybe that has something to do with all this. I don't know. You can check with anyone. Except for Julia's funeral, I haven't been to Houston all summer. Coach keeps us locked down. Whichever times those girls were killed, you ask around, you'll find someone who'll know I was here."

"Okay, we'll check that out," Noelle said. "Do you know where Jimmy is right now?

Tim answered, "He left right after practice, said he had a hot date."

"Okay. Meanwhile, if you think of anything else, call me." With that, Noelle handed him his card, and he and Lopez went back to the car as Henderson headed in the opposite direction. Noelle cranked the air-conditioning in the car full blast and got on the road. Lopez could sense his frustration and almost read his thoughts. They both knew Henderson struck them as too dumb to plan these killings, and it was easy to see that he and Jimmy had some kind of tag team going on with girls, but it was more like sport between them and not revenge.

There wasn't a whisper of a breeze, and Noelle felt like he was living inside a dog's mouth, literally and metaphorically. The only heat Noelle wished to think about was Pamela. He worried that after it finally rained again, he would have another body on his hands. Noelle needed a beer. He suggested that they check out some of the college watering holes before they left Austin to see if they might find Jimmy.

"He's in a fraternity, right?" Lopez said. "If we stake out the frat house, sooner or later he'll turn up."

Noelle cruised around the campus, where there were preppy girls and boys carrying books, but most of the students were dressed like hippies. It was becoming the fashion, even in Texas. Noelle spotted three girls wearing sundresses and lots of jewelry and stopped the car. He got out and introduced himself as a magazine reporter. He said he was doing a story on fraternities and could he get their opinion on the best. He held his notebook and his pencil, waiting. The girls looked at each other and laughed. One of them said, "You mean, most popular?"

"Yeah," he said, "or the ones with the rich kids or star athletes." The pretty brunette told him Sigma Chi. He asked her to write it down in his notebook and she drew the Greek letters. He thanked the girls and he and Lopez drove around until they found the big white clapboard house with those Greek letters nailed above the porch.

College boys came and went, carrying books, records, tennis rackets, and beer. Noelle kept switching the air conditioner on and off, but sweat dripped down his back. Finally Lopez spotted Jimmy in his side mirror, coming up the sidewalk. He was wearing blue jeans and a short-sleeved shirt all tucked in nice and neat. Noelle let him walk by the Plymouth before he jumped out of the car, pacing himself so he'd be walking behind Jimmy. He nudged Jimmy's arm as he passed him and said, "Sorry."

"No problem."

"Hey!" Noelle acted surprised. "Jimmy Brunswick. How are you, man?"

Jimmy's handsome college-boy face turned bright red. "Detective, what are you doing here?"

Noelle shrugged. "Came over here to check out the team practice. You know I'm a gambling man. Want to see how y'all are set up for the season. Lookin' good, I think."

"Thanks."

"Say, my buddy and I were just going for a beer. Want to come along? You could fill me in on the Longhorns."

Jimmy was smart and wasn't buying Noelle's story. "I'm surprised you could get away from the investigation, especially now." Jimmy's eyebrows rumpled up like he was in pain when he said,

"I'm sure there's enough to keep you busy in Houston with the whole town freaked out over these murders."

Noelle knew he hadn't learned of Jennifer's murder yet since it had only been discovered earlier that day. "I'm surprised you didn't come home for Lauren's funeral. Considering that you two were practically engaged, I'd think you'd be expected to pay your respects to the Love family." Noelle said.

"I don't know where you heard that gossip. I never proposed to Lauren; I just gave her a ring, is all. The Loves understood that I couldn't get away from practice, and everyone knew we had broken up. It would have been awkward."

"Well then, before you run off, I'd like to ask you a few questions," Noelle said in an authoritative voice. "I'm sure you want to help me. Why don't you hop in the car where I can put on the air?"

Jimmy replied, "You don't think I have the heart to kill my own sister or friend, do you?"

"I didn't say you were a suspect. You ever think someone's got it in for you or is trying to frame you?"

"My friends were raised to love girls, not kill them."

Noelle smirked. "Not even the girls that wouldn't sleep with them? Rumor has it that you're a real ladies' man."

"Detective, none of my girlfriends were so innocent or faithful either, not even my sister."

Noelle got hot under the collar. "That's not a nice thing to say about her."

"Julia and I were close. I watched her going downhill and I couldn't do a thing about it. She wouldn't listen to me. I couldn't babysit her all the time. She was a grown woman, and I had to let her go. And with Lauren, I loved her but she knew the score; we all grew up together. If I hadn't dumped her first, she would have grown tired of me sooner or later."

Jimmy put his face into his hands. Noelle waited to see if he'd cry, but he didn't. Lopez put his hand on Jimmy's shoulder. "This has to be so hard."

Good for Lopez, Noelle thought. *Stepping up to the mark and playing the good cop.*

"It is! God, Detective, it's just horrible."

"So help us, Jimmy. Who do you think could have it in for you?"

Jimmy made a disgusted face. "Man, who doesn't? In case you haven't noticed, even the rich and powerful have their problems."

Noelle sat forward and said, "Oh yeah, because you're a Brunswick, how can I forget?"

Noelle half wished Jimmy was the killer, since he'd get some satisfaction out of slapping the cuffs on him.

"Jimmy, you've got dead gals surrounding you, and we're afraid there might be others. We heard a rumor that you cheated on Lauren. We need to figure out the common denominator linking the murders."

"I don't know! I told you, there are a lot of guys jealous of me, but I don't know anyone who could commit such gruesome murders."

In a kind and quiet voice, Lopez said, "We've talked to your teachers, the girls' teachers, the gardeners. We've talked to Julia's junkie boyfriend, other drunks, junkies, hippies, nut cases, and the vagrants wandering through town. We've come up with nothing. Someone handpicked your girls, someone who hated them or you. So give us some names. Who else knew them and knows you, and who might have had it in for you or them?"

Jimmy looked down at his hands and picked at a cut on his right thumb. "Well there's Tim Henderson. At one time he was crazy about Julia, but she wasn't much interested in him. So then he got interested in Lauren but got sideswiped by me." Jimmy gave a helpless shrug.

Noelle sighed. "Let me ask you something else. Are you sleeping with Marianna de Pucci?"

Jimmy blushed. "What's that got to do with anything?"

Noelle was up to speed now, firing questions. "Maybe nothing, but it's possible that she could become our next victim. You should be concerned. What about Pamela O'Leary? Are you sleeping with her too?"

"I guess where girls are concerned, I'm pretty lucky."

Noelle couldn't figure out if he wanted to burst out laughing or slug the kid. He pressed his lips tight and said, "Who else?

Jimmy said, "There's another guy, got pretty jealous of me and Pamela once when we were together. His name's Howard Wolvensky. He's a real brain. Those are the only two guys I can think of right now! I know there must be others who got mad or jealous, but I can't think right now."

"What about Marianna? I heard she was Richard Lowden's mistress. Do you know anything about that? Is she two-timing him with you too? And when was the last time you dated Pamela? I saw you come to your sister's wake with her in Julia's car," Noelle said.

"That was the last time we slept together. When I learned that Uncle George had taken a shine to Pamela, I bowed out. I thought it would be kind of sick, almost like incest for me to keep sleeping with her."

"Sick if you slept with her after him, or the other way around?" Jimmy looked down and didn't answer. Noelle asked, "Your uncle George, did he ever take a shine to Lauren or Jennifer?"

"If he did, he never told me."

"Would he have told you? Are you close? Was he around when you were growing up? Bringing you footballs and catcher's mitts, like uncles do?"

"Not really." Jimmy frowned. "No, Uncle George never brought me footballs or other gifts that I can remember. I don't think he likes sports much except for hunting."

Noelle asked, "What about your sister?"

"He liked Julia all right. Come to think of it, he always brought her presents, but I was older and didn't pay him much mind. I even saw him read to her in her room a few times. He used to take her out on his boat too, but he never took me."

"And when Julia got into drugs, y'all never noticed anything?"

"Not at the start. I mean . . . look, Brunswicks don't like to talk much about our family stuff." Jimmy swallowed hard. "Can we keep this private, just between us?" he asked. "The thing is, Julia had problems even before the drugs. She swallowed a whole bottle of aspirin when she was fifteen, and after that she ran away a lot, mostly to Uncle George and Aunt Charlene's house. He'd bring her back home, and she'd be sorry she got us all worried. She'd go to school and be fine, and then she'd do it all again."

"How come she'd run to your aunt and uncle's place?"

"Well, they're family."

"She and your aunt, were they close?"

Jimmy snorted. "Not especially; actually, she has some illness that makes her tired and weak. She spends a lot of time in bed."

Being married to George Brunswick would make anyone ill, Noelle thought. He wondered if Charlene's illness was something she'd caught from a guy named Jack Daniels.

"On the day she was killed, Julia called someone to give her a ride back to your family's house. Was it you?"

"God, I wish it had been. She knew I was here at school and the summer session had already started. She wouldn't expect me to come all the way from Austin." Noelle nudged Lopez; Lopez made a note to check that alibi. Jimmy picked at a hangnail while thinking. "Uncle George, maybe. Look, Detective, I really do want to help, but I have to go now. I have a date that is waiting for me."

"Okay then," Noelle said. Lopez set his pen down. Noelle shook Jimmy's hand. "You've helped a lot." Jimmy looked like he was on the verge of tears and blurted out, "Please don't tell the

guys at UT I gave you their names, and whatever you do, don't tell
my parents I told you about Julia's emotional problems." Noelle
touched Jimmy's arm. "We won't."

Noelle thought that Jimmy was spoiled and soft, but he was
a Brunswick, all right, and one of these days he'd be running the
town.

CHAPTER 17

Richard Lowden met up with George Brunswick at a nearby bar after work. He shared all the gory details of the knock-down, drag-out fight he had had the night before with Priscilla and told George he was finally done and wasn't going home again. George threw his arm around Richard and congratulated him, then ordered them another round. Without any hesitation he offered Richard the guest cottage on the grounds of his estate until Richard could line up a place of his own.

After a few more rounds, Brunswick took Richard to his new digs. Richard took in the place, immediately imagined Marianna there with him, and got excited thinking about all the ways he could take her on the crescent-shaped couch curled around the modern fireplace. A well-stocked mirrored bar in the corner of this playboy's dream pad reflected his slap happy face back at him. He wondered why it had taken him so long to leave that cow who kept dragging him down.

"I can't thank you enough," Richard said. "This place is terrific. I figured I'd be living out of a cheap motel on the highway, but man, you've got a real bachelor pad with class. I can't wait till my gal gets a load of this."

George laughed harshly. "Yeah, well, enjoy it for now, because if I ever serve ol' Charlene with divorce papers, she'll definitely grab this house out from under me along with anything else we own."

Richard sighed. "Well, I don't have as much to lose if I divorce that ol' hog of mine. I'm sure she'll try to get her claws on everything she can, but she doesn't know what I've got hidden away."

George cackled. "Well, we're in Texas, boy. You know what we do with hogs here. Dunk 'em in boiling water to get the bristles off 'em, then hang them up by their fat feet, slit their throats, and skin 'em."

Richard laughed uneasily and said, "I'd give my right nut to see Priscilla hanging by her little fat feet." He didn't really want to kill his wife, but he did want her to fade away without drama. Knowing Priscilla, he knew his chances of that happening were as slim as his winning a game of poker with George at the high-roller table.

Brunswick opened the automatic drapes covering the large glass sliding doors to his patio. Richard saw the swimming pool lit and shimmering in the aquamarine lights, with George and Charlene's main mansion in the background.

George said, "Why don't you make us a couple gin and tonics and meet me outside by the pool?"

Richard was grateful that George was eager to have him along for the ride when he played with cards or women, but he got chafed when George expected him to hop to his commands. He knew it was the price for George's friendship and for this generous new bachelor pad. He should be grateful, because without George he'd be a few rungs further down the ladder at Brunswick Oil.

While Richard mixed the drinks, George took the phone with the extra-long extension cord out to the pool to call Pamela. Just after he hung up the phone, Richard joined him with the drinks.

George was in a deck chair, lighting a Havana and frowning. "Every time I talk to Pamela, I start thinking about my poor niece Julia and her friends. I loved that girl as much as my own daughter. I'd like to get my hands on the sick son of a bitch who's been killing our girls. What a waste of youth and beauty."

Richard sat down in the chair beside him and handed George his drink. "I know, it's just awful. I'm so sorry, George, especially for Julia."

George turned to Richard and said, "My big-shot brother never once disciplined that girl. I know how to keep my kids in line. Believe me, if he had paid attention to that gal, she'd never have run off, choosing to live with the scum of the earth. I feel bad for her, but as much as I hate to say it, she got what was coming."

Richard was shocked at George's comment. He just sat quietly sipping his gin and tonic staring into the pool. He must have drifted off for a second because the next thing he knew, George was jostling him. He jumped. "You want me to make another round?" he asked George.

———

The day after the detectives got back from Austin, Richard was looking forward to his next date with Marianna. He wanted to surprise her with his new bachelor pad, but she insisted he come to her place instead. She said she needed more time to pack for her summer month abroad. Richard didn't mind since this would be the first time they got to spend a whole night together outside the hotel stays on his short business trips. His or hers made no difference, because in his mind either location meant that their relationship was moving forward.

As he lay back on a lounge chair at Marianna's place, he thought about the poor suckers outside in the dog-eat-dog world of Houston's hellish summer, where sweat glued men's shirts to their backs and vinyl car seats. He'd seen grown men practically drown in the thick, sticky air just trying to take a breath. But Richard in that moment was basking in Marianna's cool oasis filled with modern class and style. It was the exact opposite of everything he had at home. He was impressed with everything about Marianna and especially pleased that she wasn't after him for money, because she'd have plenty of her own one day. It gave Richard confidence to think that it was probably his style in the sack that kept her coming back for more. He assumed that young boys didn't have the technique he had when it came to sex. He stroked her beautiful long bare leg, and she let him, but she didn't reach for him and she didn't make those soft cooing sounds like she usually did. "What's wrong?" he asked.

She sat up and reached for a cigarette out of a platinum case on the coffee table, lit it, then rearranged herself back onto the chaise longue. Blowing out a plume of smoke, she replied, "I know you said you've moved out from your wife, but I'm not hearing any talk about divorce. You know, I think you're scared of your wife."

"The hell I am! I walked out, didn't I? I'm seeing a lawyer this week. I just have to make sure things are sewn up so Priscilla can't screw me six ways to Sunday."

Marianna made a face. Richard once again cursed the day he had been born to a father with no money and no drive. He didn't like the boredom he was sensing in Marianna's attitude that evening.

"Come on," he said, stroking her leg again. "You know we belong together. I don't understand why you let your mother make so many plans for you, like this trip to Europe you're taking. Why can't it wait a while? Once I officially cut loose from Priscilla, I can take you to Rome or Paris, or wherever you want to go."

Marianna pouted like a spoiled child. "I suppose, but I don't want to wait. I hate the summer in Houston, and with all my friends getting slaughtered, I'm better off getting the hell out of here now."

"Maybe there's some way I can clear things sooner and join you over there. I'm owed some vacation time. I can tell Priscilla I'm on company business."

Marianna's eyes flashed fire. "Priscilla again. For a man who says he's left his wife, you sure drop her name into our conversations a lot. You know, Richard, I have a lot of things to take care of before I leave for my trip, so I think we better put things on hold until I get back."

Marianna stood up to her full five-foot-eight stature like Aphrodite, stubbed her cigarette out in an ashtray, and crushed all of Richard's hopes and dreams in one fell swoop. Richard was hit by a tsunami and felt he was about to drown. Gasping for air, he started to stutter, "But—but—buttercup . . ."

She interrupted him. "Keep all that gooey stuff on ice until I get back." She handed him his jacket and motioned to the door.

In a state of shock, Richard walked slowly, like he was going to his execution. At the door he turned back, took her by the shoulders, and cried, "I can't lose you. You're the one thing in my life that makes me want to get out of bed in the morning. I'll do anything you want, anything!"

She pushed him off her and said, "That's pathetic. I suggest you get a hobby. Get a hold of yourself; this display doesn't impress me at all." She slammed the door in his face.

He stood at the elevator, baffled, and pushed the call button. Immediately the elevator doors slid open and Jimmy Brunswick stepped out. Jimmy nodded at Richard and sauntered down the hall toward Marianna's. As the elevator doors closed, Richard could see him knocking on her door. Rage flared up inside him. He should have known she was using his wife as an excuse to put the brakes on their affair. In his anger all he could think of was something his father used to say to him. "In the end, either you're one of them or you're not." And he wasn't.

CHAPTER 18

Noelle still had Howard Wolvensky on his list of possible suspects to question. He was interested to learn more about the Jimmy-Howard-Pamela high school triangle from Howard's point of view. He drove to the 7-Eleven to call Pamela at Neiman's. The phone booth was next to large trash bins on the road. Noelle smelled rotting food and sour milk as he made his call, and he held his nose waiting for her to pick up. The second she heard his voice, she said, "Why, Detective Noelle, is this a personal or a professional call?"

"What do you want it to be?" Noelle answered with a thrill, flirting with her.

"Oh, personal is much better," she replied, flirting back.

"I have a little more work left to do today, but I was hoping you'd have dinner with me tonight."

"Tonight?"

A kid holding a bottle of Coke banged on the booth and Noelle surprised himself by giving him the finger. He turned back to the receiver, his voice apologetic. "I know it's last minute, but with the case and all, I can't always plan ahead."

"Oh, I didn't mean it that way," she said. "I was just thinking how much I'd like some company, and here you are, calling me. I must have conjured you up. Perfect timing! I'd love to have dinner with you tonight."

"Great," Noelle said. They agreed on a time, and he hung up. Holding his hand up to the kid still waiting outside the booth, he called to make dinner reservations at Maxim's. He crossed his fingers as he called the restaurant. He hoped that afterward he'd get to take her to a hotel.

A half hour later, Noelle drove down black tarred and cracked roads toward the place where Howard Wolvensky was supposed to live. He wondered if he had the wrong address. It was hard to imagine a UT student living in this section of town, where unkempt lawns were cluttered with rusted cars. Just about every other house looked like it belonged to a scrap dealer. An old bathtub sat in one front yard on a patch of dried brown grass, and some houses were boarded up.

Compared to these homes, Noelle thought he was living high off the hog. The whole scene brought back ugly memories of his parents' shack just off a creek flowing from the southern Louisiana swamps. Noelle had been glad to say good riddance to that home of horrors. Here he was, divorced from a hooker, no kids, always itching to gamble, and now failing at his job. Noelle still knew he had become a better man for sure than his daddy, and he held on to that thought so he could live to work another day.

He'd just arranged a second date with Pamela, and he couldn't kid himself about that either. Pamela had not been completely honest about Jimmy, but he was a gambling man, and once again he was betting on a woman who could bring him personal and career disaster.

He wondered if Jimmy had ever been out to Howard's house. Jimmy had called him a brain, so maybe Howard did Jimmy's homework. Finally he came to the address he'd been looking for:

1157 Roster. It was the worst place on the block. He pulled the car over to the side and checked his gun. He grabbed his keys and made sure the car was locked.

Noelle looked for a bell to the house but instead found an unlocked screen door. He opened it and waited a second for his eyes to adjust to the gloom. He saw a color TV and a couch with matching chairs that looked like they came from Levitz. On the end tables, he noticed *National Geographic*, *Art Today*, *Science*, and *Time* magazines. He was pleasantly surprised to smell a fresh floral scent in the house. Not a trace of stinking booze anywhere. The sound of some classical music tinkled lightly in the room.

"Anyone home?" he called.

A woman, fifty or a little younger, came out from the kitchen. She had long, straight brown hair with a touch of gray showing. Her eyes were clear blue and she had a lovely complexion, along with luscious lips. She wore a peasant blouse and blue jeans, with hippie beads looped around her neck. When she saw Noelle's badge and the gun at his waist, her lips tightened.

"John's been off weed for nearly a year now. If you don't believe me, you can go to the Alano Club on Housner; he's there, speaking at a meeting right now."

He smiled gently. "Ma'am, I'm not here about John, but I'm glad to hear he's doing good. I'm Detective Noelle. I'm here to ask your son a few questions."

"Howard? He hasn't done anything. He's a straight-A student at UT on a full scholarship there. Ask his teachers; he's the top in his class, studying biology and physics."

Noelle saw how antsy she was and worried she'd fly off the handle when he mentioned the case. "Mrs. Wolvensky, this is just routine questioning. You read about the three murdered girls?" She nodded, and he continued. "We're talking to everyone who was friends with them or friends with Jimmy Brunswick. We just need some information about the crowd of girls he hung around with, that's all."

"Howard won't know anything about that. I told you, Detective, he studies all the time and he's not that popular." She shook her head, biting her lip. Noelle could see she was fighting tears. "I wish you would leave us alone. We're trying so hard to make the rent and keep our lives together now that all John's troubles are behind us."

"Believe me, ma'am, I don't want to add to your trouble. I'm just here to learn anything; even the smallest piece of information might help us catch the killer."

She softened. "Well, I know Howard does see Jimmy Brunswick sometimes. Not here, though. Whenever he's home, he's working on his projects outside. C'mon, he's in the back working on one of his inventions."

As Mrs. Wolvensky led him through the small house, Noelle noticed how clean and organized everything was. The two bedroom doors were open, the beds made, all the clothes put away. Everything smelled like freshly washed sheets.

As he followed her from the back porch, he picked up a faint lemon scent from her hair. It had been a long time since he'd felt an attraction to a woman close to his own age. He shuddered at the thought: first Pamela and now Mrs. Wolvensky? He almost laughed at himself as he wondered how many women related to this case he could sleep with.

Finally she led him across a patch of crabgrass to a big shed. Inside, under the bright light cast by a tall standing lamp, Howard Wolvensky was on his knees between two large metal plates.

Mrs. Wolvensky knocked lightly on the doorjamb. "Howard, Detective Noelle is here to ask you some questions."

Howard didn't look up.

Mrs. Wolvensky cast worried eyes at Noelle. He knew she was afraid he'd think something bad about Howard's ignoring her like this. He wished he could reassure her.

"Howard, please stop that and come talk to the detective."

This time Howard looked up. "Mom, I'm busy." He bent back to whatever he was doing with a screwdriver.

Noelle noticed all kinds of tools within Howard's reach. He could see Howard had skills. He nudged Howard with his boot. "I need to speak with you right now."

Howard looked up at Noelle, and the boy's face was empty, like the faces of death-row inmates before their execution. There was nothing behind his eyes. Suddenly, Howard's face brightened as he came to life. He wiped oil off his hands and extended his right hand to shake Noelle's. His handshake was strong, and Noelle took note of his large muscles beneath his T-shirt.

"I'm sorry, sir. When I'm working I get so involved I block everything out. What do you want to know?"

Noelle glanced at Mrs. Wolvensky, and she said, "When Howard was little we had him tested for learning disorders. He had a super-high IQ, but he couldn't concentrate. The doctors told us he had a touch of Asperger's and attention deficit disorder. But he seems to have grown out of whatever it was. Now he has hyper-focus. That's what got him his scholarship."

Howard gave his mother a weird look and said, "Mom, why don't you let me talk to the detective? Don't you have something cooking on the stove?"

Mrs. Wolvensky excused herself and left them alone. Glad she had left, Noelle felt free to push Howard more than he would if she were in the room. "Howard, I know you know that women Jimmy Brunswick and Tim Henderson dated were murdered."

Behind his thick glasses, Howard's eyes widened. "I know; it's the worst thing that has ever happened in our lives. It's just awful."

"Can you think of anyone who could do such a thing?"

Howard's eyes twitched as he removed his glasses and polished them with the edge of his shirt. After a thoughtful pause, he spoke. "I have given these crimes some thought, and I have to admit, it's weird that Jimmy's sister and Lauren Love were murdered one after the other. It got me thinking that it was possible that the killer might be someone who resents Jimmy." Howard wiped his hands on the rag again. "Jimmy's actually a nice guy, but he has a way of alienating people."

"Could you elaborate?"

Howard shook his head. "He throws his family name around to get whatever he wants, including the most beautiful girls in Houston."

Noelle glanced over at Howard's tool rack. "Would that include Pamela O'Leary? Jimmy told me you had been jealous of him when you found out they dated back at Kinkaid."

Howard fidgeted and answered, "That's ancient history. Jimmy and I have been good friends ever since. He even hires me to tutor him with his math and science studies. He's a great jock but a little slow in some areas. Pamela and I are also good friends."

Noelle changed the subject. "I see you're good with tools."

Howard dropped his friendly attitude and glared at Noelle. "These questions are bull. I've seen what you cops did to my dad. By the time they were through questioning him, he ended up doing eight years for dealing a little pot. Just because I crushed on a girl in high school and now you see me working here with a screwdriver, you want to fit a noose around me?"

Noelle didn't like his smart mouth and shot back, "I'm not that kind of cop. I'm not interested in framing anybody just to make the case go away. I'm looking for the real killer. I suppose you can provide me with an alibi for the nights these murders happened."

"Just ask my mom. I'm home every night, working here in the shed," Howard answered.

"Just one last thing: are Jimmy and Tim good with tools like you?"

Howard laughed. "Jimmy, get his hands dirty? I don't think so. If he needed work done, he'd hire someone. But Henderson, well, he's a whiz. He worked for his dad's landscaping business, knows his way around a chain saw."

"Good to know. Well, if you think of anything else, please call me," Noelle said, as he glanced down at Howard's feet. For a small man, his feet were unusually big. Just then he realized Mrs. Wolvensky had stepped back into the shed and was speaking. "I'm sorry, ma'am, I missed that."

"I was just offering you one of my special health drinks, Detective. You were looking a little peaked."

"I'm warning you," Howard said, grinning and friendly-like, "they taste awful."

"Thank you. I wish I could, but unfortunately, I've got to wrap this up and run to my next meeting." He took another good look at Howard's mother and thought that even if her kid was a murderer, Mrs. Wolvensky was alluring. He imagined she was the kind of woman who could save and nurture him, not like Pamela or Sally, who could take him down. He smiled a crooked smile, said good-bye, and left.

As he made his way back to the car, he reflected on Howard's mood swings. It was almost schizophrenic. He wondered if that was a symptom of what his mother said he had as a kid. For his mom's sake, Noelle hoped that was all it was, but it gave him motive to dig deeper into Howard.

CHAPTER 19

The third day after Jennifer Colby's body was discovered, the police released the news of her murder. While all of Houston had their knickers in a twist over the unsolved killings, Sally was busy working hard to turn her life around. She had managed to keep her promise to go straight. She had gotten a job as a waitress at a little diner, where she wore a pink and brown uniform. After a month, she had saved enough money in wages and tips to rent a tiny furnished apartment in a run-down building in the bad part of downtown Houston. She had also found an old clunker that she could drive around town in. An older lady let her make a small down payment and Sally prayed she could keep giving her payments once a month.

In her off time, she followed Nick's cases in the papers. After weeks of keeping clean, her curves started to return and she let her hair grow out to its natural curly dark red again. She looked healthy and pretty, and she couldn't wait until the day she could prove herself worthy to Nick. She couldn't help but worry, though, that by now he might have found a girlfriend.

Her new goal verged on obsession, and the first time she followed Nick she'd been jumpy as a cat. One night she noticed him leaving his house all dressed up and managed to follow him all the way to the Galleria. She knew Nick hated shopping and wondered what he was doing there, especially since he went straight into Neiman's. She was amazed, knowing this was not his beat at all, especially when he made a beeline to cosmetics. She was even more surprised when he said a few words to the beautiful woman working behind the counter. She hoped he was questioning this woman about the case, but then when he leaned in to give her a light kiss on the lips her hopes were dashed.

Sally sank back against a pillar, feeling sick inside. The salesgirl was so young and stylish—striking in a violet dress. She felt like a fool when she realized that Nick was clearly able to attract young, impressionable girls, just like he did when they first met.

Hiding behind the pillar, she ogled the woman as she stepped out in front of the counter. She watched as Nick helped her put on her jacket and offered his arm as they started toward the exit. They passed by her, never noticing her behind the pillar. She followed them outside and watched them get into Nick's undercover Plymouth.

She thought about racing to her car to follow but fell violently ill and stopped to throw up in a garbage can. She didn't need to follow them to imagine what the rest of Nick's evening would be like; her imagination did the job for her.

Now that she knew her competition and where she worked, she knew she could return. If Nick was in love with this woman, she'd better be worthy of him. If she wasn't, Sally would figure out what to do about that.

The next day, Sally rearranged her schedule with another waitress so she could end her shift early. She put on a plain nice white summer dress and drove to the Galleria. What with the heat and humidity, the people of Houston had filled the shopping center to luxuriate in its icy-cold air, blown sweetly through the vents.

At the indoor ice rink, Sally watched the happy, innocent young girls twirling, all decked out in their best skating outfits. She couldn't remember when or if she'd ever been that innocent. Now, at the ripe old age of thirty, it was too late for her to wish for another past. She had other things to worry about. She circled quickly through the store and saw Pamela working the same counter. Sally mingled among shoppers examining some handbags and looked at a pair of shoes. She tried on a scarf and set it back and then stood by that pillar and watched the cosmetics girl gather her things. She watched another woman come to take her place and followed Pamela out of the store and to the coffee bar. Sally kept her distance as she observed Pamela, who looked like she was waiting for someone. Sally sat down quickly at a table and ordered a coffee, pulling a paperback romance out of her purse to hide her face in case the woman was expecting Nick.

A gruff voice behind Sally snapped, "Pamela, I only have time for a quick glass of wine. I told you; I can't spend the night with you tonight."

She bent down like she was fixing her shoe and saw Pamela sitting across from an older man, and it wasn't Nick. So she'd learned two things she hadn't known before: the woman's name was Pamela and she was obviously seeing someone besides Nick. A hot mix of relief and anxiety trembled through her as she sat up straight and listened as hard as she could to their conversation.

"George, why didn't you call and tell me before that we weren't going out tonight? I could have made other plans."

Pamela sounded whiny, and Sally could tell this man didn't like it one bit.

"Yeah, with that detective," George growled. "If you think dating him is making me jealous, you're wrong." His tone was harsh as he pointed out, "I know you're not the kind of girl who'll settle for a life on a cop's salary—or maybe you would if he were a dirty cop and on the take. There are lots of those among Houston's finest; I'm sure of that."

Pamela muttered, "He's a decent man and he's crazy about me."

Sally heard the screech of metal on the floor as he shoved his chair back to stand up. She could see him go to the bar. She turned slightly toward the bar and saw him bark an order for two glasses of wine to the bartender. She wished she could turn around to watch the expression on Pamela's face. She was worried for Nick, knowing this Pamela could hurt him, badly. George returned to the table, sat down, and after a moment's silence said, "Tonight I have to go home and service my wife."

Sally heard a tremor in Pamela's voice. "When are you getting that divorce?"

George made an exasperated sound. "Would you stop trying to reel me in like a fat fish? I've had it with your interrogations: when, how, why. Can't we just sit back and relax and try to enjoy this cheap-crap wine?"

Sally thought Pamela must have smiled or touched George's hand, or maybe she'd unbuttoned her blouse a little, because George's voice was suddenly huskier as he said, "Later, when I'm mercy-fucking old Charlene, I'll need to think about how it feels when I'm inside you."

Pamela laughed. "George, you're being a bad boy again."

"I can be as bad as I want," George said, with harshness in his voice. "And you'll take it as long as the perks keep coming. Drinking this cheap wine with you is giving me a taste for swill; how about a quickie in my car before I head home?"

Sally could hear tears in Pamela's voice. "If you're going to talk like that, I'm going home."

"Do that. I'm sure your mother must miss you. I'm getting another glass of wine."

Sally heard the screech and crash of the metal chair falling over, nearly hitting her. What she didn't see was the wine Pamela had thrown in George's face. She bent down again and caught the back of Pamela as she strutted like a thoroughbred down the walkway, leaving the customers at the restaurant entertained.

She expected George had gone after her, but when she turned she saw George leave the bar carrying a glass of wine back to his table. He was a big, beefy man, and the glass looked puny in his hand. He flashed a superior smile at the assorted people still gaping at him. "Show's over, folks." When he reached his table, he set down the glass and picked up the chair Pamela had knocked over.

Sally got her things together quickly, thinking she should follow Pamela or maybe tell Nick what she'd heard, but then she'd have to confess to Nick that she had been stalking him and his girlfriend.

As she passed by George's table, she could feel his eyes surveying her body. Sally's car was just a few aisles away from where Pamela had parked, and by the time Pamela was pulling out of the lot, Sally wasn't far behind.

It was easy to follow the distinctive taillights of Pamela's flashy red Mustang. It was still light outside and Sally pushed her old clunker to keep up.

She followed her out to an apartment building in a low-rent district full of sagging old houses. It was a step up from Sally's neighborhood, but not where you'd expect to find the home of a woman who looked like Pamela did behind the wheel of a Mustang and wearing diamonds. She once again considered telling Nick what she'd overheard, but knowing him, she realized that if he was in deep with Pamela, none of it would make a dime's bit of difference. Her own sordid past never stopped him from caring about her when he loved her.

She parked across the street and switched off the engine. Nick used to say that a cop's job was mostly waiting and watching. It was getting dark now, so she switched off her car lights. She must have dozed off because the rain started again. She noticed it was nine o'clock already. Huge pellets started to fall from the night sky. She thought she should leave. She had just started her car and turned on her funky windshield wipers when the one on the driver's side just flew off into the gutter. She decided to stay put and prayed the rain would slow down soon.

A little later she noticed a pickup truck stopping a few lengths ahead of her car. She ducked down in her seat. The truck engine kept running and no one got out. Sally lifted herself up just enough to look out and observe the dark space between the truck and the steps leading to Pamela's building's front door. In a flash of lightning she saw the shadow of a female figure in some kind of cape in one of the upstairs windows looking down to the street, waving to the driver in the truck. Moments later that same figure in a black hooded cape got into the pickup and drove off. Sally wondered if it could be Pamela and started to follow the truck. With buckets of water falling on her windshield, Sally could see only brake lights up ahead as the truck slowed to turn a corner. By the time Sally turned, the truck had disappeared into the dark.

Without a wiper, Sally somehow managed to make it to Nick's. She climbed the stairs, hesitating before she knocked. She knew what he'd think, her coming to him at this time of night. Before she even knocked, suddenly the door opened and he stood there.

"Sally, for God's sake! What are you doing here? I was just on my way out." His eyes narrowed as he studied her face. "You look different. You've . . . changed? You look beau—" He cut himself off.

She smiled a broad smile, so relieved that he'd noticed all her work to stay clean.

"Well, you're here," he said. "Come on in."

Once inside, she got nervous about what she had come to tell him, and she began to babble. "Nick, I've gone straight. I know you have every reason not to trust me, or believe me, but it's true and I did it for you—because I still really care about you."

Nick sat down on the end of the brass bed, motioning her to sit on his armchair. There was a mess of papers and files scattered on the floor. "That's good to hear, Sally," he said. "I'm glad for you, but I've got a lot on my plate right now."

"I know. I've been following your case in the papers. Nick, I have to tell you something important about Pamela!"

He frowned. "How do you know about her?"

"I know it's none of my business, and you'll probably hate me for this, but I've been following you."

He flushed rage red, and she started talking fast before he could throw her out. "Yes, I'm jealous, I admit it. Nothing would make me happier than to be back with you. But Nick, jealousy is not why I'm telling you this. There is just something really wrong with that girl! I mean, how well do you know her?"

"What the hell are you talking about?"

Sally felt an aching pain in her heart as she spoke. "I followed you yesterday and saw you pick her up to take her out. Today I followed her from Neiman's to the coffee bar there in the Galleria and saw her with this older man and overheard their conversation. He's obviously her boyfriend."

Nick said, "I know all about him, and none of it is any of your business. For all you know, they might both be part of my investigation."

"If that's so, then you'll want to know that I followed her home to her apartment. Something told me to wait there, so I did. A while ago, a pickup truck drove up with no lights on inside or out of the truck, and then I saw this figure all in black, wearing a long hooded black cape, get in the truck. I couldn't see if it was Pamela, but it might have been. She was about the same size. I tried to follow the truck but lost them in the dark."

"Let me get this straight. You saw a truck you couldn't recognize pick up a person you didn't recognize in a black cape—and they drove off. So what?"

"Okay then," Sally said. "She asked that man George when he was divorcing his wife. I don't mean to be cruel, but if she's got this rich man giving her diamonds and all sorts of gifts, why is she going out with you?" Nick stood up, his mouth in a scowl. "I just wanted to be sure you were okay, with everything going on in your life. When I saw you with her, I wanted to be sure she was good enough for you. You know how you used to tell me to listen to my gut; well, I thought you should know about it, that's all."

He looked off to the side a moment; she could see him thinking. A crack of thunder exploded in the night sky. The sound was so loud that Sally and Nick froze for a second, watching harsh drops of rain assault Nick's window. His mind went to worry about Pamela—wondering whether she was out in the storm.

Sally stood up to leave and saw his eyes tracing her new healthy body. They both stood there a moment, looking at each other. He cleared his throat and said, "You look wonderful. I'm really happy for you." He proceeded to ruin the moment when he said, "You really didn't come here for money?"

She felt slapped. "No, I told you I have an honest job now." She turned to leave so he wouldn't see her tears begin to fall.

"Don't leave yet; the weather is frightening out there," he said.

She didn't dare turn back to look at him.

Noelle begged, "Just promise me you'll be careful."

He called her name one more time as she closed the door and hurried down the stairs. She sat behind the wheel of her car, crying a river of tears that matched the downpour from the dark clouds over Houston.

CHAPTER 20

Sweat ran down Priscilla Lowden's face as she exercised to her Bonnie Prudden album in the living room. An hour ago, just before he left for work, Richard had kissed her, whispering in her ear, "Your eyes are emeralds. No, they're more brilliant than that!"

It bugged her that she didn't understand why Richard, after just a two-day separation, had moved back home without an explanation. He had gone on longer business trips than that. She decided to let it go and was happy when he told her he wished to make their marriage stronger. She'd just finished her last stomach crunch when the phone rang. Even though she was plumb worn out, she made herself stagger to the phone, hoping it was Richard with plans to take her out somewhere special that night. She picked it up, her breath still heaving. "Hello."

It was Nancy Love, a distant cousin of Lauren Love's father. Nancy wasn't as rich as the rest of the Loves, but she still maintained a longtime membership to the River Oaks Country Club. For that reason alone she had been an asset to Priscilla. Nancy was her go-to friend for society gossip. Nancy hesitated before she spoke. "Priscilla, maybe I shouldn't tell you this, but if you found out I knew and never told you, you'd never forgive me. It might be old news by now, but it came through a very reliable source. My friend Betty Lynn has the same hairdresser as Marianna, that beautiful stepdaughter of the Italian Baron de Pucci. She happened to be in the shop and overheard the princess Marianna telling her hairstylist about an older man she was having an affair with. My friend also told me that she actually saw your husband out with her. I think it may have been early on the same night Richard didn't come home and had no alibi for his whereabouts."

Priscilla knew exactly who she was talking about and how incredibly young and beautiful Marianna was too. Priscilla's heart sank as she sat her sweaty bottom down on the sofa. When she hung up the phone, she bent her face to her knees and wept.

So Richard was having an affair with Houston's fucking royalty. She cried even harder. Richard was a lying snake and she'd been right to be suspicious of his homecoming. He probably only came back so he could guard his money from what she might do if she got wind of his wanting a divorce.

She had to do something to stop him. If only Texas had community property, like California. If she didn't play her cards right she could end up working as a hostess again; that's if anyone would even hire her at her age. It wasn't fair. All these years, she'd helped Richard climb the ladder, and now he wanted a younger woman. She was determined to get even.

She took off her dirty workout clothes and jumped into a hot shower. As she reached for her shampoo, she thought of a scheme to wash Richard right out of her hair and screw him at the same time, and not in the good way. She'd make his life so difficult he'd regret the day he crossed her. Just maybe she would be the one doing the divorcing.

———

Later that day at the station, it was business as usual. Brennan called out from his desk, "Hey Lopez, why don't you get more ice cubes for the swamp cooler?" He pointed to the tin tray under-neath the big box fan.

"Get 'em yourself, Brennan," Noelle said. "Lopez is busy."

Lopez smiled at Brennan. "You know, after decades of picking your crops and mowing your lawns, we Mexicans have built up a tolerance to the heat." Brennan's face flushed that Irish-boy red and he lumbered out to find more ice cubes.

Noelle looked across at Lopez with a small grin. Everyone in the precinct was complaining about the heat except Noelle, for once. He was hot and sticky, all right, but happy that he wasn't car-rying so much gut around anymore, thanks to Pamela and all the work he was buried under. Once again fear about Pamela becom-ing the next victim crept into his optimistic mood. The pressure to catch this killer before it rained again was on.

He sat at his desk, sweating like a hog at auction, reading through all the tips people had phoned in. They were garbage, all of them. One lady was convinced that the killer was her mailman because he had a funny look on his face when they spoke about the dead girls. A guy who'd been arrested three times for check kit-ing called to ask for a five grand reward to lead them to the killer, whom he claimed he knew.

Noelle's phone rang, and he picked it up reluctantly, assuming it was just another loony wasting his time. It was the desk sergeant telling him there was a Mrs. Priscilla Lowden downstairs with possible info about the case. Noelle recalled the image of Mrs. Lowden at Julia's funeral, strutting about like the Queen of Sheba and throwing her weight around. "Send her up," he said.

He quickly cleared his desk and told Lopez to observe. He knew this woman and how to handle her. She entered in a low-cut fitted white suit and extended her hand like she expected him to kiss her ring. Noelle motioned to the seat opposite his desk.

"Detective Noelle, is that right?"

"That's right, and you're Priscilla Lowden, married to Richard Lowden, who works for Brunswick Oil."

"Yes." She looked down at her hands and licked her lips.

"And you have information about the murders?"

She took a deep breath. "Detective, I trust this information to you alone. I may know someone who might be involved. I'm not sure, though, and don't want to waste your time; it's just—well—something fishy is going on."

Noelle introduced Lopez and told her he'd be taking notes as they spoke. "The person I'm thinking about goes out most nights and comes home very late, even in this terrible weather we've been having."

Noelle smirked. "What else is fishy about this person besides the fact that he's not afraid of getting wet?"

Her eyes filled up. "I know he's married too and must be having affairs with young women, probably with more than one. You know the baron's stepdaughter Marianna, the one who's friends with the dead girls?"

He had known she was talking about her own husband, but not that she knew about his mistress. Noelle commented, "Stepping out on a wife doesn't exactly make a man a murderer, but the connection to the baron's stepdaughter may be a point of interest to us. Can you give me the man's name?"

Priscilla paled and twisted her hands together. "Oh, I don't know. The thing is, I'm not a hundred percent sure. What would happen to me if this man finds out I told on him? Couldn't he come after me if he were the killer?"

"This will be strictly between you and me, I promise." Noelle smiled and patted her hand, adding, "But if it ever looks like you're in danger, you'll have full police protection."

She smiled a weak smile. "Oh, Detective, I'd feel so much better knowing you were looking out for me."

Noelle said, "So tell me, who are we talking about?"

Priscilla looked down at her hands again. "He's always been such a handsome man, Detective. I suppose that's why all the young ladies like him. I liked him, too, when I was . . . well, let's just say slightly younger than I am now."

Noelle grew impatient but kept his poker face tight. "Mrs. Lowden, I'd hate to be in your shoes if there's another murder and it turns out you could have stopped this killer but didn't."

"I'm afraid you may think I'm just a bitter wife and don't know anything at all." Priscilla balked.

"Then why are you here?" Noelle barked to shake her up. "All you're telling me is that some married man is having affairs. That could be more than half the men in Texas. Either give me a name or quit wasting my time."

Priscilla started to cry. Noelle handed her a handkerchief. "Detective," she said, between muffled sobs. "The man I'm talking about is . . . is my husband, Richard."

Lopez made a big show of writing that down. "Good. Now what exactly have you seen or heard that makes you think he's involved in the killings?"

Once she started talking, she kept piling more and more on. She told him about the cruel tasks Lowden performed for George Brunswick, like paying off women George had hurt. She told him about a problem at the oil fields outside El Paso, where Richard had had to arrange to take care of the Mexican workers making trouble for Brunswick Oil and how she'd overheard her husband on the phone discussing plans to get rid of them. As she rambled on, Lopez wrote it all down. If Richard Lowden had arranged for someone else to hurt or kill Mexican workers, it still didn't make him a guy who would dirty his own hands. "Tell me, does your husband do a lot of work around the house? Is he good with tools?"

"Why, yes, he is. He's always fixing something or building shelves and that sort of thing in the garage."

"Thank you, Mrs. Lowden. We will look into all these leads you have given us. Now just return home and act normally when you see your husband next. You don't want to send a signal about what you've told us or what you might think of him. You just be a good loving wife, like I'm sure you have always been."

Noelle stood up to signal that it was time for her to leave. "You've been very brave coming here. If anything progresses toward violence at home, just give us a call immediately."

"I love my husband, but I'm not sure of the man he's become." She stood and cast her eyes down, like all of a sudden she was shy. "I hope I'm wrong, and if so I hope I haven't caused him too much trouble."

Noelle kept himself from laughing. He knew right well she sincerely hoped she'd caused Richard Lowden a whole truckload of trouble.

After she left, he turned to Lopez and said, "I'm going to Donnelly with this to get him to authorize a trip out to El Paso."

"Please count me out of that if you can. I hate that place," Lopez said. "They murder spics for sport out there."

Moments later he found Donnelly sitting at his desk with a head of wet hair dripping on his shirt. "I dunk it under the faucet. If your head's cool, so is the rest of you. You should try it."

"No thanks, I have a reputation as a hothead to live up to. Besides, I gotta keep my hair looking smooth for the ladies."

Donnelly smirked. He wasn't sure he liked this new side of Noelle. "Marry someone already—then you won't need to worry about the ladies. So what have you got for me?"

Noelle filled him in on Priscilla's information. "I want Lopez and me to get some info on the murder of a Mexican worker that Richard Lowden might have set up, according to his loving wife."

Donnelly wiped off the dripping hair with his handkerchief and said, "El Paso? That's time and money. Can't you call the local cops to get what you need?"

"Maybe, but if it turns out that Lowden's our killer, and we didn't bother checking it out ourselves, the papers will crucify us. Tell you what—I'll go alone. Lopez can stay here."

That was all it took. Donnelly got on the phone and got the ball rolling with paperwork and expense money, and his assistant booked Noelle a flight out.

———

On her drive back home, Priscilla got nervous over what she had just done. Noelle had managed to put a real scare in her. Her fingers shook, and she felt like her mama used to when she had the low blood. She was afraid to stop to take the time for a snack. If that detective called Richard and he figured out she'd gone to the police station—why, she didn't know what he'd do to her. Last time they quarreled he said he'd shoot her. What if he really was the killer?

She parked her car in the garage and hurried into the house, running through the kitchen and living room and into Richard's office looking for his gun, but she didn't find it. She rifled through the drawers, but there wasn't anything interesting except for a receipt for sapphire earrings. She fumed, knowing they were not for her but for that rich-bitch baroness who could afford to buy plenty of her own jewels.

She shoved the drawer shut and wrestled through the cabinets, searching for his safe. Finally, she found it behind a framed poster of a Miró. In happier times, he'd told her the combination and she'd never forgotten it. That was an ace she'd kept carefully up her sleeve.

There was a thousand in cash inside the safe. She counted it again, just to make sure, liking the thick wad it made. She'd show him. She would buy her own little gift in gold—but then she thought twice about it. If she took the cash, then he'd know she'd been in his safe. There was no way Richard wouldn't miss a grand. Regretfully, she put it back. She pulled out all the files and ledgers, sat on the floor, and read through them one by one. Richard thought she was stupid, but when it came to money, she was sharp as a tack. She ran her finger down long columns of numbers, adding quickly in her head.

After reviewing all the bank statements, passbooks, gambling wins, brokerage accounts, tax refunds, and sales proceeds, she saw that Richard had more money than he let on. She could keep the house and buy all the clothes she ever wanted, have her hair done at the salon every day if she felt like it, and even join the Junior League. She might even get a sporty little Mercedes and never drive that crappy Fairlane again.

The main thing was, she couldn't let Richard squirrel it all away where she couldn't get at it. He was going to fight hard. Somehow she had to copy all these papers and ledgers and put them back before he got home. She checked her watch and saw it was only eleven thirty. It felt like hours since Nancy had called and turned her life upside down. Richard wasn't ever home before six, so she called the downtown lawyer Nancy Love had recommended. He told her to bring the papers right to his office. He'd have his secretary copy them. The lawyer would keep that set nice and secure while she returned the originals to Richard's safe.

She was so excited at the prospect of becoming free of Richard and still getting at least half of his money that she wasn't even hungry.

CHAPTER 21

Muffins could have baked under the sun in the oven of El Paso, but Noelle was glad it was desert dry, unlike the wet, muggy air of Houston.

He drove out toward the oil field, fifty miles east and thirty miles north of El Paso, stopping first in a little nothing town to meet with Lupe Ortiz, Brunswick Oil's field man. They met at a dim place where Noelle stuck out like a sore white thumb on a hand of brown digits. Noelle bought Lupe a beer, and Lupe told him about how Pedro Angeles had died a few nights after rallying the Mexican workers at the Bella Oil Field to strike for the right to be paid the same as the white workers. A month ago a bunch of Hells Angels stormed into the King Bar. One thing led to another, and Pedro was shot dead after taking a severe beating.

"You think it was a setup?" Noelle asked. He drank his beer straight from the bottle.

Lupe's dark eyes shifted away from Noelle's, as if it were too dangerous to look straight at him. "*Sí*, yes. I think it was planned out by the big boss. Pedro was a danger to him."

"Who's the big boss?"

Lupe's gaze shifted to Noelle and then away again. He hadn't touched his beer at all. Lupe glanced down at his callused, scarred hands; Noelle looked at them too. They were hands that had worked hard out at the field. "Only the Mexicans get the brutal work. We handle the hot pipes before the oil spills on the ground. Push the machines through the dry plains when it's hot as jalapeños out there, something like a hundred and twenty degrees on the thermometer. Even the snakes hide under the rocks. Our pay is next to nothing and all of us too scared to say a peep, except for Pedro. Pedro made us speak up."

"Okay, Lupe. Thanks for your courage."

"Please, Detective Noelle. *Por favor*, do not speak my name, no tell I talked to you."

Noelle stood and clapped Lupe on the shoulder, "Man, that's the last thing I'm gonna do. You're a good man." Noelle marched out to his rental car.

Out at the Bella field, there was a set of low buildings, white-washed stucco with small windows. He searched for the office of the manager and found the sign at the only building built from wood. He saw two air conditioners sticking out of the larger windows. He parked his car, and as soon as he stepped outside, the heat from the rigs blasted straight through him. Noelle climbed a small set of stairs and knocked on a closed screen door.

A fortyish man in a golf cap appeared. "Detective Noelle? I'm Randy Holte. Come on in."

Noelle shook Holte's hand, surprised to see a fancy gold watch and a diamond pinky ring. Holte pointed Noelle to a visitor's chair and sat behind his desk with a syrupy smile on his face. "So what can I do for one of Houston's best?"

Noelle said, "I know you've heard about Julia Brunswick's murder, and the other girls too. We've been working on a hunch that it might have started with someone holding a grudge against a

Brunswick or the company. When I heard you'd had some trouble out here, I thought I'd best see if there was any connection."

Holte's pale blue eyes lit up. "You mean the Mexicans?" He sat back in his chair, thinking. "It could be. They've been causing all kinds of trouble, actually staged a riot and shut down production for a few days. We just got Bella up and running again." He smiled flatly at Noelle. "These things happen; it's a dangerous world. I think that's a good reason to drink. You wanna join me with a beer, Detective?"

"Sure, thanks."

Holte reached into the ice chest he kept to the side of his desk and opened two Dos Equis, passing one to Noelle. "To good luck in this hot, cruel world."

Noelle lifted his own beer. "And to the Hells Angels."

Holte laughed. "If that's what they were. Who knows? I guess no one's been able to find the guy who put down Pedro." He shrugged his wide shoulders. "Biker dudes come and go, and believe me, they take care of their own. No way is anyone going to snitch on them."

"Let's get back to the idea of a grudge against Brunswick Oil," Noelle said.

"Yeah, the Mexicans. Sure, I guess one of them could have snuck off to Houston. Killing their rich white women is one good way to get even with the boss man."

Noelle asked him about records. Did he have any workers who'd gone missing for a couple of days, and who did Holte report to?

By now Holte was happy as a clam, drinking his second beer. He was having a good old time, chatting about his ambition to get promoted up to Houston like Richard Lowden did. "Lowden's the guy I report to. We don't speak much since he's pretty busy doing George Brunswick's work, but the guy complains an awful lot. He told me that his promotion to junior VP is all hype and not much more money. I think he was afraid I'd be envious or something. He has no idea how good he got it and how hard my job is. When Pedro bit the dust, I had an army of those spics around my family's home."

Noelle drank from his beer, thinking that if Lowden had arranged for Pedro Angeles's murder, the order had come down from George himself. He finished his beer and let Holte ramble on a while longer. Finally he stood and thanked him for his time and for the beer, wishing him good luck with his promotion.

Noelle wanted nothing more than to get out of the hellhole of Brunswick's fields in El Paso, but first he would visit the bar where Pedro Angeles had been killed. The King Bar was in the seediest part of El Paso, close to the border. Lupe had told him the bartender was a guy named Stormy. Noelle waited until it got late enough for the place to empty out some and Stormy would be free to talk. Close to two a.m., he got out of the car, hitched up his pants, put on his don't-fuck-with-me stance, and went inside. The door swung open, Western-saloon style, and smoke clogged his sinuses as he nearly slipped on spilled liquor on the floor. A few drinkers were still hooting and hollering, but eventually they began to leave.

"Stormy?" Noelle said, as he approached the bar.

The bartender raised his hands as if in surrender and said, "No, sir, I am not Stormy. I got his job about two weeks ago, after Stormy disappeared. I'm Danny." He had the kind of long shag haircut and shiny vinyl vest that made him look queer in Noelle's eyes. Noelle couldn't figure how, if he was a homosexual, he could manage this joint every night without getting a beating.

"I'm here investigating a murder."

Danny's whole face slammed shut. "I don't know anything about that. I wasn't here." He turned and began washing beer glasses in the sink, his hands shaking violently.

"So who was here?"

"Like I said, it was that Stormy guy, but he's gone and left no forwarding address. Just up and disappeared. That's how I got the job, and I need to pay my way through school. I don't know anything, and I'm sure no one else does either. That's the way things work around here."

"Yeah, I figured." Noelle knew pressing Danny would do no good. He knew it took a lot of juice to shut the mouths of an entire bar and to make a bartender, a biker, and his entire gang disappear. He also knew that more than likely George Brunswick had given the order and Richard Lowden had been the matchmaker.

Noelle spent the night in a cheap motel out by the airport and took the first early-morning flight back to Houston. He thought about how he would approach Lowden. Even though Priscilla Lowden had made an accusation, they had no hard evidence to bring him in.

———

Just as Noelle's flight was landing in Houston, Richard Lowden was boarding another flight to El Paso. After Holte had reported Noelle's surprise visit, Richard made the mistake of telling George. Brunswick ordered Lowden to get out there immediately to deal with the aftermath. Richard Lowden hated El Paso even more than he hated his wife, and he was furious that he had to fly out there because of that idiot Randy Holte.

The long drive out to the field from the airport got his blood boiling. When Lowden entered Holte's office, the stupid bastard didn't even bother to get up from his seat. He just swung around in his chair, kicked the lid of the ice chest off with his boot, and handed Lowden a beer. Lowden got more irritated, feeling that Holte wasn't giving him the respect of his position. He took a seat, and even though it wasn't past ten a.m., he accepted the beer, took a big swig, and said, "You fucked up, Holte."

Holte's face flushed. "Boss, I swear, I gave that cop nothing, and you know better than me that we've got all the parties' concerned lips sewed tight. They're all either paid off or running scared. I'm telling you, that detective doesn't know a thing."

"Oh, he knows, all right. He just can't prove it."

Holte shrugged. "So what's the problem then?"

"I don't know, but old George got his tits in a wringer over this. He made me come all the way out here when you could have told me that over the phone. Like I have nothing better to do than take an hour flight, rent a car, and drive longer than that to have a cold beer with you. He's just pissed about that dick snooping into Brunswick business."

Lowden slumped in his seat and drank more of his beer. He was dead tired from all the running around and from George treating him like a trained dog. And if all that weren't enough, Priscilla was going crazy on his ass, and Marianna, the love of his life, had pulled the rug out from under him. He wanted out of El Paso, out of his marriage, and out of Brunswick Oil. He'd love nothing more than to let Randy Holte take his job. Then he could say a big *fuck you* to George Brunswick and to his wife and go someplace far away from Texas, maybe Hollywood, where the girls were as pretty as Marianna. Lowden couldn't think of anything else to dump on Holte, so he downed his beer and stood up.

"Okay, Randy, if any cop ever comes around here again, don't give him any beers, and for God's sake don't joke with him about Mexicans. Never, and I mean never, say one damn word about me or George, you hear me?"

Holte finally got off his ass and said, "Yes, sir, I'm sorry. Please tell Mr. Brunswick I didn't mean to cause any trouble."

Relieved that his useless visit to El Paso was over, Lowden took the next flight out. On the plane he let the icy air-conditioning dry his sweat, but his blood still boiled every time he thought of Marianna treating him the way she had.

It was mid afternoon when Noelle made his way to Lowden's office. The sun was shining off the Brunswick Oil building, a monumental architectural delight in downtown Houston. Noelle was amazed that the mirrored surface reflecting the scorching sun didn't set off a five-alarm fire.

Noelle stepped off the elevator on the ninth floor into a maze of modern Plexiglas cubicles surrounded by some larger offices behind closed doors that faced out to a view of the city. Noelle wondered why Lowden, a junior VP, was working on the same floor as the clerks. He flashed his badge to the receptionist and told her that he was there to see Richard Lowden. The gal, young and tan with a Twiggy haircut, widened her big brown cow eyes. "Yes, Detective?"

Noelle answered, "Is there anything you can tell me about Mr. Lowden?"

She kept her voice low as she told him that Lowden had just come back from El Paso in a terrible mood. He was yelling at everybody after lunch.

He thanked her and asked her not to tell Lowden he had a visitor. He followed her directions and made his way to Lowden's office. Since his door was cracked open he quietly walked in.

Noelle watched Lowden for a second. He was jumpy as a cat, pacing back and forth along the twelve-by-twelve steel-gray carpet, staring out at his view. Noelle cleared his throat, and Lowden stopped pacing and turned around. His face drained when he recognized Noelle.

Noelle got right down to it, "Mr. Lowden, I need to ask you a few questions."

"I'm happy to answer your questions, Detective, but I don't know how I can help you." Lowden sat down at his desk; his hands were shaking and he attempted to hide them in his lap.

Noelle sat down and said, "Just doing my job. So you just got back from El Paso, I hear. Is that right?"

Lowden shook his head. "A terrible tragedy out there, but what can you do? The men get liquored up and sometimes they fight. My man out there told me you paid him a visit yesterday. That's pretty far off your beat."

"I heard Pedro Angeles was beaten to death by a Hells Angel. What I wonder is why a biker gang would do their drinking at a Mexican hangout?"

"I don't know, Detective. They probably drove up to the joint by accident. Must have been a gang from another city or state even. You know those Hells Angels; remember that incident where they started trouble at a Rolling Stones concert and someone ended up stabbed? Shit happens."

Noelle watched sweat bead up on Lowden's forehead while he fiddled with a pencil on the desk. The guy was a lousy liar. Noelle thought back to that night he saw him with Brunswick at Sam's. He wished he could have sat opposite him with a hand of cards; he'd probably get to take Lowden for every cent he had.

"So who else around here knew about the trouble out in El Paso?" Noelle asked. "Did you tell your girlfriend about it?"

Lowden flushed a bright red. "I'm a happily married man, Detective."

Noelle snorted. "Don't mess with me, Lowden. I know you have a bit on the side. I've seen you with her at Sam's. I even saw how itchy you got when Marianna sat behind you and your wife at the Brunswick funeral."

"I don't talk about Brunswick business with outsiders, especially women."

"You consider those country club girls outsiders? And what about Julia? She was a Brunswick, or did you think of her as an outsider too?"

He was stone-cold sure Lowden had arranged Pedro Angeles's murder, but he knew they could never prove it. It was one thing to arrange a bar fight and cover it up, but a whole other thing to slice up beautiful women. Noelle was still convinced that Lowden must have known something about the murders.

"Well, I suppose you can provide us with witnesses for your whereabouts on all three nights the victims went missing," Noelle said.

Lowden took out his day planner and said, "Well, let me see what those dates were."

Noelle rattled off the dates and watched him go through the motions of looking at his calendar.

Lowden said, "Well, it looks like I was out of town on Brunswick business on the night Julia was killed. Marianna de Pucci, my mistress, as you already know, was with me, and I'm sure she'll vouch for me. But you'd better speak to her soon. She's due to leave the country in the next day or so. On those other dates I was out late with Mr. George Brunswick."

Noelle stood. "Mr. Lowden, I'm sorry to have taken up your work time. I'll check out your alibis, but don't leave the state in case I have more questions for you."

"You don't have to worry about that, Detective. They keep me really busy here. No rest for the weary, as they say."

As Noelle left, he turned in the doorway and saw Lowden picking up the phone. He'd bet a high-stakes bankroll that Lowden was calling good old George Brunswick.

CHAPTER 22

Sally couldn't help herself. On the nights she didn't have to work and felt lonely she continued to follow Pamela. She would follow her to restaurants, in the store, and to her apartment. She could not wrap her head around why Nick still wanted Pamela, even knowing that she was sleeping with another man.

The way Nick lit up whenever he saw Pamela made Sally crazy. Sally was standing in the bedroom of her tiny apartment, putting on her peach lipstick, when the idea came to her. She'd go to Neiman's and have Pamela do her makeup. She wasn't like the rich customers there, but her money was as good as theirs.

She changed into a pretty sundress with an expensive label that she'd bought at Goodwill for a few dollars. The dress matched her peach lipstick. She checked herself in the mirror, leaning in close to look at her eyes. For the first time in a long while, her green eyes were clear. She had gained just enough weight to look curvy again. She brushed her hair, stuck her wallet back in her purse, and nearly ran down the stairs, suddenly feeling happy. It was a hot Saturday afternoon and her car's air conditioner was busted, so she rolled down all the windows and let the hot, wet breeze ruin her hair.

Only a block from home, her makeup started running down her face. At the Galleria, she parked close to Neiman's, checked herself in her little pocket mirror, and tried to clean up her eye makeup and smooth her hair.

She had second thoughts about her plan. She tried not to stare at the haughty women milling about in their fashionable clothes. She felt self-conscious in her own Goodwill sundress, knowing it was out of date. She thought these women could see right through her, but she was on a mission. She moved from one makeup counter to the next, searching for Pamela. Finally she saw her packaging something up for an older lady with blue hair. This close she could see how striking Pamela was in a fashionable gray silk dress. Her blond hair curled to her shoulders and her eyes were perfectly made up. The closer Sally got, the better Pamela looked.

Pamela was nearly finished with the blue-haired lady, so Sally sauntered over to her counter with confidence. "I'll be with you in a minute," Pamela said. She smiled, revealing her overbite. So Pamela wasn't so perfect after all, Sally thought.

Pamela handed the blue-haired woman her packages and slowly strolled over to Sally. She smiled again and asked, "What can I do for you?"

Sally's palms were damp, and she was afraid Pamela could see she didn't belong there. Sally worked hard to keep her voice from shaking, "I need a—a lipstick—like yours. But, uh, what I really need is a makeover." She smiled, shrugging. "I never learned how to put on makeup the right way."

Pamela offered her hand to Sally, introduced herself, and asked Sally's name. Pamela stared into Sally's face, causing a cold sweat to break out on her forehead. Pamela told Sally she had great bone structure and beautiful lips and eyes, and that she'd need only a little makeup to look fantastic.

Sally wanted to hate her, but she couldn't. Pamela seemed so understanding and kind that Sally couldn't help liking her. Pamela had her sit on a stool beside a table and a mirror while she busied herself picking out foundation, mascara, eye shadow, several lipsticks, and a sponge. "Now, don't put this base on until you have a good cream on your skin and under your eyes. You're still young, but protecting your face is really important."

Her hands fluttered around Sally's face, smoothing the base over her skin. Her touch was soft, and she smelled of flowers. Sally closed her eyes a minute as Pamela fluffed powder over the base. It felt good to be tended to like this. No one had really done that kind of thing for her before, except Nick, when he rubbed her feet or played with her hair. It gave her shivers down her spine.

"A good powder is important too," Pamela said. "It will make the base last for the day and keep you from having a greasy tone." She offered Sally a hand mirror. Sally saw how evenly toned her face now looked. Pamela took the mirror back and said, "For the rest, no peeking until I'm done."

"Okay." Sally trusted Pamela to treat her well. Pamela picked up a blush and a brush and tapped it lightly on Sally's cheekbones. "Just a touch is all you need. You never want your cheeks to look like a clown's."

Sally knew just what she meant. She couldn't help but laugh. Sally realized if their circumstances had been different and Nick weren't between them, they could have been friends—maybe Pamela could even be a good girlfriend, something she'd never really had.

Pamela penciled Sally's eyes with black eyeliner. "You can use this both on the eyelid and under your eyes, because your eyes are so big. And all you need is a light touch of mascara. A lot of the girls like colorful eye shadow, but not me." As Pamela worked, Sally's eyes began to water. Pamela handed her a tissue. "Just blot," she said. "You never want to rub your eyes if you have mascara on. For the finale, let's pick simple icy pink lipstick. This shade's all the rage right now."

When she finished, she gave Sally the hand mirror again. "Ta-da!"

Sally was so excited when she saw herself: livelier and warmer. If only Nick could see her looking this good. "Oh, thank you, thank you, Pamela," she said. "I have never looked so good!"

Pamela laid three tubes of lipstick on the counter. "These are the three shades I think you should buy."

Instantly Sally flushed with embarrassment. "I can only afford one." She was afraid Pamela would be angry and feel she'd wasted her time. Pamela only smiled and said, "Then choose whichever one you want."

Sally considered the different shades of pink and peach. Finally she picked the icy-peach shade.

Pamela said, "You bought the best one." As she wrapped up the lipstick, she said, "Here, I'm adding a bunch of samples. You can try them at home."

Sally handed her the money for the lipstick. When Pamela counted out her change, she said, "I hope you come back." Her eyes glowed with warmth and sympathy. "Don't worry, I'll make you up, and you don't have to buy anything."

Pamela's kindness took Sally by surprise. She'd been so wrong, thinking Pamela was sneaky, manipulative, and maybe even cruel, using Nick and Brunswick. She was kind, gentle, and understanding. In that moment, Sally wanted to confess that she'd come to tell Pamela to leave Nick alone. Just then another customer started to impatiently tap her fingers on the glass to get Pamela's attention. Pamela winked at Sally and moved to assist the lady of leisure.

When Sally got back to her clunker in the parking lot, she just sat in the stifling air and began to cry. If Pamela really loved Nick, Sally thought she had no chance to get him back, and if Pamela was just playing Nick, Nick had no chance. Pamela was just too . . . too much, too good, too classy. As Sally backed out of her parking space, she saw in her rearview mirror that her tears had smeared the mascara.

———

The next week, Sally wiped down a table at the Dime coffee shop, pocketing her tip and setting the salt and pepper shakers back where they belonged. By the clock on the wall, she had fifteen minutes until her shift was over. This had been a good first job for her, but she was hoping to get a better one soon, somewhere she could earn more money. When she read the want ads, she couldn't believe that they were hiring at Sam's. She knew she would be taking a chance if anyone remembered her there from the time before Nick, but she wanted that job. Maybe she would see Nick there?

She hung up the dishcloth, untied the little apron, and transferred her tip money to her wallet. She clocked out and went into the restroom to change into a little black dress and a pair of high heels. The dress was bargain basement, cut simply enough to look classic and not cheap, and her shoes were barely used by some debutante before she donated them to the Salvation Army. She checked herself one more time in the mirror. She was aiming for a classy hostess job and headed to interview at Sam's, where she heard they were hiring.

She drove in her wreck through the summer afternoon, praying to any god who would listen. She hesitated in the doorway, pushing down her negative feelings about not being good enough. Once inside, she saw a man who she assumed was the owner or manager. He was holding court at a brown leather booth next to the bar. He looked snazzy in a dark suit and crisp white shirt with a wide patterned tie. Sally sat at the other end of the bar and ordered a white wine to build her confidence. She observed the line of women standing around this man as he looked them up and down. She got really nervous when she saw him coldly dismiss a plain woman, even though she was dressed to the nines. He shook his head and said, "No, you're not our type."

Sally's confidence dropped a few more notches. She immediately feared that the man would see through her cheap little black dress to the hooker she'd been. She watched as the next woman—tall, thin, with beautiful dark eyes—strolled up to him, kissing him on both cheeks like an old friend. "Oh, Sam, it's so good to see you after all this time."

Sally knew when she heard his name that he must be the club's owner. She noted their friendship and thought she should just quit and leave now.

As she expected, Sam was nodding yes to this woman. "Can you start at six tonight?" he said, then called over his assistant to get his friend sorted out with paperwork and whatever else she might need.

So that was it; Sam had the hostess he needed.

Sally paid for her wine and turned to leave. Sam noticed her and called over to her. "You—at the bar. Young lady, come over here."

Sally trembled as she walked over to stand before him. Sam looked her up and down, just as he had with the plain woman. "Did you come here for a hostess job?"

Sally nodded. "Yes, sir."

Sam laughed out loud. "What the hell, were you just going to walk out? I don't bite."

Sally smiled that sweetheart of a smile. "Yes, sir, I thought you had already picked someone and wouldn't need another hostess."

Sam studied her. "You're perfect for this job," Sam said. "Do you have experience?"

Sally felt a rush of victory. She relaxed and fudged the truth. "I've been working at the Dime coffee shop. I'm from Alabama, and I don't have any family there anymore, so I moved here. Unfortunately I can't pay my rent on the tips I make at the Dime. I heard you were hiring from one of my customers. She said this was a good place for girls like me to work."

Sam paused a moment, then said, "You do know that our hostesses take care of the high rollers here, right? And we have more than one hostess position open. The job entails a bit of social entertainment. But rest assured I will never make whores out of our ladies."

Sally smiled shyly. "Well, it's good to know that, sir."

Sam waved to his assistant again and told her to set Sally up too. He shook her hand, smiling. "I can see you're an innocent. Not gone out for many jobs, have you?"

When Sally shook her head, he stuck a finger beneath her chin, laughed again, and said, "Well, now you know I don't bite. Do you know how beautiful you are?"

Sally smiled uncomfortably, realizing that Sam had the hots for her. She hoped it wasn't going to get in the way of her holding on to this job.

"I'm going to give you a different name," he said. "Sally's a little plain and country for my establishment. Since I like you so much, I'm going to give you the girl's version of my own name. From now on, you're Samantha." Sally kind of liked the idea of playing a character instead of being herself at this new job. And Samantha sounded like a classy name.

———

After getting her first paycheck from Sam's, Sally went back to Neiman's to buy a second shade of lipstick from Pamela. Pamela offered to make her up, and Sally accepted. As Pamela worked on her, Sally told her all about her new job at Sam's and how grateful she was to be making some good money for the first time in her life. She even had enough to put a deposit on a better apartment than the room she'd been renting by the week. Pamela was intrigued by

Sally's poor-side-of-the-tracks story and invited her to lunch the next day. The invitation surprised Sally, but she jumped at the offer to get to know Pamela better.

The next day, Sally dressed in her simple black dress and wore the bronze watch Nick had given her. She wasn't sure why Pamela was being so nice to her, but she was eager to find out. Was it possible that Pamela was looking for a friend too? She did just lose three of her good friends.

Sally arrived early and sat at the bar, feeling uneasy. She got scared, thinking that perhaps Nick had felt so close to Pamela that he told her all about his ex-hooker wife to get her sympathy. With her raw nerves and the stream of cold air blowing on her from the vent overhead, she started to shake just as Pamela rushed through the door, looking like a million bucks. Sally knew her outfit had no style in comparison to Pamela's—a loose designer hippie dress and floppy hat that were the latest fashion trend, along with matching platform shoes. At least Sally was happy to have a brand-new pair of platforms too; they were all the rage. But clothes on Pamela looked so cool. She dressed like the cover of *Vogue* and not like a girl doing makeup at Neiman's. Confidence was what Sally lacked. She realized that what she didn't have gave Pamela her edge and all the self-assurance in the world.

Sally felt better knowing that Pamela was cut out for a wealthy man like George, and not someone like Nick who could only give her the simple things in life. She got up and joined Pamela. "Hey, Pamela, I'm here."

Pamela smiled. "Hi, Sally. Wow! Look how good you clean up!"

Sally felt insulted even though she knew Pamela meant it as a compliment. The maître d' rushed over as soon as he spotted Pamela. "Oh, Miss O'Leary, we have your table by the window. Please follow me."

Sally guessed the maître d' was going all out because he knew Pamela was George Brunswick's mistress, and he must have brought her there a lot.

Once the maître d' left, she whispered across the table, "Pamela, I haven't gone to many nice restaurants like this. You've been so kind to me."

Pamela laughed and reached across the table and took Sally's hand. "I know exactly how you feel. Before I got my scholarship to the Kinkaid School, I was always ashamed of where I came from. I had to learn everything about style, beauty, and manners because my mother certainly didn't give me any."

"Then we have something in common."

Pamela had let go of her hand and picked up her menu. As Pamela studied the menu, Sally noticed that she seemed a million miles away. Sally looked at her menu and asked, "What's foie gras?"

Pamela smiled. "It's from the liver of baby ducks. It sounds dreadful, but it's actually good. My boyfriend George forced me to try it, and I actually kind of like it now. Go ahead and order some if you want. I keep a tab here that my gentleman friend pays for. Personally I'm ordering light today, because I have a date tonight."

With Nick or with George? Sally wondered. "You are a lucky girl," she said, and smiled at Pamela.

Pamela sighed. "Not really. I'm going out with a married man who despises his wife. He says he'll divorce her, but it's never the right time. That's why he pays my tab."

Sally felt sure that Pamela was using Nick to make George jealous. Her stomach growled so loudly it made Pamela laugh. "Please don't eat lightly because I am. Order whatever you're hungry for."

The only thing Sally recognized on the menu was filet mignon. "I love filet mignon, but what do you think? It's so expensive. Is there anything else you think I should try?"

Pamela just waved a hand. "Order the filet." She lifted her chin, and Sally could see how proud she was saying that.

When the waiter came to the table, Sally ordered the filet and Pamela ordered a good bottle of wine and salad for her lunch. Throughout the meal Pamela talked makeup, clothes, shoes, and jewelry. Every time Sally asked a personal question, Pamela avoided answering, and she in turn didn't ask anything personal about Sally.

As Pamela signed for their meal, Sally said, "Please, let me at least chip in," and took out a ten-dollar bill from her wallet. Pamela rolled her eyes and said, "No way, this is on me."

Sally felt herself go pink with embarrassment. Pamela stood and said, "It was great seeing you again. Maybe we can do it again sometime." She left as quickly as she had rushed in, so fast it created a vacuum in the room.

Sally still could not figure out what Pamela wanted from her, and her instinct told her that she would probably never find out.

CHAPTER 23

Noelle could barely breathe as he drove to Neiman Marcus on his way to see Pamela. She had called him at the precinct, telling him she wanted to see him again. Grateful that he'd won big at Sam's the night before, he was planning to go all out and spring for a room at the Warwick Hotel.

When he pulled up in front of Neiman's, she was waiting for him. She looked so classy, in a long white summer dress and white platform shoes. As she strolled slowly toward his car, he could see the tiredness in her eyes, after a long day at work. He jumped out of the Plymouth to open the passenger-side door for her, and she lifted the hem of her dress and slid into his car. He moved quickly around to get in behind the wheel, turned toward her, and said, "How does Tony's sound?" He was so proud that he could surprise her with dinner at a place like that. He started up the car and headed into the Houston traffic.

She reached over and ran a finger along the edge of his pants leg, giving him a smoldering glance. "I'd rather go straight to a hotel if you don't mind. We can order room service, right?"

With her hand so close to the inside of his thigh, he let out a long breath and said, "How about the Warwick?"

"Perfect," she purred.

The desk clerk gave him a key to a room on one of the top floors. Noelle asked him to send a bottle of champagne up right away. He and Pamela rode the elevator up. Noelle unlocked the door and stepped back like a gentleman so Pamela could go in first. The room was bigger than his entire apartment, filled with a four-poster bed heaped with pillows, two armchairs, and a pair of heavy drapes on either side of a picture window. He closed the door behind them and immediately pulled her to him and ran his hands through her hair and down her back. "I've been thinking of this night since forever."

"Me too."

He kissed her and she tasted of strawberries and cigarettes. Her scent of flowers filled his nose, and for a millisecond he worried he'd forgotten to use his aftershave. He loved how soft and slender she was in his hands. He scooped her up in his arms and carried her to the bed. Just as he was about to lie down beside her there was a knock at the door. It was the champagne. He quickly tipped the bellboy and dismissed him.

As he popped the cork and poured two glasses, she sat up to remove her stockings. He handed her the bubbling champagne and studied her long, beautiful legs, excited to know that in moments they would be wrapped around him. She took a small sip, then put down her glass and lifted her dress up over her head and dropped it onto the floor. Even the cool bubbly couldn't tamp down the heat that surged through him.

He took off his jacket and his shirt; she smiled over her glass as she sipped the champagne. "Oh, this is good," she said, giggling. "You've gone all out for me, Detective."

She quickly drank down more than half her glass and lay back on the bed, naked, her head propped up on a heap of pillows. "Nick, I want you in me right now."

He lay down on top of her, sinking into luscious scents of softness. He kissed her and whispered her name as she moaned, "You're a perfect fit."

It amazed him that they were perfect together. He hadn't felt this way since Sally. He took his time, teasing her nipples with his tongue, kissing her mouth as her breathing became jagged and she whispered to him, "Nick, I'm coming, I'm coming."

He let himself come at the same time she did, wave after wave shuddering through him. He lay there, collapsed on top of her, and inhaled deeply that intoxicating scent of flowers, now mixed with the earthy smell of sex.

He pulled himself off her and drank the last drops in his glass. Pamela had finished hers too, so he got up to refill both glasses. They folded down the bedspread and slid between the sheets, propping themselves up side by side on the pillows, drinking the champagne and talking about nothing: his game at Sam's, the new shades of lipstick she'd ordered. After a while, Pamela set her empty glass on the nightstand and turned to him again. "Kiss me."

He couldn't believe he was ready again so soon. He pushed his hands through her hair, down to her breasts, inching himself down her body, kissing her rib cage, sucking on her navel, sliding down further, opening the folds of her sweet pink spot.

Pamela sighed, crying out, "Please, don't stop. Don't stop, Nick." This time when she came, she was damp everywhere, her skin glowing with sweat.

Noelle held himself over her, propping himself on his arms, entering her, rocking slowly and coming again in one long shiver.

They both lay silent for a few moments. He pulled himself off her to lie beside her and asked her if she was hungry. She smiled and said nothing, looking like she was a million miles away. She yawned and whispered tenderly, "I think I need to sleep now. Just hold me, please."

He opened his arms while she slid against him, resting her cheek on his chest like a child. In the silence and afterglow they both fell into a heavy sleep.

He didn't know what time it was when he woke, hungry and thirsty. "Pamela?" he called out. He got out of bed, checked the bathroom, and saw a note on the sink.

Nick—

You're a great man and the best lover ever. I don't deserve you. Sorry I had to run. If I'm not home before my mother gets home there'll be hell to pay.

P.

———

The following morning, at the precinct, Noelle fumbled through files on his desk, distracted by his crazy thinking about George Brunswick. The thought of George touching the same places he had been on Pamela's body the night before made his skin crawl.

Across from him, Lopez sifted through the files again, looking for anything they might have missed. The next logical step after Lowden's interrogation would be to follow up with George Brunswick, since his name was given as Lowden's alibi.

Donnelly had made it clear eight ways to Sunday that he had to stay away from the Brunswicks, and he had already violated this order by questioning Jimmy in Austin and using that trip to El Paso to rattle Richard Lowden. All of a sudden Noelle blurted to Lopez, "What about George Brunswick's wife?"

Lopez looked at him strangely and said, "What about her?"

"Donnelly never said she was off limits, did he?" Lopez gave him a funny look as Nick leaned back in his chair to think about how he could approach her.

He thought about George Brunswick's reaction when he found out he had questioned his wife. Noelle thought he could slip information about George's cheating to her. That would kill two birds with one stone: shake George up and drive a wedge between him and Pamela.

"Come on, Lopez. There's nothing for us to do here. Let's take a joyride." Lopez shook his head wearily as Noelle picked up the keys to the Plymouth, then followed him out of the station.

By the time Noelle drove up the long, winding driveway through the magnificent gardens up to the Tudor mansion, it was too late to stop him. Lopez was freaked that they were at the Brunswick home. "Boss, I thought this was off-limits." Noelle just gave him a look and said, "I've had my fill of Cullen and Donnelly putting the brakes on my instincts. My gut tells me there was something fishy about George Brunswick's relationship to his niece, and I'm going to get to the bottom of that slimeball's story, even if it kills me."

Lopez got jumpy. "The last thing we need to do is confront George Brunswick where he's king of his castle. Donnelly will have our badges." Noelle made a beeline to the door, and Lopez dragged behind.

At the door, they were greeted by a lovely black woman with glossy black hair pulled tightly into a bun at the crown of her head. She inquired, "Who can I say is calling?" and flashed a million-dollar smile at Lopez. Noelle arched an eyebrow, signaling Lopez that the maid seemed smitten with him.

"Mrs. Brunswick is expecting us. I'm Detective Noelle and this is Detective Lopez," Noelle said as he showed his badge.

The maid seemed starstruck as she opened the door to them. "I'm Darlene Flowers. I remember seeing you both on the evening news talking about the murder of poor Julia. It's such a sad affair, but I'm happy to make your acquaintance." She glanced over at Lopez again and continued to beam. "It's so good to see men of color doing good work on the police force. We need more of us in honorable jobs like yours."

She pointed to the badge clipped to Lopez's belt. Noelle cleared his throat, hoping Darlene might be an asset to them later.

"This way, detectives." She motioned for them to follow her.

She led them along a long, dark corridor toward a grand staircase, where the only light came through stained-glass windows tinted red and blue and yellow. Except for the stained glass, the place was as gloomy as the set of an old vampire movie.

At the staircase she opened a door into a large living room filled with damask-covered couches and chairs. The size of the room and all its fine things took Noelle aback. He'd never get used to how much stuff these people had. Every lamp in the room was lit, creating scattered pools of light and thick shadows along the walls. Seated in the shadows in a wing chair in front of the fireplace was Charlene Brunswick. Her hair was gray and styled in a French twist, and she wore a beautiful dress embroidered in red roses. Noelle didn't know much about fashion but could only guess this dress had come off the Paris runways that spring.

Despite her style, she was plain, thin, and frail, and she looked older than her husband. Almost old enough to be his mother, Noelle thought. Charlene beckoned with an impatient hand. "C'mon in, detectives. Have some sherry with me."

At once Darlene went to the bar and poured two glasses of sherry, handing one each to Noelle and Lopez. She carried the bottle carefully over to Charlene and refilled her glass.

"Sit down!" Charlene commanded, and pointed to the other wing chairs in front of the fireplace. She spoke to Noelle, ignoring Lopez entirely. "So, Detective, what do you want to know?"

Noelle thought it was a refreshing change of pace to interview a willing participant. "Mrs. Brunswick, what can you tell us about your husband's relationship with his brother James?"

She smirked. "There's no love lost there. James keeps George on at the company because he pities him. Their daddy never took much of a liking to my George, and as far as I can tell, George does nothing all day but flirt with his young secretaries. After work he passes the time with some other girl. He never lies to me about any of it. I have to give him credit for that."

Noelle knew from experience that if he kept quiet, a woman who had something to say would start talking, and Mrs. Brunswick didn't disappoint.

"George did tell me he was getting a little sick of that girl because she's hell-bent on getting George to marry her. You see, Detective, I don't fear my competition. I know George will never leave me. It's my money that supports his playboy midlife crisis, and he's not a stupid man. His daddy didn't leave him much of an inheritance, and that's all tied up in trusts for our daughter and son. Basically, James Jr. keeps George on the job in spite of his uselessness."

Noelle felt relieved and furious that George was stringing Pamela along. He gulped at his sherry. The stuff tasted foul, but he needed that alcohol to steady him. Since the maid had left the room, Charlene turned, pointed a crooked finger at Lopez, and said, "Detective, please refresh our glasses, would you?"

Noelle saw Lopez's face flush. Noelle slightly rolled his eyes, so Lopez would know what he thought: the woman was a witch, but they had to stay on her good side to get more information.

Lopez went to the bar and poured a small amount in Noelle's glass. "Oh, please," Charlene said, "Detective, there's plenty more. No need to be stingy. Fill the glass all the way up." Lopez filled the glass to the rim and filled Charlene's glass too.

Once Lopez was again seated, Noelle said to Charlene, "Has your husband made it clear to this girl that he won't marry her?"

Charlene twisted her mouth into a grotesque smile. "He told me he's trying to let her down easy. Quite frankly, he gets bored easily, and I think he's reached his limit. He'll soon replace her with another, and I hope he does. I'm getting bored too."

Noelle almost choked on his sherry. "What do you mean?"

Charlene waved a languid hand. "Detective, we live in modern times. Just because my husband no longer wants me doesn't mean I'm not, shall we say, entertained by his appetites for sex."

Noelle could not believe his ears. Was old Charlene getting off on her husband's sex acts with women? He didn't know who he wanted to punch first, her or him. It was bad enough thinking about what George might do with Pamela in the sack, but to think that he shared the sordid details with his wife made him want to vomit.

He could see, too, that she was amused by his shock. He wondered if George had told her that Pamela had dated him too. Her sweet-and-sour smile made him sick. He tried to drown it out with a hefty swig of sherry. He dared not look at Lopez for fear of seeing what he was thinking. He figured Lopez was secretly clutching the rosary beads in his pants pocket and saying the Hail Mary a thousand times over.

More than ready to change the subject, Noelle said, "Let's talk about Julia."

Charlene took a long drink and wiped a drop from the corner of her lips before she spoke. "Julia, my unfortunate niece, had mental health problems. Her parents were useless, so we tried to help her, and George was as patient as a saint with that child. She needed a firm hand, someone to tell her yes or no. George did the best an uncle could do, but a girl needs the firm hand of her daddy, don't you agree? Julia never learned to curb her impulsive nature. She craved excess."

Noelle thought, *If that's not calling the kettle black, nothing is.* He couldn't stifle his outrage. "What about the other girls who were killed? Were they excessive too?"

Charlene didn't answer and massaged her forehead with one hand, frowning. "Oh, for God's sake. I feel one of my headaches coming on." She opened a box sitting atop the antique table beside her chair and pulled out a gold pillbox. She swallowed two pills with her sherry and dramatically lay back in her chair. She crossed her arm over her eyes and in a slower, dreamier voice said, "I think we've finished this interview, Detective Noelle. Thank you for bringing me some diversion on a bad day. As you leave, please ask my maid to come help me upstairs, will you?"

"Of course, and thank you for your time," Noelle said.

They couldn't get out of there fast enough. When Lopez and Noelle stepped into the hallway, they found Darlene waiting outside the door. Once again she gave Lopez the eye. As she started to lead them down the corridor, Noelle lagged a few paces behind to give her privacy when he saw how closely she brushed up against Lopez's arm. Noelle was hoping she might suggest a further meeting with his junior detective.

"I can't talk now because Mrs. B expects me right back, but can we meet another time?"

"What? When?" Lopez was obviously shaken by her strong come-on.

Noelle jumped in and said, "Lopez, perhaps you can meet Miss Flowers after work. You might take her out for a coffee or a meal; charge your time and expenses to the department. I'm sure she might have a lot to share about the Brunswicks."

"Saturday. I get off at three," she offered.

"I-I," Lopez stuttered.

Noelle knew he was thinking of his wife and daughter, of their weekends together. He cleared his throat so that Lopez would get the hint.

"Yes," Lopez said. He handed her his card. "Call me and tell me where you'd like to meet."

Outside again, Noelle realized he was fuming and disgusted with these Brunswicks, but he kept his mouth shut, even to Lopez. He wanted to confide in him beyond what he put into the files, but he felt Lopez's morality would condemn him if he knew about his affair with Pamela. It was bad enough he was asking Lopez to date the maid to get more dirt on George, or any Brunswicks, for that matter. After what he'd just heard from old ugly Charlene, he wouldn't put anything past them. For all he knew, the whole damn family could have committed these gruesome killings.

CHAPTER 24

When the local TV news and the papers weren't talking about the murders, they were broadcasting the weather. After days of boiling heat, it had rained all night, and both Lopez and Noelle were antsy. At the precinct, Noelle reminded Lopez it was time for him to keep his date with Charlene Brunswick's maid.

Lopez took the precinct's Dodge to River Oaks. The neighborhood was like a foreign country to him, and he sensed danger at every curve of the winding driveway. What if Charlene Brunswick found out he was there again? If she reported him to Donnelly, it would be his ass on the line.

The rain was coming down hard as he followed her instructions to drive behind the Brunswick house to an employee parking lot. By the time he made it to the back door, he was soaked. Darlene had been waiting by the door for him. She opened it and grabbed the sleeve of his raincoat to pull him in.

"Shh! We must be quiet," she whispered. "The cook will be back at five and no one else is here right now. Mrs. B is sleeping one off upstairs." She pointed to another door and pushed him into a storage room.

"I'm sorry I couldn't meet you outside the premises, but Mrs. B insisted that I stay until the night shift girls come on at five p.m. She hates to be alone. We can talk in here." The room was cluttered with furniture and boxes, and Lopez started to sneeze from the dust. There was one grimy window, very high up, and Darlene led him past a couple of small tables to a sofa that seated two. "I know you will believe me when I tell you about how badly we are treated here. I wasn't sure I could trust the white cop or if he would even care. I'm the only black maid here and all the rest of the help are Mexicans—mostly illegals."

Darlene smiled at him, and Lopez felt guilty noticing how pretty she was with her paper-sack-brown skin. She was a light-skinned Negro who could pass for Mexican if she wanted to. She even had a small splash of freckles on her cheeks. She had beautiful plump, rosy lips too. She wore a loose uniform that hid her voluptuous shape.

She smiled again, and Lopez wondered if she even had any information at all or just wanted to date him. He thought she just might be looking for a guy with a good job to take her away from housekeeping.

"This is a treacherous place to work since both Mr. and Mrs. B have bad tempers. The old man has a one-track mind, with sex on it all the time. That's why I wear baggy uniforms, to try to cut down his lurid remarks," Darlene said. "And I would never tell Mrs. B; she is an evil woman. She would say it's my fault, and she'd find a way to punish me."

"Has Mrs. Brunswick done something bad to you?" He kept his voice and his facial expression businesslike so she wouldn't get any ideas.

"Not me, but she fired the maid whose job I do now. No one ever saw that maid leave the house, and she left everything here: her jacket, all her pictures, and even her purse. Two weeks later someone called the police but didn't say his name to report the missing girl. The police came out to question Mrs. B about the maid's disappearance, but Mrs. B told the cops to leave. I heard her screaming, 'How dare you question us?' She told the police the maid was illegal trash who wanted to blackmail Mr. B. She said she threatened the girl by telling her she'd called INS, and she told the cops the maid got scared and ran away to Mexico, leaving all her belongings behind."

"Did you tell the police that the woman didn't even take her purse or wallet?"

"I wanted to, but I was afraid I'd be fired, or worse. Besides, those police don't care about illegals; they are happy to have them return to Mexico on their own accord. Makes less work for them. You see, I have a very sick mother and I'm trying to get my degree at college."

Lopez's heart went out to Darlene, but he was feeling worse thinking about Mrs. Brunswick calling Chief Cullen if she caught him there with her. Darlene suddenly paled when from beyond the high window they heard the rumble of a van. "Oh, shit! I forgot the caterers were coming."

She hurried Lopez out of the storage room and back through the kitchen to the door. There, Lopez stopped. "Are you suggesting that Mr. or Mrs. Brunswick could have something to do with the murders?"

"It's possible, don't you think?"

"She's very fragile," Lopez said. "She would have had to hire men to do that."

"Let me tell you, Detective Lopez, Mrs. Brunswick plays weak, but she is not. I have seen her take the stairs two steps at a time when she thinks no one is watching. She could afford to pay anybody to do anything. Please don't tell your partner, the white detective, what I told you. He might be in on it. Mr. B is real chummy with the bigwigs on the force. I'm afraid of all of them. I don't want my poor mother left alone if I should disappear one night."

She closed the door behind him. Lopez got into his car, escaping unseen by the caterers, who were busy unloading at the back of their van.

———

While Lopez had been busy with his covert assignment, back at the precinct Noelle was putting in some overtime when Donnelly came to his desk with the face of a boiled ham. "Noelle! We got another one, down at Kinkaid! The killer left her mutilated right there on the football field."

"Shit, I was afraid of this." Noelle wasted no time rushing to the crime scene.

He called Lopez on his car radio and gave him the bad news. He told him to meet him at the Kinkaid School. Noelle barreled through the rainy streets in the Plymouth, jamming down the 610 to Memorial. It was common knowledge that all the victims had gone to Kinkaid, and it was looking like the killer had too. Noelle got there at the same time Lopez arrived. They parked side by side next to the squad cars lining the football field.

Noelle greeted Lopez with a sour face. Lopez offered his take on the situation: "Maybe we've been looking at the wrong workmen; the killer might have worked at the school. He could be a disgruntled janitor or something."

Noelle smirked. "Lopez, you mean that sassy maid told you the butler didn't do it? I think you've read one too many murder mysteries."

He and Lopez found the senior officer and got a mile-a-minute update.

"We found her on the far end of the field, but there's not much to see. This girl was ripped apart," he said.

Out on the field Noelle and Lopez found the photographer clicking away. Lopez shielded his eyes from the horrific sight of the slaughtered girl as Noelle moved in close. He recognized the new victim as Marianna de Pucci, Richard Lowden's playmate.

Noelle sank into remorse. He had been so worried about Pamela becoming the next victim that he'd overlooked Marianna. She fit the profile much more closely than Pamela had. He should have insisted on getting protection for her, but he thought she had left town.

Two killers, together or separately, was the thought that popped into Noelle's head. Lowden and Brunswick, together or apart, and what about Charlene's hired help as the assistant? The whole case was a jumble of *ifs* and *maybes*. There was not a shred of evidence to link anyone to any of the crimes, and everybody had witnesses to vouch for their whereabouts on the nights of the murders.

Noelle knew for a fact that Jimmy knew more about Uncle George and Julia than he could admit even to himself. Also, it would have been easy for George to return Julia's Ferrari to the Brunswick estate without anyone thinking a thing about his presence there.

According to Pamela, it was possible that George had dated her girlfriends before she got her clutches on him. Maybe Lowden got Brunswick's castoffs, and when they were done with a girl, they killed her. Maybe the whole damn thing had to do with one big sick sex ring headed up by old crazy Charlene Brunswick to get her jollies. He shuddered at the thought of Pamela being passed down to Lowden next, and then what?

The rainstorm had done its job. Noelle, Lopez, and the other cops found the same boot prints, but this time there was a Wrigley's gum wrapper near them. Noelle gingerly lifted the soggy wrapper off the ground. It could have had the killer's prints on it if only it hadn't rained all night.

Lopez, at the far end of the field, called over to him, "Noelle! I found some truck tracks over here!"

Noelle hurried over and instructed one of the forensics guys to make a plaster cast of the tire tracks. Even he could see they were deep, probably from a pickup. Finally, something new to work with!

Back at the precinct, Noelle's thoughts about the tire tracks were confirmed. They were ten-year-old B.F. Goodrich tires that fit a heavy pickup truck. Now all they had to do was run a report on everyone who owned an old pickup truck in Houston, which was just about everybody. Noelle felt more hopeless than ever. He could feel his life about to be flushed down the rainstorm drain with all the rest of his hopes and dreams.

Later, Donnelly was gnawing on a Hershey bar when Noelle gave him the details about victim number four, Marianna de Pucci. "That puts you close to Richard Lowden, but not Brunswick," Donnelly said.

Noelle nodded. "I'll talk to Lowden again, but first, we've got to let the girl's parents know." Noelle sighed as he left Donnelly's office. He was becoming an expert on how to tell parents their daughters had been hacked to pieces.

On the way out to River Oaks with Lopez, Noelle scoffed. "I'll bet you a thousand to one this so-called baron doesn't have a dime to his name. Royalty my ass; his last job was probably washing spaghetti off plates in some restaurant in Italy. Seeing the ugly rich American tourists probably gave him the bright idea to come over here and marry one. A Houston oil heiress would do just fine—he gets her money while she gets to play baroness because she never got to be homecoming queen."

"Boss, you're a very cynical man."

"You will be too, soon enough, I promise."

Noelle drove the Plymouth onto Lazy Lane in River Oaks. The houses here were enormous. He pulled up into the circular drive-way. "Okay. Here we go again," Noelle said.

They walked up to the chateau and rang a large bronze bell. The arched wooden door looked so heavy, Noelle half expected it to drop down like a drawbridge over a moat. An English butler in formal attire opened the door. "What can I do for you, gentlemen?"

Noelle flashed his badge. "We've come to see the baron and baroness."

The butler opened the door wider to let them into a stone hallway. It looked even more like an ancient castle on the inside.

"I'm afraid only the baron is available, as the baroness has taken to her suite. Follow me, please," the butler said.

He led them into the library. Noelle was startled to see the baron, a distinguished silver-haired man, rise quickly, letting go of the hand of a much younger man sitting very close to him on the couch.

Noelle glanced at Lopez with a look that spoke volumes. *Not only without a dime, but a pansy to boot*, he thought.

"Detectives," the baron said. "May I offer you a drink?"

Noelle shook his head, while Lopez surprised him and accepted the offer. *Lopez must really be rattled*, Noelle thought. Wealth, infidelity, promiscuity, royalty, a date with a black maid, and now homosexuality was probably just too much for him.

The baron instructed the butler to bring Lopez the beer and quietly introduced the young man at his side. "This is our dearest family friend, Ernesto. He's been staying with us for a while. I'm afraid, detectives, we know why you are here. We have a friend on the force. We suspected something when our chauffeur went to pick Marianna up for her flight to Rome and she was nowhere to be found. Our friend on the force told us they found another dead girl this morning. As soon as the baroness heard, she took to her bed. Please, detectives, you must tell me: have you come to confirm our greatest fear?"

"I'm sorry, sir, but it's true." The baron's expression showed that he was already mourning Marianna. "We found the body at the Kinkaid School, and yes, I regret to say we've identified your daughter, Marianna."

The baron and Ernesto both bowed their heads a moment. "Oh, my poor little darling; it's too dreadful to think of her in that state."

The baron went on to explain to Noelle that he loved Marianna as if she had been his own. He and his wife, Cynthia, had been married only ten years ago, and up until recently, Marianna had lived with her father.

"When she turned nineteen, she came back to us. At that time she legally took my name, de Pucci." The baron continued talking a streak about his stepdaughter. He told them that Marianna had been an A student at Cornell, but she left school to return to her mother.

"Her real father could not provide her luxuries like we could. I'm afraid we may have spoiled her. She began dating men who weren't at all suitable or men too old for her. Julia was not the only girl taking drugs, you know. We were hoping a trip to Europe would straighten her out. We even had hopes of finding Marianna a suitable husband on the Continent. Oh, my poor Cynthia, I don't know if she will survive this."

The butler brought Lopez his beer. Noelle pulled out his notebook and his pen. "Have you met any of the men Marianna dated, and do you have any idea who may have given her drugs?"

The baron sighed, looked over at Ernesto, and gave him what Noelle guessed was an encouraging look. "The only names I know are James Brunswick's son, James III, and some boy named Henderson; both boys, as they say, were big men on campus. Her mother found out that Marianna was carrying on with an older man named Richard Lowden. Marianna swore she broke it off with him recently."

The baron surprised Noelle and wept as he spoke. "If only her flight to Rome had been a few days earlier, this would have been averted." Ernesto reached into a pocket and handed the baron a handkerchief. Noelle wished the baroness were present.

Through his tears, the baron went on. "This kind of thing never happens where I come from. No one would dream of harming a beautiful girl like this. No—in Italy we worship youth and beauty."

Lopez set down his beer and shook his head. "This is pure evil, the work of the devil."

The baron wiped his eyes. "Yes, you are right. I am a spiritual man myself, and I see your soul knows the truth, as I do, Detective. Pure evil. It must be stopped."

The baron gazed at Ernesto a moment, as if Ernesto would know the answers.

Noelle handed the baron his card and told him they'd definitely want to speak with his wife when she was able. In the meantime, if he thought of anything else, he should call.

Once outside, Lopez sighed. "It seems like rich people have a lot of problems. I'm not sure I'd want all that money."

Noelle smirked. "I'd be glad to take the dough off their hands. I've got a lot of problems that money would fix just fine."

CHAPTER 25

Marianna's murder was not announced until two days later, on Monday. Richard Lowden sat moping at his desk, watching the sheets of rain streaming down the big window in his office. He froze when he heard some secretary shouting out that there'd been another murder. He heard the office chatter about the girl's body found cut up on the football field at Kinkaid. Her name was spoken loud and clear: Marianna de Pucci. He ran into the men's room and started to vomit violently. He locked himself in a stall and wept. By the time he came out, the workday was over and everyone was gone.

He couldn't move or even think of driving home in his grief, and the last thing he needed was to face his crazy wife. Images of Marianna and the gruesome horror done to her beautiful body by a chain saw made his stomach turn again.

His phone rang and he lifted a receiver that felt like a ten-pound weight and stifled his weeping. "Lowden here." From the other end he heard his lawyer say, "Richard, you owe me big-time. I put this on hold for awhile. I should have called you sooner, but

I have been in the middle of one helluva court case. Divorce is messy."

In a fog, he replied, "Why's that?"

His lawyer said, "Because your wife thinks I'm her new divorce lawyer. I have all the copies of your financial statements stored here in my office. She thinks I'm keeping them safe for her to use against you when she files for divorce."

Lowden thanked him and hung up the phone. Thank God for his squirrelly lawyer and for his wife's stupidity, not knowing that Brunswick Oil had every lawyer in Houston on its payroll. He shuddered as he poured himself a drink, and the self-pity began to flow. He felt damned to a life without love, with a thug for a boss and a fat, crazy bitch for a wife. Marianna had been the only one who brought him joy and comfort. Now all he had left was the Southern Comfort he kept in his desk drawer. After several more drinks he had braced himself for the evening ahead with his wife and thought of a way to ease his pain.

———

Priscilla had just come home from the beauty salon, giddy over the gossip about Marianna. She felt sorry for the de Pucci family but could not help enjoying her victory over the dead girl. The husband-thieving bitch wasn't young and beautiful anymore, she thought. She looked into the mirror in her hallway like the evil queen in *Snow White*, and asked, "Who is the prettiest of them all now, *bitch*?" But she wasn't happy with the mirror's answer staring back at her. Even though her new haircut was in fashion, straight and with no hair spray, she still felt like a very old cow, a complete failure as a wife and a woman. She had never been ready to have children. She didn't want any extra expenses. She hadn't succeeded at anything, not even her diet. She had no one now. Priscilla trudged upstairs to her bedroom as if she had chains on her feet. She looked at the mirror again and saw only her fat face and those dark circles under her eyes. Richard was right. She was hideous and useless.

She fell down onto the bed and wept into the pillow. Richard didn't love her, and now she didn't have a single friend. No one from society would receive her anymore; even sweet pathetic Nancy Love was avoiding her calls.

She wanted to die. She was sobbing so hard, at first she didn't hear the phone on her bedside table ringing. The phone kept on ringing until finally she rolled onto her side to pick up the receiver.

"Hello, my love." It was Richard, and his voice was trembling.

My love. Priscilla inhaled sharply. "Richard," she whispered, her throat painful from crying.

"Baby, I've been feeling just terrible about how I've been so hard on you lately. With all the insanity happening in this world, I realize life is too short. I know what really counts, and I want to make it up to you. After all has been said and done, you are really the only woman I have ever loved. How about I take you to Tony's tonight? Can you be ready by eight?"

Priscilla sat up, excited. She couldn't believe her ears. She would do anything for a chance to start over. "Really, Richard, you mean that?"

Richard's tone was smooth. "You know there's never been another love for me. I even picked up a little present for you."

Priscilla stood up and her stockings snaked down her legs. "Oh, Richard, you remembered our anniversary."

He made a kissing sound into the phone. "Of course I did. Just be ready. I have another surprise too." Priscilla's heart fluttered. "I'm getting a raise, and James Brunswick himself told me to give my wife something that lasts a lifetime."

Priscilla couldn't help squealing. "What is that?"

Richard answered, "But honey boo, that's the surprise I'm showing you later. Now you'll just have to be patient. I'll be at your side before you know it. Go and pretty yourself up for me."

———

An hour later, Richard came through the door with a bouquet of two dozen yellow roses. They had been Priscilla's favorite ever since he had sung the popular song "The Yellow Rose of Texas" to her on their first date. When he saw Priscilla dressed in a tight blue dress with a plunging neckline, he flashed his brightest smile.

She held her arms out to him, laid the roses down on the coffee table, and rushed into his embrace. He snuggled her a bit and pulled out a tiny black velvet box from his jacket pocket. "Here, honey, present number one. Open it."

Priscilla's green eyes got big when she saw the glittering diamonds on a circle of gold. Tears slipped down her plump cheeks. "It's lovely," she sighed.

She slipped it on next to her gold wedding band.

She threw her arms around him and nestled into his shoulder, and he felt her body shaking with sobs. "I thought you hated me. I wanted to die."

He stepped back, lifting her chin so they were eye to eye. "Starting tonight, it will be good between us again." He checked his watch. "I hope you don't mind. I moved our dinner reservations to a bit later, so I can take you to your next surprise. I just can't wait to show it to you." She smiled that smile that had gotten him to propose, all those years ago. "Sweetheart, can you pour us some champagne while I clean up a bit before our hot date?" he said and then dashed upstairs.

In their bedroom he quickly packed a change of clothes, a towel, soap, and aftershave into a gym bag. While Priscilla was busy cutting the thorns off the roses in the kitchen, he sneaked back down to the garage and put the bag in Priscilla's car trunk.

By the time Priscilla carried the vase back to the living room, he was at the bar, holding a glass of champagne out to her. He lifted his in the air. "How about a toast to loving each other eternally?"

"To us." They clinked glasses, and she drained her champagne quickly. He smiled, pouring her another.

"Drink up, baby." He sipped from his own glass. "With my new prospects, we're going to the tip-top of Brunswick Oil!"

He could see how delighted she was. She tossed back her champagne and nearly danced around the living room. "I can't believe how depressed I was, and now I'm so happy."

They spent less than fifteen minutes finishing the bottle, beaming at each other as Priscilla kept glancing at the new ring twinkling on her finger.

"Well, let's not waste any more time," Richard said, after they'd drained the bottle. "Let's go see your big surprise."

Priscilla refreshed her lipstick. Richard said, "Oh, I forgot. My car's out of gas. We'll have to use your car, Priss, is that okay?"

"As long as you don't mind a snub from the parking attendant at Tony's," she said.

"Honey, don't worry your little head with such trivia. You know how I tip big; they wouldn't dare. Besides, it won't be long before you'll be driving your own Mercedes. I know you'd like that."

She laughed as he opened the car's passenger door for her. "You can be a real gentleman when you put your mind to it."

"Baby, you got that right. I can do anything when I put my mind to it. Baby, I'm putting my mind on you tonight." Richard drove out into the rainy night, along Allen Parkway to River Oaks. When he turned a sharp corner, he noticed Priscilla leaning her head against the window. "Are you feeling okay?" he asked.

She looked at him with sunken eyes and put a hand to her mouth, and he saw the effort she was making to swallow. "Richard, you might want to pull over to the side of the road. I'm so sorry, but I'm feeling sick to my stomach." Richard kept driving though the heavy rains and the occasional gust of wind rocking the car. "Honey, it's not like you to get carsick."

Priscilla bent her head over her knees. "Richard, my head," she moaned. "I feel faint."

He reached over to stroke her hair. "Hold on, sweetheart, we'll be there in a minute. It's just around the bend."

Priscilla tried her hardest to sit up, but her chin sank down onto her chest. He could hear her slow breathing, finally one long pause, a rattling inhale, a heavy exhale and another long pause, one more breath, and then nothing: a great silence finally from the chattiest woman he had ever known.

He pulled up onto a stretch of land on the bayou at the back of River Oaks where there were no houses. He switched off the headlights and carefully opened his car door. He scanned the area to make sure no one else was around, then crept around to the passenger side. As he opened Priscilla's door, her body leaned into his arms. He maneuvered her head until it rested on one of his forearms, and with his other hand he pried one of her eyelids open. He could see that her green eye was frozen in stillness. She was too heavy to lift, so he dragged her by her arms down the slight and muddy hill to the bayou, straining his eyes to look out for any sign of snakes or alligators in the dark.

She looked almost innocent as he laid her out flat on the ground. He remembered when they first started dating what a pistol she had been—so full of fun, with a big bright laugh and a sexy body that now was buried under flab. Soon it would be buried under mud. All she ever wanted was for him to love her. He was sick to his stomach with the horror of what he was left to do. He pulled a shovel from the trunk of the Fairlane and began his work. His uncontrolled weeping surprised him. Was he weeping for Priscilla or for Marianna or for all the unlucky bastards like himself who had no options but to work under rich tyrants?

He buried her as best he could in the mud, trudging back up to her car. He stuck the shovel back in the trunk, pulled out his gym bag, and put it on the seat next to him. He drove a bit away from where he'd left her. When he was almost out of the area, he pulled over at the top of a ridge. He took his bag off the seat and got out. From outside the car he reached in and released the emergency brake. He walked to the rear of the car and gave it a little push.

As he watched the old Fairlane roll slowly down the hill into the bayou, he felt pleased with a job well done—Oh God, he remembered he'd made a big mistake. He forgot the new ring he had planned to return to the jeweler. He'd buried Priscilla still wearing it. That ring had cost him a pretty penny, but it was too late now. When he thought about it he realized it was a fair price to pay for evidence that he loved his wife and had no motive to kill her.

George was expecting him at the Warwick that night. He had to be very careful never to let George suspect what he'd done. He still had the key to George's guest cottage, and he knew if he hurried he could get there on foot in a half hour.

He used a hose in the garden to wash off most of the mud that the rain had missed. He went inside to shower properly and change his clothes. He put all the dirty clothes into his gym bag and planned to drop it in a city dump outside of town later. The rain had stopped, but a strong breeze had picked up. He poured a drink from George's aged cognac to steady his nerves and called a cab to get back to his own car parked in his garage.

———

George got a kick from the tawdry feeling of taking Pamela to a suite at the Warwick under a fake name. He had just had his way with her, and Pamela was limp on the sheets of the big luxurious bed when the phone rang. George picked up, and the desk clerk apologized profusely as he told him a gentleman, "Mr. Aces," insisted he was expected to join him.

"That's right, send him up," Brunswick said, chuckling to himself that Richard had used the nickname George called him whenever he starting losing at Sam's.

Lowden looked drunk when he entered the suite and collapsed into one of the chairs. "George, I think something's happened to Priscilla. She wasn't home when I got in after work and hadn't come home yet when I left to meet you here."

Brunswick poured cognac into a snifter. "Is that necessarily a bad thing?"

"No, it isn't. It's just—the police. What if she doesn't show up and I have to call them to report her missing?"

"What about them?"

"What if they ask more questions? I don't think either one of us wants that."

George swirled the cognac in the snifter, inhaled the fumes, and took a long sip, thinking. "You know, you may be right. Perhaps it's better if you avoid the police. You haven't had a vacation in some time. Take a trip out to Austin and shack up with some hooker for a few days. That way you'll have an alibi if something bad did happen to your wife."

Lowden went very still. "If Priscilla goes missing it will look like I had something to do with it, especially after what happened to Marianna. Noelle knows I was dating her too."

"Richard, it's probably wise if we don't communicate for a while. I'd hate for the police to have the wrong idea about anything you might have done and connect it to me."

Richard looked desperate. "You think I had something to do with killing Marianna?"

While George liked a certain amount of desperation in women, he despised it in men. "Of course not. I know you were sweet on Marianna, but if it turns out something really has happened to Priscilla too, we need to get on with our lives. You read me?"

Richard exhaled a long jagged breath. "Yes, boss."

"Richard, I have to cancel our plans for Sam's tonight. See yourself to the door, will ya? I have to get back to Pamela. That little tamale is just itching for another good screwin'. She can't get enough of me tonight."

Once Richard left the suite, George went back into the bedroom and slid into bed with Pamela. He had planned to let her down easy that night while driving her home, but the conversation with Richard had left him feeling testy.

She'd been asleep and when he woke her, she yawned. "What time is it?"

"Still early," he said, "and I'm not done with you yet." He rolled her over and took one nipple in his mouth and bit down hard on it. Pamela let out a nervous laugh. Then he turned her over on her stomach, mounting her from behind. "Honey, I think it's time I remind you of who your daddy is before I send you home to Mama." George kept slapping her ass while anally pounding her. She bit her lip not to cry out and whimpered under his weight until he finally came. He climbed off her and said crudely, "Pamela, you got what you wanted; now I think it's time for you to get up and out of here."

Pamela moaned. "George, I can barely move. Please help me get up."

George hated victims. He grouched, "Okay, but we need to talk." At the bar, he filled a water glass full of brandy and ordered her to drink it. "Here, this will heal what ails you. Now get up!"

Pamela drank two-thirds of it and tried to stand, with tears leaking from her eyes. He watched her look go from sad to fierce and she yelled, "George, Julia told me all about how you'd been raping her since she was seven years old. I didn't believe her at first, but after tonight, I think I believe it. Maybe Julia was about to tell the truth about you and when you found out, you took her to the bayou and murdered her."

George went cold. "That's an interesting theory you've got there, Pamela. But you really don't know me. What about the other girls? Can you concoct a motive for my killing those bitches too?" He looked at her threateningly. "If you really think I killed any girl, don't you know it'd be just as easy to eliminate you too?"

Pamela hissed, "Oh really, I'd like to see you try. What you don't know is that Detective Noelle is sweet on me, and he's even watching over me right now. He probably knows I'm here with you, so I'd be careful if I were you."

George grabbed her around the throat and was about to squeeze the life out of her but stopped. "Go put your clothes on before I do something I'll regret."

As Pamela dressed in the bathroom, George thought about Lowden and the pathetic state he was in. He'd bet a billion that Lowden had had something to do with his wife's sudden disappearance. If Richard was capable of covering up his own wife's murder, perhaps he could get him to keep Pamela quiet in case she started trouble.

When Pamela came limping out from the bathroom, he gritted his teeth and lied. "Pamela, look, I am sorry. I was angry, and I took it out on you. I got jealous when I found out you were dating that cop. I don't like it one bit. You see, Charlene and I had words about you earlier. I know now that I have to divorce her. I do want you to myself, you and you alone. I promise I'll be a kinder lover once all this stress is off my shoulders. I am so sorry I hurt you tonight. As for Julia, you've got it wrong. That was a rumor she started when I tried to get her to quit the drugs and leave that junkie. I could never kill her; I don't know how you could even think that. She was like a daughter to me. I'm sure she was as high as a kite when she made up those lies about me. She could be vindictive when she didn't get her way, you know."

Pamela finished her brandy and sat down slowly on the bed. George could see the pain he'd caused her. He offered her one of his Valiums but secretly wished he could give her an overdose. He went to her and handed her the pill and the brandy. He whispered, "Here, take this and close your eyes, darling; you'll feel so much better in the morning."

Pamela stared up at him innocently, still weeping a little. "Are you leaving me here alone?"

George gritted his teeth again, hating every moment of this charade. "No, sweet darling, I will spend the night beside you." The thought of being near her now made his skin crawl, but he smiled back. "You just relax and let Daddy take care of you."

CHAPTER 26

Although the rain had stopped, the weatherman reported a slowly moving hurricane off the gulf. People lined up to buy batteries, canned soup, propane canisters, and masking tape, just in case the storm made its way to Houston.

Noelle, at his desk, began going over the autopsy reports and the interviews with the victims' friends and family and all the servants of their rich families. Again and again, Noelle tried to make sense of the few clues: the stogie, the Girl Scout medal, the gum wrapper, the boot prints, and the plaster cast of the old truck tires. He paused at the photos of Marianna's body, missing both legs and arms, as it brought up a memory he had about a doll with no arms and legs his mother had kept from her childhood. He'd never asked her why she'd hung on to the old thing and wished he had.

He remembered his mother had been a Girl Scout, and whenever she made Creole food she'd sing a Girl Scout song. The words of that song were glued in Noelle's brain: *She's got a G for Generosity. She's got an I for Interest too. She's got an R for responsibility. She's got an L for loyalty.*

Noelle reflected on the words: generous, interested, responsible, and loyal. Was the killer trying to send a message?

She's got an S for Sincerity; she's got a C for courtesy.

She's got an O-U-T for outdoor life. She's a real Girl Scout.

Generous, interested, responsible, loyal, sincere, courteous, and outdoorsy.

Noelle snorted. It didn't sound like any girl he'd ever known, but it did remind him of a dog he once had.

Feeling just as frustrated as his partner, Lopez spoke out. "Are we ever going to catch a break?"

"I feel for you, man," Noelle said. "All we really have is this cigar butt and a Girl Scout pin. But I do see one stone we haven't turned: the boot prints. We need to check the shoe sizes of all our likely suspects."

"But we need warrants for that, and you know that's not going to happen; maybe with that Howard or that Tim kid, but forget about the others."

"Wouldn't matter anyway, they're all alibied up. Let's call it a day. I feel like my brain's on drugs." Noelle grabbed the keys to his truck and headed out.

That night at home, Noelle was in his armchair drowning his thoughts of Pamela with shots of good ol' Jack when his phone rang. Noelle was afraid to answer, in case it was the precinct reporting another hacked-up girl. "Noelle here."

A male voice with an Italian accent whispered, "This is Ernesto Maurizio, the baron's friend. The baron doesn't want to get involved with this, but I was helping his maid clear some boxes from Marianna's room."

There was silence on the line. Noelle got impatient. "Yeah, and?"

Ernesto's whisper got gritty. "I found some pictures of Marianna with her friends, including some of the other girls who were murdered."

It was common knowledge that Marianna was a part of the clique of murdered girls, and it was no surprise they'd be in pictures together, Noelle told him.

"But the girls are pictured with a man who holds a certain reputation around town."

Noelle's interest perked up. "Don't tell me—George Brunswick, right?"

"Yes, I'm afraid so. The baron said to throw them away, but I thought they might be of some interest to you."

"You got that right. I want to see them as soon as possible. I can drive right over."

"No, you mustn't come here. I don't wish to upset the baron and baroness. I will bring them to you. Is there a place we can meet in private?" Noelle gave him directions to a spot in Memorial Park. They agreed to meet there in forty minutes. He hoped that the pictures would finally give him some leverage to get permission to question Brunswick.

Noelle sat in his truck at the edge of Memorial Park and watched as the winds picked up, stirring the massive oak trees. Sweat rolled down from his armpits; he was so antsy that he tapped his thumbs on the steering wheel, checking his watch every two minutes. Finally a fancy Porsche zoomed up and doused its lights. Noelle leaned over and opened the passenger door for Ernesto to climb inside. Even in the dark, he wore sunglasses. Noelle thought he looked like that Italian movie star Marcello Mastroianni. It used to bug him when Sally mooned over his pictures in movie magazines. Noelle teased her by telling her that all her favorites were fags to cover up his jealousy.

"So?" Noelle prompted, nodding at the packet in Ernesto's hand. "What have you got to show me?"

"Promise me, Detective, the baron and baroness will never find out I showed these to you."

"Come on, if you willingly withhold evidence and this guy kills again, you can be implicated."

Ernesto's face filled with horror, "Oh, no, Detective." He handed over the packet while Noelle switched on the overhead light.

The photos were Polaroids, but Noelle could see them clearly—the colors were still sharp. In the first one, George Brunswick was looking smug with Marianna on one arm and Jennifer on the other. Lauren Love was in another with him. Another one of the pictures was of all three girls in tiny bikinis on a boat, looking like they were having the time of their lives. Pamela was in one shot too, but she was not smiling. She wore a sundress instead of a bathing suit.

Noelle could recognize the blue waters of the gulf off Padre Island in the background. He assumed they were sailing on Brunswick's yacht.

Noelle wasn't surprised about the yacht, since Jimmy had told him how Uncle George used to take Julia sailing on it as a kid. He also assumed that he had been in the company of these very women because Pamela had said as much.

When he flipped to the next photo, they were on land and George was carving up a goat. George held a heavy knife dripping with gore, and the entrails lay in a heap of slime at his feet. There was even a blood smear on Brunswick's square, tanned jaw.

A *cabrito*, Noelle knew, was a Mexican feast where goat meat roasted for hours.

In other shots, the girls held champagne flutes and Marianna had her eyes covered with one hand; in the next, Jennifer was making a sickened face with her hand at her throat while Lauren was accusingly pointing a finger at George.

The next picture was a close-up of George, with an ugly leering look, holding the goat's heart on the tip of his knife.

Noelle assumed Pamela had been behind the camera, since she wasn't in any of these shots. If not Pamela, then who? Lowden, maybe, but he was never seen in any of the photos.

In the next set of pictures, George and the girls, including Pamela, were eating the goat meat. There were more pictures taken at night with a flash. In the close-ups he could see that George had a plate full of what looked like the goat's entrails. The photographs were disturbing not because Brunswick had gutted a goat for dinner; it was the expression on his face and the way he flaunted that goat's heart in front of the girls. Even so, no one would have given it any thought if it hadn't been for the fact that all three of those girls had been slaughtered like the goat.

Ernesto pointed his manicured finger at Brunswick and said, "This man is pure evil."

Ernesto left after Noelle explained to him that he might need him again for questioning. Ernesto hadn't been happy about that, but Noelle had a lot more to worry about than his feelings. With these pictures he hoped to put pressure on the big brass to allow him to question old George. If that didn't work, at least the shots would be a good excuse to contact Pamela again. He just could not get that girl out of his head. He was a hurting fool for love and felt fueled with this new evidence to lure her away from him. With the coming storm he also had a good excuse to protect her. Even if it meant keeping her holed up in a hotel all night if he had to.

———

Noelle sat in his truck, waiting and hoping Pamela wouldn't stand him up. She had promised to meet him at eight p.m. and she was already a half hour late. He was worried. Suddenly there she was in a pair of jeans and a blue blouse with a scarf over her head. She seemed nervous, looking all around as she climbed into his truck. "Where did you get this heap?" she asked with a sour look.

Noelle's gut twisted. "Sorry, I didn't have time to pick up my work car." He pulled out onto the dark street, feeling the wind tugging at the truck's body.

It started to rain. Pamela sighed. "Great, I didn't bring an umbrella."

Noelle told her he had one, and she sat back quietly with her arms crossed over her chest as he drove to Mort's, just off Dunlavy. He parked and reached under his seat to dig out the umbrella. He walked around to open her door. Pamela hopped out and snatched the umbrella and rushed away from Nick and the truck like she was ashamed to be seen in it with him. Noelle followed, getting wet in the rain, wondering why he even bothered. He caught up to her outside the door and, grabbing her hand, walked her into the dim, smoky bar. A jukebox played country music and Pamela almost groaned as he led her to a leatherette booth with a torn seat.

She sneered, "This is the place you were in such a rush to take me to? It's so dirty."

"I know you don't like slumming, but the burgers are the best in town. Sit down, it won't kill you," Noelle barked at her. As she sat, Noelle noticed she was careful not to let her hands touch the seat or the table. "What do you want to drink?" he asked her.

She untied her scarf and took it off. "Something strong, strong enough to kill the germs in here."

When the waiter came over, Noelle ordered two martinis, hoping the drink would soften her mood. Pamela added, "Hurry with the drinks; I don't have a lot of time." The waiter nodded and rushed off to the bar.

Pamela gave Noelle a smirk. "And you wonder why I date a man with money? You'd never catch George dragging a lady to a dump like this."

Noelle pulled out the packet of Polaroids and threw them down on the table. "No, but you don't mind his other low habits, do you?"

Pamela glanced at the photos. "What are you talking about? I remember these—I took most of them." The waiter brought their drinks and set them down. He asked to take their order. "No thanks, I'm not dining here," Pamela said. Noelle told him to give them a minute.

Pamela quickly plucked out the olives to suck at them. Noelle watched her spit the pits back into her drink, and for the first time he was seeing Pamela's flaws. "That's not so ladylike," Nick teased as he took a slug of his martini. "Look," he said, "I'm here for one reason, and that's to warn you about your sugar daddy, George. These photos bring new evidence that George may have had something to do with the killings."

Pamela's eyes burned. "You're lying. I know for a fact George could never do something like that. He's a man's man and loves the sport of hunting, but he is a good-natured man and always a gentleman. It was my idea for him to take me and my girlfriends to Padre Island for Cinco de Mayo."

Noelle took another hefty slug to keep his fists from clenching while forcing himself to speak in a quiet tone. "Look, Pamela. I'm just trying to protect you because I care about you. The killings all took place in heavy rains, and there's a hurricane warning out. It's going to hit Corpus Christi soon. I want to be with you so you are safe." He wanted to shake her blind eyes open. "I interviewed George's wife, and for your information, she knows all about you. She even had the nerve to tell me that George entertains her with details about what he does in bed with you. Mrs. Brunswick is quite a storyteller, and there was no hint of a woman scorned in her tale. She wasn't worried one bit that George would leave her. Can't you see, Pamela, he's playing you—and in case you didn't know, George is never going to divorce that crazy witch because she's the one with all the money."

Pamela's eyes welled up. "You're making all this up so you can get me for yourself." She finished her drink in one long swallow and pulled her scarf over her head, knotting it at her throat. "I will never love you, Nick Noelle, not like that."

He watched her walk out of the bar, her head held high and her long legs scissoring in quick, angry steps. Nick let her go. He figured she wouldn't get too far in those heels, so he rested his forehead on his two fists and thought, *What was it with women like that who had sway over him?* He thought of Sally, hopefully asleep in her bed safe and sound and not out on the streets in this stormy weather. He summoned the waiter over and asked for a double shot of Jack Daniel's, hoping Pamela would have to come back and wait for him to take her home or at least call a cab. When Nick finally left the bar he saw no signs of Pamela anywhere. He worried at first but then thought she had probably walked over to the Mexican cantina across the street and called a cab from there.

CHAPTER 27

George Brunswick moved stiffly, scanning Sam's with the eyes of a predator as he walked through the room. Sally could tell that this man with the slicked-back hair and wide forehead was a high roller by his fancy suit and tie. She could sense that he was in some kind of mood; she had enough experience with men to recognize when a man was hiding anger. Sally stood at the bar, watching his savage eyes survey the tables of the men playing cards and the glamorous women in their sexy dresses and rich jewelry. Suddenly she remembered that face. She was caught off guard when those creepy eyes landed on her. She suddenly recognized him. He was George Brunswick, Pamela's sugar daddy from the Galleria.

Her mouth got dry and she crossed her arms over her chest in a pose to protect herself. The cold air-conditioning blowing down from the vent above her made her shiver. Sam, the owner, noticed Brunswick's immediate interest in Sally. She was the only new girl George had yet to meet. He went up to Brunswick and took his hand, ushering him over to Sally. She forced a smile as they approached. This was her job: to make the men at Sam's feel good about spending and losing money, or to help them celebrate when they won. Sam had promised Sally when he first hired her that she didn't have to sleep with any of them to do her job. His place was classier than that, he assured her. Up until this night, all she had to worry about was keeping Sam's hands off her.

She had her long wavy auburn hair wrapped in a ballerina bun at the nape of her neck and had lightly made up her dark green eyes and thick black lashes. Thanks to Pamela she knew how to look classy now, and the important thing was that no one—not Sam or this millionaire—ever figured out how fake she felt. Working at Sam's was not only bringing in more money but turning her into a good little actress.

"This is Samantha," Sam said, introducing her to Brunswick. She gave George a proud smile, offering her hand as he introduced himself to her. His eyes stared down at Sally's chest as he said, "Sam, you always know how to pick 'em."

Brunswick took her arm, waltzing through the tables like he owned the joint and her too. Sam signaled a waiter to follow Sally and Brunswick. The waiter carried a silver tray and a decanter of cognac. Sally counted the steps to the private room to calm herself. Even if Brunswick was rich enough to make Sam jump, he was still just a man. She could tell he was one mean customer, but she had had enough experience to handle him, as long as she stayed on her toes.

George and Sally entered the private room with rich wood paneling that smelled of cigar smoke and money. The seats were upholstered in dark leather. Travis, a dealer, was already waiting at George's lucky table. The waiter set down the tray and the decanter. After a nod from Brunswick, the waiter poured the cognac into a snifter. Brunswick held the drink under his nose for a moment. Sally noticed his big hands and long fingers with buffed nails. "Hmmm, not bad," he said. He took a sip and said, "Pour some for the little lady too."

Travis, tall, thin, and in his midtwenties, had shared some laughs with Sally on the job, and as the waiter handed her the snifter he caught her eye, flashing her a look of concern. "Go on, take a drink," Brunswick growled. She did as she was told, but the cognac went down hard, like hot fire in her belly. Sally had never really liked alcohol. It always made her a little sick, oddly enough, when heroin for the most part didn't. Brunswick frowned as he watched her take tiny sips, forcing her smile. He grabbed the snifter and filled her glass to the brim. George leaned in and whispered to her, "If I were you, I'd take a drink, unless you want your boss to know about how you spent your nights on the streets." He then playfully pinched her nose, holding it until she opened her mouth. George poured the liquor down her throat. She almost choked but took it all. Travis looked away, unable to bear Brunswick's savage behavior.

Looking at Sally like she was a special meal, Brunswick held her chin and tilted her face toward him while whispering, "Honey, I'm going to show you how a real man plays the game of baccarat, not like your deadbeat dick of an ex-husband."

Sally was more bruised by his knowledge of her past than the pain lingering where he squeezed her. Brunswick commanded, "Now sit down, and don't talk. You better bring me some luck tonight."

Brunswick took a seat, and Travis dealt two cards facedown. Brunswick placed a thousand in hundred-dollar bills in the middle of the table. He said, "Punto"; then Travis turned over the cards, and Brunswick smiled like a crocodile. "So far, so good." He drained his snifter and glared at Sally, demanding, "Drink up; I like my gals nice and loose."

Sally's eyes moved toward Travis, who held her gaze to say how sorry he was for her. Sally knew it would mean the end of his job if he spoke up against Brunswick. She was afraid, and deep inside she longed for Nick to come and rescue her.

As she sat there quietly thinking about Pamela, she felt for her, knowing how desperate she had to be for a rich life that she would cling to this monster.

Travis dealt more cards while Brunswick laid out more money. When Sally finished the cognac, Brunswick laughed. "Travis, fill her up again so I can fill her up later." Cringing, he poured more cognac in her glass. With a dizzy head, Sally gazed at the pile of cash growing higher and higher in front of Brunswick. She blinked, trying to steady herself.

"You're doing your job," Brunswick said. He wrapped an arm around her shoulder and squeezed her tight. "A little more good luck and I think I'll be about done. No need to get greedy."

At some point, Sam had slid into the room to watch. When Travis filled her snifter again, Sally looked at Sam pleadingly. Sam only gave back the slightest shrug, suggesting that she was on her own. To keep the room from spinning, Sally stayed focused on one spot on the paneled wall. Finally Brunswick scooped up his winnings and turned to Sam. "Well, Sam, guess who's the winner tonight?"

Sam shook Brunswick's hand. "You keep having nights like this and you'll put me out of business."

Brunswick looked down at Sally and told Sam, "Yeah, took the bank, and now I'm taking this little filly as well." He helped Sally stand up; her knees wobbled. She grabbed hold of the back of her chair.

Sally knew that she didn't have to go with Brunswick, but if she didn't, that would be the end of her job.

Sam said in a smooth voice, "George, Samantha's new at this hosting job; perhaps we can get you a more seasoned gal."

Brunswick slung his arm around her shoulder. "This one suits me just fine."

Sally knew she was in over her head as Brunswick pushed her in front of him through the tables to the private back door, where a valet opened the passenger door of a Maserati for Sally as Brunswick got behind the wheel. George threw some money in his face and gave Sally a drooling kiss, slightly biting her tongue. Maybe she could still get out, run away—and then what? Back to the Dime coffee shop or even worse, the streets?

Brunswick fired up the air conditioner until goose bumps covered her skin. He drove through the city streets talking to her like she was a child who needed discipline. "Now, baby girl, these are the rules. You don't say a thing to me, not one word, and just do what Daddy tells you. Got that? I'm sure you've played that game with some of your tricks before. When we get to my place, I'll tell you everything you need to do, and you will do it if you want to keep working at Sam's. If you're any good, there will be a nice reward at the end of our game."

Sally turned her face to the window so Brunswick wouldn't see the tears rolling down her cheeks.

He growled, "Answer me, girl!"

In a broken voice, she said, "I understand, Mr. Brunswick." She could barely breathe; her chest ached. She didn't know if she'd been in his car for hours or only minutes when he pulled up in front of his apartment building.

A parking valet came for the Maserati, and Brunswick pushed a big bill into his hand. He grabbed Sally by the arm and said, "Quit acting like a virgin." He pulled her alongside him into the lobby and into the elevator. On the way up to his penthouse he pressed his lips and teeth into her mouth, hurting her.

When the elevator door opened he pulled away. She tasted blood on her gums.

She was numb; Brunswick had to drag her to the door. Once inside, he shoved her onto a deep couch. From where she lay, she could see the cloudy night sky through sliding glass doors. Her mind drifted up to one star in the sky peeking out behind a cloud. She stared out at it, dreading what was to come, and told herself she would not feel, no matter how much it hurt. She had trained herself since childhood, when her own father would sneak into her room and force himself on her; she knew how to go to that place where she would feel nothing, only empty darkness.

Brunswick tore her dress and yanked off her slip and underwear. He bit at her breasts until she couldn't stand it anymore and cried. Then he pushed himself inside her while hitting her until she went silent.

As Sally's consciousness traveled up into the clouded dark skies, her last fleeting thought before she went to black was a hope for a heaven beyond the stars.

CHAPTER 28

Sally woke up with the sunshine beaming down through the floor-to-ceiling window. The room was huge and she lay in a king-size bed under disheveled sheets, aching all over. Terrible pains shot up from her inner thighs, vagina, and anus as she forced herself to sit. She glanced around at the mirrored room and began to bawl as the face of George Brunswick surfaced in her mind. She touched her swollen, tender lips and ran her fingers through her tangled hair. In the mirror at the dresser she could see the bite marks around her nipples and the dark bruises from her neck down. The only place she had no bruises was on her face.

She had to hold on to the headboard to stand up, and she made her way to the bathroom. In the toilet, blood ran down from her burning vagina as she passed urine.

She sobbed uncontrollably, thinking of the hard work she'd done to go straight, and in all her years of hooking, no john or street pimp had ever hurt her as badly as George Brunswick had. Her survival instinct kicked in, and she stopped sobbing and began to think about getting out of there. She wrapped a large towel around her and moved as quickly and quietly as she could through the bedroom, peering into the living room to make sure Brunswick wasn't there waiting to hurt her again. She didn't smell that heavy cigar-and-cologne odor or see him, but she saw a note on the coffee table.

Samantha,

You were good, REAL good last night. Here's some money. Buy yourself something pretty.

You'll find some ladies' clothes in the closet if you want. Yours got pretty torn up, you wildcat. Let yourself out as soon as you can. I have the cleaning lady coming at noon. Hope to see you real soon.

Sally's blood boiled when she read between the lines. He implied that she had asked for what she got. Under the note was an envelope with six hundred-dollar bills inside. Her pride made her want to leave it, but she couldn't. She knew she would need it since she could never, ever go back to Sam's again, and yet it still wasn't enough to compensate for what he had done to her.

After dressing she stepped into her shoes, which she had left at the door, and limped out of the penthouse to the elevator. Outside, she looked up at the yellow sky. The hot winds dazed her, and her first thought was of Nick. She knew better than to make a formal police report of rape. No cop except for Nick would believe her story about Brunswick. She raised a hand to hail a taxi to Sam's, where she picked up her car in the parking lot. From there she drove to Nick's with mixed feelings. Would he trust her or reject her again?

———

Sally's car was parked in front of his apartment when Nick pulled up. When he saw her car, he wanted to turn around and leave, but he could see her head slumped on the wheel. The wind was blowing furiously as he stepped out of his truck, trying to remember how much cash he had in his wallet.

When he knocked on her window, Sally rolled it down and, seeing the bills in his hand, cried out, "Nick, I didn't come for money. I had nobody to turn to and I have some information that might help you with the case."

Noelle saw the smudged mascara and her swollen mouth and the bite marks on her neck. Something hot and fiery boiled up inside and he jerked her car door open. "Sally? What the hell happened to you?"

Big tears rolled down her face as she grabbed his hand for help to lift herself out of the car. "Nick." She whispered his name like a prayer. He helped her stand up.

"I will kill whoever did this to you." She limped a few steps toward the Victorian building, trembling. He knew she'd never make it up his steps, so he picked her up and carried her.

Inside, he laid her down on their brass bed. He got out two glasses and poured them each a drink. She took small, cautious sips. He remembered how she didn't like to drink much, but he could see she needed it. "Go on," he said. "It'll help."

Some color came back to her face and her fear eased up. When she seemed steadier, he asked, "Okay, Sally. Can you tell me what happened?"

"Last month I started working as a hostess at Sam's. I was happy to be earning more money than I ever could at the Dime, but mostly I was thinking I'd get to see you there."

Nick shook his head and said, "Why didn't you ask me about the place before you went to work there?"

"Because I knew you'd tell me not to. Sam himself assured me that the girls who worked for him never had to do anything they didn't want to do," she said.

More tears slid down her face. "It was fine, at first, until George Brunswick showed up last night. He threatened me because somehow he knew I am your ex-wife and had been a hooker too."

Noelle felt a pang of guilt when he realized that Pamela had most likely passed down that information to George about Sally. When he'd confided that secret to her from his past, it was in a moment of vulnerability; it hadn't occurred to him that Pamela would ever use it against him.

Noelle's fiery rage boiled up in him. "George Brunswick did this to you?"

Noelle was so agitated he paced the floor. He noticed Sally barely able to lift her leg trying to get up. He rushed to get some Darvon Compound from the counter, next to his Jack Daniel's. He poured her a glass of water and handed her two pills. "Here, take these," he said.

She looked up with those beautiful sad eyes and said, "If I do, I won't be able to drive home."

Noelle lightly touched her cheek and felt a tinge of bittersweet sorrow.

She gripped his hand. "I'll never go back to Sam's, and I'll never ever go back to the streets, I promise you. For the past month it's been good to look into the mirror and know I was clean and earning an honest living. I can't believe I was too naive to see that Sam was just a high-class pimp."

He sat down beside her and touched her hair. "Sally, I'm proud of you." As Nick uttered those words, he remembered that short-lived sweet time when she'd planted a garden around their cottage and the effort she made to be a good wife. He wondered if she'd really be strong enough to stay straight this time.

After Nick gave her the pills, he helped her out of her clothes and pulled down the sheet and blanket for her. She sank into the big brass bed that was always meant for her and Nick. He tucked her in like a child. He couldn't deny it; he still felt something so strong for her, and for that moment, he allowed himself to believe in her promises of a clean life. Nick hated to leave her, but he had work to do. He knew now there was no way anyone was going to stop him from confronting George Brunswick. With the pictures and now evidence of his violence toward women, he felt like he had a good case to put Brunswick at the top of his suspect list.

———

Hours later, Sally woke up still hurting and heard the sound of rain hammering the roof of Noelle's apartment. Her stomach churned and her head throbbed. She couldn't remember if Nick had slept next to her. It would be a sign that there was still a chance for them.

She struggled to sit up and was mortified when she saw that the cuts and bruises on her body had darkened to a purple shade. She hobbled as fast as she could to the toilet to throw up. She washed her face with cold water and gargled with his mouthwash. She tried to use a comb to smooth her long hair, but it was too tangled. She stepped into the shower to shampoo it, wondering where Nick could be. She made her slow way to the kitchen, and on the table beside the refrigerator, she saw a note.

Hi, Sally,

There's a bag of donuts and some cold coffee you can warm up on the stove. Feel free to take as much pain medication as needed, but be careful not to take too much.

I'm working out a way to interrogate George Brunswick and to get him arrested and prosecuted. Don't go anywhere.

Just stay there for now so I know you are safe. I'll be back as soon as I can with some healthy food for you.

Love, Nick

She read the note three times, each time focusing on that one word, *love*. It made her heart hurt to think about how she'd never loved another man as much as she loved Nick. Even if she thought he might be out there with Pamela, she would wait right there for him. She ached like she'd been beaten with hammers. She forced herself to eat a stale donut, then gulped down two pills with a few sips of cold coffee and got back into the bed.

Sally sank deeper into the pillow, with confused thoughts about Nick's attraction to Pamela and his caring actions toward her. In the center of her spinning brain was a worry about finding another job that would keep her off the streets. Once the pain pills kicked in, all fear and worry dissolved; she was out like a light again.

———

Sally woke again the next day, still exhausted but restless. As far as she knew, Nick had never come back the night before, unless she was so out that she slept right through it. She got back into her dress, pocketed Nick's pain pills, and left him a note. Rain came down in spurts as she drove back to her tiny apartment. By now she hoped he might have questioned Pamela and arrested George Brunswick. Sally put on a pot of water and scooped out a tablespoon of Folger's, adding a second tablespoon to stay awake.

Sally didn't have a phone at home, so she wouldn't know if Nick was trying to reach her unless he came by. Then she remembered that Nick didn't even know where she lived. The water on the stove started to boil and she pulled herself together, realizing she

had no time for self-pity. She drank the strong cup of instant coffee, ate a banana, and swallowed another one of Nick's pain pills.

Fortified with caffeine and Darvon, she dressed carefully in a
simple pair of pants and a blue cotton blouse. She draped a scarf
around her neck and décolletage to hide all the bruises and teeth
marks. She locked her apartment door and inched her way down
the stairs, groaning with every step. She figured Pamela would
be at work, so she drove slowly, cautiously, through the wind to
Neiman's. With storm warnings everywhere, there were few customers in the mall or at Neiman's. Sally walked stiffly to Pamela's
makeup counter, and as she approached, she could see that Pamela
did not look happy.

When Sally appeared before her at the counter, it took Pamela
a second to recognize her. "Oh, Sally, sorry but I can't help you
right now; my shift's ending. We're closing early due to the storm
warnings. They say it's going to be the worst we've seen this summer. I have to leave right away."

"I just need a moment of your time. Can I buy you a drink at
the Galleria?"

Pamela lifted her chin and her voice got snooty. "I have plans
with a good friend."

"Pamela, look." Sally unwrapped her scarf, pointing to the
bruises and cuts on her throat and chest. "This is what your lover
George Brunswick did to me."

Pamela's eyes widened as she gasped out loud. "Why would
George Brunswick put his hands on low-life trash like you?"

Sally felt slapped but came back at her. "It's because you knew
that I was Nick's ex-wife and you told him. How else would he have
ever known?"

Pamela scoffed. "Why else would I pretend to like you?
Otherwise I would never be seen in public with a whore like you.
Blame it on curiosity; I just had to check out the competition."

Sally stared her down. "It's because of you and your big mouth he did this to me, to get even with Nick for dating you."

Pamela came out from behind her counter and yelled, "Just stay away from me. I don't want to hear anything more about George Brunswick cavorting with white trash like you."

Sally inhaled sharply. "White trash, huh? It takes one to know one."

Pamela yelped, "If you don't leave right now, I'll call security." She turned with her fists clenched. "I will! I fucking mean it!" Pamela walked off, so mad she looked like she could burst into flames.

Sally was filled with anger and shame, thinking how foolish she had been to imagine Pamela could have been a friend. Outside Neiman's, Sally trudged toward the parking lot with her head held high. For the first time she knew she had come too far to go back to her old life ever again.

CHAPTER 29

A jacked-up Noelle pulled into the Brunswicks' driveway, parking his truck behind a freshly minted Mercedes. Even though he was afraid to lose his cool with Brunswick, he was hell-bent on confronting him while the Houston police were preoccupied with extra work over the approaching hurricane.

Even if that storm didn't hit Houston dead-on, they were still in for some heavy wind and rain. A Maserati buzzed past him in the driveway and pulled into the garage. It was George Brunswick behind the wheel. Noelle got out and cornered George as he stepped out of his car. "I have some questions to ask you about the murder of your niece Julia."

With a sly look on his face, Brunswick answered, "I've been expecting you. Follow me; we can talk in my library, away from inquiring minds."

George led Noelle down a long, dark hallway through a set of double doors. When they stepped inside the library, the first thing Noelle saw rattled him. A huge stuffed grizzly bear met him eye to eye. Every wall was decorated with hunting trophies: the gawking dead eyes of an elk, a pair of tusks from a huge elephant standing upright on either side of a big stone fireplace, and too many deer heads to count. Noelle wondered just how much venison one family could consume.

As a kid Noelle had been forced to kill for food or starve, but Brunswick could get the best table at any restaurant, so what was his excuse? It was obvious that George just liked killing. Brunswick had a wicked smile, and his eyes were black holes that could suck anyone into oblivion.

"Well, Detective, why don't you take a load off? Let me pour you a double Scotch and let's have a chat like gentlemen." George poured two drinks, gave one to Noelle, and took his seat in a big leather club chair beside the fireplace. Noelle sat on the couch and pulled out his notebook. In a flat voice, acting like he didn't know about what George had done to Sally, he said, "Mr. Brunswick, what do you know about the people around your niece before she was killed?"

"Well, Detective, I can't really answer that. The girl had a death wish ever since she was a teenager. From that time on she was pretty much absent from my life and her parents' and brother's too. I understand she'd even fallen out with her girlfriends. She probably met up with the wrong guy. It's that simple."

Noelle's jaw tensed as he held back the anger and disgust festering inside him. "How did you know Julia was falling apart?" Noelle asked, making notes on his pad to keep everything routine.

"I saw it at family functions. I heard about it."

"Who'd you hear about it from, her girlfriends?"

Brunswick ran a hand through his hair. "Why don't you ask me flat-out what you really want to know?"

Noelle shifted. "Okay, then. Tell me about the social times you've spent with her girlfriends."

"You've seen me with Pamela, and I know you've questioned her about me too." Brunswick tried to turn the table on Noelle. "So,

Detective, do your superiors know that you saw me with Pamela? Do they know about your frequent visits to Sam's?"

Noelle smiled a wide fake smile. "Yep, I'm a gambler, and a pretty good one at that, it's no secret. So what else did Pamela tell you about me, and when and where did you first meet her?"

Brunswick was grinding his teeth. He got up to pour himself another drink, and with his back turned, he said, "I don't know what that has to do with anything, but it was at Jimmy's twenty-first birthday party."

"Did you meet any other girls that night?"

Brunswick turned and smiled, baring his shark teeth. As he sat back down in his club chair, Brunswick said, "Oh yeah. I met most of Jimmy's castoffs that night too."

"Including the girls who were killed," Noelle said.

Brunswick drank from his glass. "Yeah, I knew them all, most of them since childhood."

Noelle kept making notes on his pad. "Did you date any of them too?"

"No, Detective. The girls in question were trouble, and besides, I socialize with their parents."

At that, Noelle pulled Ernesto's photos from the pocket of his jacket and spread them out on the coffee table. "You look pretty chummy with the girls in these pictures."

Brunswick plucked a pair of reading glasses out and lazily sauntered over to the coffee table to examine the photos. "Yes, I remember that day. Pamela begged me to take her girlfriends out on my boat; she wanted to impress them. We cruised out near Padre Island—ever been there, Detective?"

"As a matter of fact, yes, I've fished those waters. But I never slaughtered a *cabrito* over there. It looks like you know a lot about it."

Brunswick laughed out loud. "Oh come on, it was Cinco de Mayo, and just because I know how to clean a goat doesn't mean that I know how to cut up girls."

Noelle scooped up the pictures and put them in his pocket.

"I just find it interesting that you could do it so well. I imagine it takes practice." Noelle flipped a page in his notepad. "Okay, a few more questions. What were you doing on the night of May thirty-first?"

Brunswick sat back down, "Well, let me see, I have to think. That would have been the night before you found Julia's body, right? I was at the Houston Ballet's charity ball with my wife."

"Is there anyone other than your wife who can verify that?"

Brunswick laughed. "Are you serious? My brother and his wife and all our friends were there."

"Were you there for the whole night?"

Brunswick sighed. "We left early—my wife's indigestion."

"Were you with your wife for the rest of the night?"

"Charlene took some medicine and went to sleep, and I stayed up late reading right here in my library."

Noelle made a note. "I suppose you can get your servants to verify that, then? And what about the night of Lauren Love's murder?"

Brunswick almost spit as he answered, "Detective, since you've bungled this case so badly, are you trying to pin these murders on me now?"

Noelle noted beads of sweat on George's big forehead. "No, sir, these are just routine questions we're asking everyone connected to the victims. It's a big list and we have to go through it all. I'm sorry for the inconvenience."

Brunswick drained his drink in one long swallow. "Well, I'm not your killer, I'll tell you that right now. I don't know how anyone could cut up a beautiful woman."

Noelle put down his notebook. "Maybe not, but I have first-hand evidence that you are good at roughing up the ladies."

Brunswick's eyes sparkled and he countered, "I was wondering when you were going to get around to that. You screwed my ho, so I had to screw yours. I knew it would get your attention. And for your information, she was begging for it."

Noelle threw his drink across the room and hit George right in the middle of his forehead. Before Brunswick knew what hit him, Noelle was on his feet throwing a punch, hooking him square in the jaw, knocking old George on his ass. On his way out, Noelle yelled, "You're not the only good shot in town." He rushed out to his car before Brunswick could even pick himself off the floor.

As Noelle gunned his truck down and out of the Brunswicks' driveway, he knew he could not go back to work. By now he was sure old George had called his buddy Cullen at the precinct. Suddenly the sky cracked open and just that fast, rain poured down and the wind whipped his truck from side to side on the freeway. He had wanted to tear Brunswick to pieces, but not before he could prove he was the killer. He decided to head back to his place to check on Sally.

CHAPTER 30

George picked himself up off the floor and brushed off his bruised ego. He then called his good buddy, Cullen, the chief of police. After reporting Noelle's police abuse, he cleaned up to keep his standing date with Pamela. Later in the evening, George lay in bed at the Warwick Hotel next to Pamela. Even though his jaw was swollen, George was tight-lipped about the sucker punch Noelle had given him. Pamela was holding back too by not bothering to mention one word about Sally's visit to her at work and her story of George raping her.

Instead of using his words, George took out his humiliation by Noelle's hand on Pamela. He was extra rough with her during round one of their sex play; he even left fresh bruises on her inner thigh. After it was over, Pamela lay back in the bed and watched George in his silk robe pacing the room while drinking a cognac. He turned to her and said, "I promised my wife I'd be home early tonight. You better get up and dress." Pamela sat up and laughed, "Your wife? You must be joking."

He shook his head. "Charlene is making life difficult. Divorce is off the table for the time being."

Pamela stuttered, "But—but you promised! I've taken a lot of shit from you—but now you've crossed the line. Sally told me about your little tryst with her. She even showed me your signature marks to prove it. I put up with your kinky play with me, but with that white-trash whore—I won't stand for it."

George laughed. "You're beginning to sound more like a wife every day."

Pamela jumped out of bed and started to punch him. George grabbed her wrists and dragged her back to the bed. "Where do you get off giving me orders? I get enough of that at home. On second thought, I'm not quite through with you yet." He pushed her down and yanked her hair so hard it sent shooting pains down her spine. He bit hard into her nipples and threw her to the floor. He stepped on her belly until she cried out, begging him, "George, please stop, I love you! You know there is nothing you can do to me that can hurt me more than you not keeping your promise to marry me."

George's rage calmed a bit. "Pamela, I need more time. Charlene had me sign a prenuptial agreement before we married. My lawyers are looking for loopholes, but I can't rock the boat just yet."

Pamela sighed. "But you told me you had plenty of your own money stashed away on foreign shores. Couldn't we go there and live in peace together?"

By the time George dropped her off at home that night, Pamela was dazed and numb. It was dark, wet, and windy outside, and bits of trash and palm fronds blew up in her face as she walked to her door. As she pondered Nick's warnings to her about George, they began to make sense. How had she been so blind as to allow George to con her into thinking that she would get the Brunswick name and money once they married? The truth was more painful than any marks George had ever left on her body. That she had let him treat her like a whore, all for nothing, was enough to make her want to kill herself.

The wind was whipping Pamela into a frenzy as she wobbled up the stairs. She wanted to scream when she thought of how she let her bitch of a mother control her and how stupid she was to obey her when Maggie insisted she forget Jimmy and go after the older Brunswick, since he'd be an easier catch. Facing her mother and admitting failure now was the last thing she needed.

Jimmy Brunswick had been the only boy she'd ever really loved, and she knew now that there wasn't a chance in hell that she could get him again. She was at her breaking point, and not knowing what wild storm was waiting inside, Pamela paused and stood in the pouring rain. She dreaded the thought of facing her boozy mother and her mom's loser boyfriend, Michael, but she had nowhere else to go now that all her friends were dead. She placed the key in the lock, hoping that Maggie was in her happy drunk state or, better yet, out with Michael. Her worst fear was that Michael had stood Maggie up, as he had done so often before. That scenario meant that Pamela would have to listen to her mother bitch and moan about all the asshole men in her life, including Pamela's long-gone daddy.

Pamela quietly opened the front door and tiptoed through the living room, and was caught off guard by Michael, who sprung up off the couch stark naked with a semierect penis. "Hey, pretty lady, I was just thinking about you," he said, looking like the cat that ate the canary.

Pamela screeched, "What the fuck! Where is my mother?"

Michael moved toward her and slung his arm around her. "Maggie's sleeping one off. The old whore was so sloshed, she couldn't even wiggle that fat ass of hers. It was like fucking a corpse. But lucky for me, you're home early."

Pamela pushed him off her and shouted, "Go put your clothes on before I have you arrested for exposing that ugly old-man body to me."

"Oh come on, girl, your mama told me how your daddy gave ya the taste for older men. I'm in better shape than that rich ass-hole you keep company with. And I bet I'm a better lay too. Just ask your mother. This old man keeps her pretty satisfied—when she can stay awake, that is."

Pamela suddenly got real friendly and said, "Okay, Michael, just relax; if you want me, let me get in the mood first. Why don't you treat me like a lady and pour me a drink?"

Michael grinned again. "Now you're talking." He moved to the coffee table and poured her a drink of his cheap whiskey. While he did that Pamela moved over to the kitchen counter and reached for the long, serrated bread knife. She held it behind her back and moved toward him as Michael summoned her to sit next to him on the couch. Just as he extended the drink to her, Pamela revealed the knife and, with one fast move, she sliced his throat from ear to ear.

Just then Maggie stumbled into the living room and saw the blood spurting everywhere. She saw her daughter standing over Michael, laughing hysterically, holding the knife in the air. Maggie screamed, "What the fuck did you do?"

Before she could utter another word, she vomited at the sight of all the blood spilling from her near-dead boyfriend, jerking spasmodically as he bled out. Maggie stepped backward, away from her daughter, who was still holding the knife. Pamela just watched Maggie as she tripped in her own vomit, hit her head hard on the edge of the coffee table, and then fell to the floor. Pamela put down the knife and laughed out loud again. "That's what you get, you old cunt. You can both go to hell together now."

Pamela picked up her purse and ran into her bedroom. She took off her bloodstained clothes and showered. Afterward she packed a large suitcase with as many of her good clothes as she could fit and also filled her overnight bag with all her cosmetics and jewelry. She applied some makeup and checked out her face and hair in her dresser mirror. She smiled at the image staring back at her. She grabbed her bags and carefully tiptoed around the blood as she moved through the living room. She didn't bother to stop to see if her mother was still breathing. It made no difference to her one way or another. She turned out all the lights and locked the door behind her. She knew she could never go home again.

CHAPTER 31

When Noelle got home dead tired that night, he found his bed empty and a note from Sally. In it she assured him that she was all right and would go straight home. The rain outside was coming down hard, and since he didn't have her phone number, he gave his problems a rest and poured himself a hefty shot of Jack. One drink led to the next as he pondered his dilemma. Noelle knew that in his past years on the force, he had been the best homicide detective they had, but he also knew that his temper could be the end of him. He realized if he didn't crack the case soon, he'd be a goner. That night he passed out in his old chair to the sound of pouring rain and didn't move until the insistent loud ringing of his phone woke him after ten a.m. The first thing he saw was a sharp laser beam of sunlight coming through the window as he picked up the phone. It was Donnelly screaming that Cullen was in his office waiting for a meeting with him and Lopez. He showered and hit the road.

As he stepped outside his apartment, he realized that Houston had been spared the worst of the storm for the time being. The sun was out again and the beautiful oak trees and tropical plants could fool a tourist into thinking that Houston was a paradise, except for the stinking garbage and a rancid smell of dead fish blowing off the gulf. The locals were used to bad summer storms, but this season's rains put the smell of murder in the air.

He pulled into the parking lot at 61 Reisner and saw Lopez getting out of his car. Noelle felt pity for Lopez, and responsible for dragging him into his troubles. Noelle quickly parked and hurried to catch up to him. He saw that his face was knotted with worry. "Man, the chief sounded pissed."

"Lopez, if you saw what Brunswick did to my ex-wife, Sally. That son of a bitch raped and beat her! I went to his place to confront him; I couldn't help myself. Even you would have lost it."

Lopez frowned, "*Madre mia*, you hit Brunswick?"

Noelle laughed. "Cheer up, buddy; you should be proud of me. Last night I punched out the devil."

Lopez waited until they were safely in the elevator before he said, "Boss, I'm afraid they're gonna tie our hands tighter than before."

Noelle put his arm around Lopez. "Buddy, that's the least of my problems now."

The elevator doors opened. Chief Cullen and Lieutenant Donnelly were there waiting. Noelle quickly whispered to Lopez, "You haven't done anything, so let me do the talking." Donnelly waved them into his office and shut the door. He sat behind his desk and Cullen perched his butt on one corner of the desk, almost crushing one of Donnelly's Hershey bars. Donnelly grabbed it and threw it in a drawer. He said, "Well, Noelle, what do you have to say for yourself?"

Noelle shrugged, and Cullen shook his head and added, "What did you hope to gain by punching George Brunswick in the jaw? In all your years on the force you've never done anything so asinine!"

Noelle nodded. "Yes, I was stupid, all right, stupid not to see how friendly you and Brunswick are."

Cullen flushed red and spit out his words. "Goddammit, Noelle, you're not making it any easier on yourself. You went too far this time. I'm taking you off the case, and Brennan will take over. I should have put him in charge in the first place. For now, consider yourself suspended."

Noelle sat up straight as Donnelly frowned. "I don't get it, Noelle; you must be nuts to screw Brunswick's mistress, telling that girl and us that she was helping the investigation."

Noelle kept his poker face, knowing he had no excuse for Pamela. "Look, I only have one thing to say: Lopez had no knowledge of any of this and took no part in anything that wasn't aboveboard. I hope you don't take him off the job. He's a good man and hasn't caused any trouble. Besides, he knows the case inside and out. Let him work with Brennan."

Donnelly gave Cullen a look of agreement. "Okay, Lopez, you work with Brennan. Noelle, don't leave town. If Brunswick decides to press charges, we'll need to call you in."

Noelle stood up to leave. "I'll be around."

Cullen said, "Aren't you forgetting something? Your badge and gun, please."

He placed his gun and badge on Donnelly's desk, shook Lopez's hand, and wished him luck. He went to his desk, grabbed his files, and tossed them over onto Brennan's desk. He walked with his chin up and his shoulders squared; without looking back, he left the building.

———

Later that same day, George Brunswick lay on a chaise longue in his backyard, puffing his Cohiba cigar, and staring at the water shimmering in the oblong pool. It was a great day, he thought, as he blew smoke rings up toward the sky. He was feeling pretty cocky about himself. He'd gotten Noelle off the case, he'd put Lowden on ice, and he let Pamela know who wore the pants in their relationship. Now all he had left to do was figure out how to get rid of Charlene. He was fed up with her holding the purse strings.

Beyond the pool, water splashed in that god-awful fountain Charlene had installed. He felt so good that he didn't even mind looking at its tacky winged cherubs and angels. She said it reminded her of the great fountains of Rome. George thought, *Rome my ass.* This was Houston and no splashing fountain could drown out the chatter of tree frogs and cicadas. He wouldn't even be surprised if a water moccasin or an alligator hid out in that monstrosity.

He tamped out his cigar and closed his eyes. The memory of the night he'd had with Samantha/Sally brought a sick smile to his face, and he fantasized about repeating his brutal performance with her as he began to drift off. Suddenly he was jolted from his fantasy when he heard a loud whacking sound and a palm frond crashed into the statue. The sound repeated, but this time it came from behind him.

As he turned and was about to give hell to whoever was making the racket, he was shot with a hot pain in his arm. Dumbfounded, he looked at his elbow and saw that his forearm was gone and blood was spurting out all over the cement and into the sparkling pool.

When he saw the ugly smile on the face of his assailant, he wanted to shout, but the pain, shock, and awe silenced him. He could only stare at the blade in the killer's hand, knowing what was coming next. He whimpered and began to weep and beg for mercy.

———

After Noelle left the station, Brennan sat for hours poring over Noelle's files. From what he could gather, Noelle was right about George Brunswick being the closest thing to a real suspect. The chief had made it clear that there would be no repeat performance of questioning George Brunswick, or anyone in the Brunswick family at all, for that matter. For the first time Brennan sympathized with what Noelle had been up against and wondered if he could find a way to get around the chief's hands-off policy. The only thing he knew for sure was that he wouldn't let himself be compromised by a pretty girl. Besides, he was at a loss about what to do next.

Across from him, Lopez looked up and didn't smile. Brennan knew Lopez was true-blue to Noelle and could probably see that he was out of ideas. Lopez took pity on Brennan and from across the desk said two words: "Richard Lowden."

"George Brunswick's sidekick?" he asked Lopez.

"That's right."

Brennan thought Lowden would be the one who had to clean up Brunswick Oil's messes and no doubt do George's personal errands too. Somewhere along the way, Lowden must have done something squirrelly. Brennan would find out and use it to pressure Lowden into spilling whatever he knew about George.

Donnelly, pale as paper, stepped over to their desks and said, "You aren't going to believe this, but Cullen just called me. He said that Charlene Brunswick found her husband dead out by their pool only ten minutes ago. Apparently someone hacked him to pieces, the same way our other victims got it."

"Noelle was right when he said the killer was more and more insane each time. It's pretty brazen to do that in broad daylight, and at his home, no less," Lopez said.

Brennan, in shock, remarked, "But, Lieutenant, that makes Noelle's theory all wrong and takes Brunswick off our list of suspects."

"Should we call Noelle and let him know about this?" Lopez asked.

Donnelly shook his head. "No way, we don't give him anything the public doesn't know. Got that, Lopez?"

Lopez nodded yes, but Brennan could see he wasn't happy.

Donnelly tapped a pencil against his desk and said, "As a matter of fact, now we have to consider Noelle as a possible suspect, at least in the Brunswick murder. He did just punch the man's lights out yesterday."

Lopez raised his voice. "Oh come on, Lieutenant, that's crazy."

"Crazy like a killer," Brennan said.

Donnelly remarked, "Cullen's going to talk to the press in fifteen minutes. He won't say anything about Noelle being a suspect, not yet anyway, but it's going to get worse once the press gets the details on this Brunswick killing. Cullen told me it was especially gruesome. You'll see when you get over there."

By the time Brennan and Lopez reached the scene, uniformed cops had already taped off the Brunswick manor. George's body, what was left of it, lay on the concrete by the pool with a black halo of flies and mosquitoes swarming around him. Brennan almost gagged on the thick bile that came up from his stomach.

Blood was clotting in thick pools everywhere that showed that Brunswick's death had been slow and had happened just a short while ago. They were lucky that Charlene had gone out for her afternoon dip and found the body while the evidence was still fresh. This fact gave Brennan and Lopez hope that good evidence would be found to catch the bastard this time. Careful to avoid any of the blood pools, Lopez pointed out two sets of footprints, one large and one small, just like at the other scenes. At least now they knew it had to be the same killers that murdered the girls.

This time the killer had left the weapon, and it wasn't a chain saw. A scythe lay propped against a palm tree, and Brennan noticed something impaled on the tip of the blade. He suddenly understood exactly what Donnelly had meant by gruesome aspects: the lump of flesh was Brunswick's penis.

When they looked back at the torso again they could see that Brunswick's pants had been ripped open; at his crotch was a bloody hole with flies buzzing all around it.

Brennan was so faint that he helped himself to the water flowing from the jug held by a fat cherub in the fountain to wet down his face and the back of his neck. According to the blood loss, most likely Brunswick had been alive when his dick was sliced off.

Charlene Brunswick looked down upon the crime scene from the second floor of her Tudor mansion. She kept her eyes on all the details and watched the coroner tending to her husband's mutilated body. Neither Lopez nor Brennan could understand why she did not turn away from the horror. Any other wife in these circumstances would be knocked out cold with the help of a doctor's prescription by now.

Lopez had been overseeing the casting and measurements of the footprints. Now he held an evidence bag up to Brennan. "Well, we found something—another Girl Scout medal."

Brennan examined the medal closely. It looked as old as the other one, though he couldn't be sure. "What does it mean?"

"I don't know," Lopez said, "but with what happened to Brunswick's private parts and now this—I'm thinking the killer could be a woman. It's hard to imagine a man doing that to another man, unless he was a jealous homo or something."

Brennan shook his head. "What about the wife? Does anybody know if she was a Girl Scout?"

Lopez said, "She'd be too old to own this pin."

Brennan said, "I could see a woman angry enough." He pointed at the roses and the azalea bushes. "Look, he or she not only hacked up Brunswick, but went after the garden too; what would a Girl Scout have against flowers? I thought they liked nature."

"We have to take a real close look at Richard Lowden. He might have hated Brunswick enough to hack him up like this," Brennan said. "What if Brunswick did kill those girls and Lowden found out? Lowden was having an affair with Marianna de Pucci, and this could be his revenge."

"But the Girl Scout medal, Brennan?" Lopez questioned. "How would Lowden get that and put it here? How would he even know about it? The Girl Scout medal connects this murder to the Love murder."

"Shit. I don't know." Brennan looked up at the sky starting to darken with clouds and felt a light sprinkle coming down. "Let's go talk to Lowden, right now. If we're lucky, we'll get to him before he gets to wash all the blood spray off."

Brennan called in to the station to let Donnelly know where they were headed. Donnelly put a stop to their plans when he said, "We got another body, down at the bayou again. This one has been dead a while, at least a week. You and Lopez get down there as fast as you can."

On the way to another crime scene, Lopez just sighed. "I wonder who else Jimmy Brunswick has slept with."

Between the rain and the alligators, both detectives would be surprised if they found any evidence, let alone the corpse itself.

"Hey, Lopez, why do you think Pamela O'Leary's not dead yet?"

Lopez said, "Maybe because she'd been dating Noelle and the killer knew it?"

Now Brennan began to worry. If Noelle had so much trouble with this case, how was he going to do any better? The whole thing was fucked up, every which way.

Rain was pouring heavy again, and within minutes the gutters were sweeping up candy wrappers and torn scraps of newspaper and flooding all the green lawns with muddy rivers. When they got to the bayou, the water was already rising. Brennan and Lopez sloshed across the swampy ground to the body. Lopez looked down at the bloated, soggy corpse and right away noticed two things: her dyed black hair and a big fat ring shining next to a gold wedding band on her bloated ring finger. Exhausted and sad, he looked at Brennan.

"I recognize that carved gold band. This woman came to the precinct to see Noelle and make an accusation about her husband. That's Priscilla Lowden. I recognize that dyed black hair too."

CHAPTER 32

After he left the precinct, Noelle, from the safety of his armchair, poured himself the first of many drinks from one of several bottles of Jack he'd picked up at Eddie's Liquor Store. He was worried about Sally since he hadn't heard from her, but he didn't know how to reach her. With each slug of booze he reflected deeper on how his life was unraveling.

Even though Cullen had taken away his job, he knew he would not give up. It just wasn't in his nature to quit the chase for the killer. He took another slug and thought of Pamela and how she had aided in his self-destruction. He realized that he no longer felt that rush of lust when thinking about her. Now when he closed his eyes, the face of the new, beautiful version of Sally engulfed him. But he had a chaser of doubts about her too. From experience, he knew he couldn't trust her, and he worked himself into a state thinking how he could never trust any woman ever again.

Noelle refilled his glass and suddenly thought of Lopez, who had shown him only kindness. Juan Lopez, the Holy Roller partner he'd thought he'd never get along with, had proven him wrong. It got him thinking that he'd been wrong about a lot of things. The first quart of Jack was almost gone and Noelle leaned back in his armchair, worn out from thinking and drinking. He wiped a tear that rolled down his cheek and let his hands fall limp to his sides, drifting into sleep and dreaming.

In his dream he was at the death site in the bayou near Ima Hogg's. Three men were with him, one of them a small man holding a chain saw with gloved hands. Noelle couldn't see the other two, but he knew they were there. One of them said something to Noelle about carving up goats, but when Noelle looked down on the ground there was a girl carved up. The girl was Sally in her worst days, all bony and ugly, with beady eyes and a battered, broken nose. The skinny man began to tear hunks of hair out from her head, piece by piece. Blood spurted while Noelle watched the killer stabbing Sally in the heart, and the blood spattered all over Noelle's clothes. He was alone beside Sally's body on the muddy ground, screaming for help.

He jolted awake drenched in sweat, and his arm jerked, knocking his glass off the table and spilling the last few drops of whiskey and melted ice left in the glass. He checked the clock and was disoriented when he noticed it was just coming on to six p.m. With his fingers shaking, he poured himself a fresh drink. The dream had rattled him like no crime in real life ever had. It felt so real, like he had actually been there with poor Sally. He was so creeped out that he started wondering if he had had something to do with these murders in one of his alcoholic blackouts.

The image of Sally dead in the mud was so fresh it pushed him to put down the bottle and wobble into the shower to sober up. He had to find Sally and make sure she was all right. After his cold shower he drank down a quick cup of Folger's as he thought about where she might be at this time of evening. Sally never did tell him exactly where she was living, and he knew she would not have gone back to Sam's, unless she was crazy. He remembered that Sally had told him one of the dealers at Sam's was her friend. He'd find him and see if he knew where she was. He needed to know she was alive.

———

Noelle stood reeling in the parking lot outside Sam's club. Even after that shower and the Folger's, he was still drunk, and Sam's was not a safe place for him to be. By now he imagined that Cullen had told the press that he was suspended from the force and had been taken off the case. He took a deep breath and ducked inside, hoping not to run into Sam or anyone else who knew him there. He sat down on one of the stools closest to the exit. The bartender came right over to him. "Hey, Detective, how ya doing? I heard you're off the case?"

"Yeah, that's what we want the public to think, but can I trust you to keep it to yourself? Get my drift?" Noelle winked.

"So, what can I get for you?"

The last thing he needed was another drink, but he couldn't sit there and order nothing. "Irish whiskey," he said.

The bartender poured a shot and put the glass on the bar in front of Noelle. "Can't believe George Brunswick was murdered. That's sure going to put a dent in Sam's income." Noelle nearly choked on his drink but tried to hide his surprise at the news. His thoughts were all over the place as he wondered what had happened. Did that mean he'd been wrong about Brunswick too? He knew that Lopez and Brennan were probably tearing their hair out right about now.

Casually, Noelle said, "You know I can't talk about the case, but listen—I'm looking for a guy who works here, a dealer named Travis."

"Oh, sure, Travis, he's on at nine. You don't think he's involved with the killings? He used to deal for Brunswick at the high-roller tables."

Noelle took a sip of whiskey. "He's not likely the guy we are looking for, but as I said, I can't talk about the case. Do you have Travis's number?"

"I'm not allowed to give employees' info out. Sorry."

Noelle managed to pull a card out of his pocket. "Look, when you see him, please give him this. He's no suspect, I'll tell you that much, but I need to ask him some questions about someone else he knows who might know something."

Just then, a drunk at the other end of the bar crashed down onto his back on the floor. "Shit!" the bartender said. "That old drunk always does this and I always have to clean up after him."

Noelle stood. "I'll help you." The two of them pulled the old guy up by the armpits and dragged him over to a booth.

"Tell you what, Detective; since you helped me out, here you go." On the back of Noelle's card, the bartender scrawled Travis's phone number and address. "Let's keep this just between us, okay?"

"You got it, thanks so much." Noelle left a big tip on the bar and hurried off.

The winds were getting fierce; Noelle pulled his truck over to a phone booth and ran through the elements to call Travis. It took some persuasion, but Travis agreed to give him the address where Sally was living. It just happened to be in the same building where Travis lived.

Twenty minutes later, Noelle hurried from his truck up the small metal staircase to Sally's apartment. Noelle ran into Travis on the stairway. Noelle thanked him by pulling out a hundred-dollar bill.

"Oh wow, Detective. I sure wish I could take that, but I care about Sally, and besides, now that you lost your job, you probably need that bill as much as any of us."

"Yeah, I guess I do." Noelle stuck the hundred in his pocket. Travis looked at Noelle with sympathy and said, "You really care about her, don't you?"

"I really do; she's been through hell and back."

"Be kind to her. She loves you; she told me so." Travis smiled innocently, showing his sweet dimpled cheeks. Noelle thought, *This kid is so good looking,* but he didn't feel an ounce of jealousy because he could tell Travis was probably gay. He'd never taken kindly to homosexuals before, but he was really grateful that he'd met this one who cared about his Sally and would look out for her too.

Noelle's chest swelled with a rush of hope at the same time his fingers began to shake. Noelle felt remorse for not trying harder in their marriage. He should have figured out how difficult it was for Sally to change her whole life so fast. He should have given her more credit for trying to make that change in the first place.

He looked down at himself and saw that he had to get it together for Sally's sake if not for his own. He tucked his shirt-tail back into his pants and smoothed his hair over his bald spot, wondering what the new Sally would see now when she looked at him. He took a deep breath and knocked on her door. Something moved in her apartment and he rapped harder.

A small voice, shaky with fear, called out, "Who—who is it?"

"Sally, it's me. Nick."

"Nick? Prove it's you. Tell me what kind of bed you bought us before I unlock the door."

Nick felt so bad that she was that frightened. He remembered the day her whole face lit up and how she fell back onto that bed laughing, not one bit afraid of anyone or anything. Now he thought she might have even been scared of him some of the time too: afraid she wouldn't live up to his expectations, afraid she'd ruin it all. But in reality it was he who'd broken it all. His voice, filled with emotion, said, "Sally, please open the door. You don't have to be afraid now. George Brunswick is dead. As for our bed, it was a big old brass one and it's been empty without you in it ever since you left me."

Sally swung open the door wearing a flowery flannel nightgown, her dark red hair longer falling in waves past her shoulders, longer than he remembered it. Her deep green eyes welled with tears as Nick came through the door.

In a glance he took in the clean, fresh space with the bare floors and a colorful rug and plush used sofa. She'd even hung a few pictures of flowers on the wall. Her new environment had the essence of innocence that she was newly discovering.

He spotted the teddy bear on her bed, and he couldn't help it anymore—tears ran down his face. "Sally."

All kinds of expressions showed; he wasn't sure what they meant.

There wasn't any stopping him now as he pulled her toward him and held her body close to kiss her. She melted into him.

Noelle carefully moved the teddy bear from Sally's bed onto her dresser and made sweet love to her.

––––––

The next morning, Sally woke up and stretched her limbs like a cat, feeling warm and sleek in her new skin. Strong in her body, whole and clear in her mind, she knew that Nick loved her, and she loved him, and they were finally going to have a life together. She relished the heat of his body still warming the sheets where they'd slept.

"Nick?" She figured he must be making coffee, or maybe taking a shower. She got up, checked the bathroom first, and padded into the room off the bedroom that was both a kitchenette and living room. He'd made a pot of coffee and left it for her with a note.

My dearest love,

Last night, I finally figured out what I should have known all along. You were always the one. I have always loved you, and I always will. I saw the pure heart inside you, still there even though evil men have tried to desecrate you.

I wanted to stay until you woke up, but I have to go find this monster. Please, Sally, I need to know you're safe. I'll be back as quick as I can. I promise.

I love you,
Nick

She knew Nick had been taken off the case, so she didn't understand what he was about to do. Sally worried. She went into the bathroom to get ready. She had planned to return to the Dime coffee shop to see if they would give her the waitress job back. As she was putting on the lipstick she'd bought from Pamela, she wondered if Nick still had feelings for Pamela. She thought about how Pamela must be feeling now too, knowing that all her friends and now her lover George was dead. She was probably terrified, and Sally almost didn't blame her for wanting Nick around to keep her safe. Sally thought again and remembered how Pamela never seemed worried about her own safety, how she really was only sweet when she wanted something from someone.

She put down the lipstick and was stunned by the thought that followed. Could Pamela be the killer? And if she was, why would she kill her friends, or George Brunswick, her meal ticket? If Pamela was the killer, and she knew that Nick was done with her for real, Nick might be next.

Sally felt somewhat foolish thinking those crazy thoughts as she finished getting ready to leave the house. Later, at the Dime, Sally was immediately put back to work, but that same train of thinking about Pamela nagged her throughout the lunch shift. By the time she finished up at work, she remembered the black truck and the black-cloaked woman coming out of Pamela's apartment the last time she followed her. A cold shiver blew through her heart, and her worry over Nick blotted out her fear for her own safety. The chilling thoughts didn't stop her when she decided to find and follow Pamela again.

———

Noelle jumped in his truck and drove as fast as he could through the storm. Palm fronds swung wildly and oak leaves shredded away from their branches. *You don't need a weatherman to say which way the winds blow* was a Bob Dylan lyric that popped into his head. He could feel the hurricane a-comin'. He knew by now Donnelly would have made him a suspect in Brunswick's murder. He imagined his face plastered on the six o'clock news. He had to move fast and lay low at the same time. He was a man on a mission: find the killer, get his job back, and start a new life with Sally. As long as the idiot cops thought he was the killer, he couldn't be anywhere near Sally. He feared that Donnelly might send men to her place with guns loaded, and there was no way in hell he could put Sally at risk. He drove to a small town outside Houston, where he traded his truck for some cash and a smaller car, bought a few supplies, and turned back to Houston, thinking the whole way that both George and Richard must have been in on the murders. As soon as he was back in Houston he would search for Richard Lowden. He suspected that after Marianna's murder, Lowden had hit the breaking point.

He wished he could trust Brennan and Lopez to figure it out and crack the case, but he knew he couldn't. Lopez had come a long way under his mentorship, but he just didn't know about Brennan. He suspected that Brennan could be on the take like Cullen or Donnelly. And if that was so, Noelle would have to stay clear of them all. He drove through Tanglewood and parked down the street from Lowden's place. He pulled out a pair of electrician's coveralls and a toolbox from his trunk, throwing the coveralls on over his clothes. He walked right up to Lowden's front door like any other workman who had been called out on the many power outages happening from the heavy winds. He ducked around to the back and put on a pair of gloves to cut the telephone wire. He wrapped a towel around one of the hammers from his toolbox to keep the noise down and used it to break out a small windowpane in the back door. He reached his hand through to unlock the door and climbed inside.

Immediately the hair rose on his neck when he smelled that familiar odor. He made his way through the kitchen, stepping quietly, listening while he checked the living room and the dining room. Seeing no signs of a struggle, he moved down the hallway to the study, cautiously opening the door into the dark room. When he switched on the overhead lights he saw Richard Lowden's body lying on the floor in a pool of blood, with a gun near his hand. At his side was a note, sticky with blood. Noelle tried to pick it up with two gloved fingers, but it stuck in the blood and started to tear. He squatted down, careful not to step in the blood, to read it.

The only person Noelle had thought might have some answers was dead, but obviously not butchered in the same way as the other victims. Most likely it was suicide, but it could have been staged to look that way by the killer. In the note Lowden confessed to killing his wife Priscilla and said he could no longer live without love. Noelle thought that Lowden more than likely had nothing to do with the other murders, because if he had, he would have confessed to those while he was at it. Noelle peeled off the bloody gloves and backed out of the room, making sure he left no tracks while he switched off the light. He trotted briskly back to his rented car, hoping no one had seen him come or go.

CHAPTER 33

After spending hours in the bayou at Priscilla Lowden's crime scene, Brennan and Lopez made their way to Richard Lowden's house to inform him of his wife's murder. In Brennan and Lopez's book, all fingers pointed to Lowden for his wife's death, but Donnelly and Cullen were casting aspersions on Noelle. Cullen even had the nerve to suggest that Noelle might be psychotic enough to commit that gruesome murder too.

Lopez was at the boiling point, and Brennan was looking forward to seeing how Lowden would react to the news. He drove, struggling to see through the heavy rains cascading over his windshield. Lopez sat quiet and pensive. He hadn't said more than two sentences since Donnelly had told them to keep an eye out for Noelle, and if they saw him to bring him in.

Brennan, frustrated by his silence, slammed his hand on the steering wheel and said, "Goddammit, Lopez! How can you just sit there? Don't you have anything to say?"

Lopez's dark eyes were thoughtful and sad. "Noelle would have cracked this case if he hadn't let that Pamela bewitch him."

Brennan sighed. "Yeah, we know Noelle was a smart cop, that's for sure, as long as he thought with his big head and not his little head. Too bad the guy couldn't keep it in his pants." The light turned green and Brennan jumped out ahead of oncoming traffic. "You don't know him like I do; he had to have real feelings for that girl," Lopez said. "But the few times I saw her, she seemed so cold; never showed any emotions over her friends' murders either. I didn't know God created girls without feelings."

Brennan thought about Lopez's observations and then said, "Jealousy is a powerful motivator. How can you be so sure Noelle had nothing to do with Brunswick's murder?"

"Noelle may be a hothead and he's had a hard life, but he's solid. He's a good cop with a big heart, even if he keeps it up his ass most of the time."

Brennan asked, "So you think Lowden killed Priscilla?"

Lopez shrugged, then nodded. "Well, he is the husband, so probably."

"You think he might have killed the others too?"

Lopez shook his head. "I doubt it. I can't figure how Priscilla's murder relates to any of those others." Suddenly a big palm frond snapped in the wind and crashed down on the road. Brennan swerved the Plymouth, missing it by an inch. Lopez made the sign of the cross and spoke softly under his breath. "It's what happens when people worship this world and not God. It invites pure evil."

Brennan was relieved to pull into Lowden's driveway still in one piece. The street was quiet, and Lowden's house was dark, no lamps lit or masking tape around the windows to keep a predicted hurricane from smashing the glass. Brennan noticed that all the houses were without lights. He and Lopez dashed through the rain to the front door and rang the bell again and again. After pounding the door, they waited only a few seconds before Brennan tried the knob and found it unlocked. As they entered, the smell of decomp hit them like a shovel in the face. The air-conditioning was off, the humidity was as thick as the Amazon, and there was a loud buzzing coming from down the hall.

They both drew their guns as they made their way into the living room, where the scent grew more unbearable. Brennan noticed Lopez had taken his tie off and pulled it across his nose. Brennan did the same. Lopez went first for the doorknob and when he opened it, the noise from the buzzing flies sounded like a fire alarm.

Lowden's body lay in front of a leather couch with chunks of his brain scattered on the carpet. One hand was stretched out on the floor and next to it was a piece of paper stuck in a clotted pool of blood. A gun lay on the other side of Lowden's body.

Brennan shook his head. "Goddamn motherfucker killed himself?"

"Looks like he's been dead awhile too, maybe even before Brunswick."

He and Lopez quickly checked the house to make sure no one else was there before they approached the body. Back in the study, Lopez pulled on a pair of gloves and squatted beside the body, easing the piece of paper from the blood pool. Lopez handed Brennan the note. Brennan, embarrassed to admit it, said, "I left my reading glasses back at the squad. You read it to me."

Lopez held it carefully by one corner and read aloud.

To Whom It May Concern,

I, Richard S. Lowden, am taking my life because it never amounted to anything. The girl I loved left me and then she ended up dead. George Brunswick only befriended me so he could use me. Now he's dead. I've ruined everything I ever touched. The only girl who never laughed at me was my wife, and I tore her apart. I killed the only person who loved me and now there's nothing to live for.

Lowden's signature was an inky flourish beneath those pained lines.

Sweat beaded up on Brennan's forehead as he moved to the window and looked out at the rain battering Lowden's tidy landscaping. "Lopez, there's a hurricane headed right toward us."

Lopez didn't answer. He'd picked up the phone and set it back down again. "The phone's dead. We have to go back to the car to radio this in."

"So, Detective," Brennan said. "You think this is it? You think Lowden's death closes the case?"

Lopez shook his head. "He only mentions his wife in the note. He confesses to tearing up the person who loved him—but not the others. I think he was just a weak and sinful man who ended up in a bad place and couldn't see a way out."

"All right, then. Let's get out of here. I can't take much more of the smell."

They waited outside in the car, beneath the beating rain, for the forensics team.

"Lopez," Brennan said, as the windshield quickly fogged up, "I can see you're getting to be one hell of a detective."

Lopez flashed him a quick smile and looked down at his hands. "Noelle taught me everything I know. But if Lowden didn't kill Brunswick, this only makes things worse for Noelle."

———

When Brennan walked back into the precinct, he was plain worn out. The last twenty-four hours of horror had been more than he could take. He'd seen George Brunswick's penis on a scythe, Priscilla Lowden's bloated body covered in mud, and now Richard Lowden with his brains blown out. He wondered how poor Lopez had been able to hold up with all that he and Noelle had seen too. He was at a loss as to where to go next.

Lopez made a phone call to the coroner's office, then took off for the evidence room. Brennan sat at his desk reading through Noelle's notebook again and started to copy over Noelle's chicken-scratch handwriting with all the important information, including phone numbers for damn near everyone he and Lopez had talked to. He went through the motions like a kid writing his punishment on the blackboard at school over and over again.

No one believed some crazed serial killer had just rolled into town at the start of the summer rains and started hacking up pretty rich girls. All around him other detectives in the squad took phone calls, got up and left, came back, drank coffee, and wadded up paper to toss in the trash basket. With every move, they each cocked an eye at Brennan, wondering if he was going to solve this case. They probably had a pool going, and Brennan thought for sure that they were all betting against him getting the job done. He tugged at his already loose tie and made himself concentrate on Noelle's notes.

Noelle had written ideas about everyone, except for Pamela. There was nothing but her home phone number and her work number and extension at Neiman's.

She was the only one in the girl gang left. It was way past getting late in the day, and Lopez had returned from the evidence room and called Maria to see if she needed him to pick anything up on his way home. When he hung up, Brennan said, "I'll be heading out in a bit, but there's something I want to check out on my way home." Lopez gave him a funny look, but Brennan only shrugged. He didn't share with Lopez that he was about to pay Pamela a visit, not yet; he wanted to see this girl on his own.

Lopez eyeballed him, thinking that perhaps Brennan kept secrets just the way Noelle had. The last thing Lopez needed or wanted right then was to know what Brennan could be up to. All he wanted was to get home, where his good, wholesome life remained. He knew his beautiful wife and daughter would be waiting for him, and there was nothing more he wanted to do but to protect them and make sure they were safe.

———

Brennan switched on the car radio, heard the country station Noelle liked, and quickly turned the dial until he found a station playing some good old rock and roll. Now that was his kind of music. The Rolling Stones' "(I Can't Get No) Satisfaction" blasted above the pounding wind and rain. He thought he was going to do his best to do just that: get some satisfaction before his day was over. He had to!

He didn't have time to circle the parking lot, so he pulled up in front of the valet outside the Galleria's hotel, stuck his head out, and called over to the guy in the red jacket, "Hey! Over here!"

The valet took one look at the Plymouth and curled his lip, then shook his head. "Sorry, guests only."

Oh, yeah? That got his Irish up, and Brennan stuck his badge out the window. "Get over here, now!" He was glad to see the valet run right up to the car, carrying a big umbrella for him, and apologize. "Park this for me," Brennan told him, "and don't make me wait when I come back. I'm on serious police business here."

He got out of the car and the valet slid in and drove off. Brennan hurried into the hotel lobby, where he took a second to straighten his tie, smooth down his suit coat, and run his hand over his fiery red hair. He saw himself reflected in a giant mirror and thought to himself that he didn't look half bad. Better and younger than Noelle, and not so weather-beaten. Face of an angel, his mother used to say. Brennan had grown into his full height at age thirteen: six foot one, a hundred and ninety-five pounds of righteous anger. His mother used to tell him God made him sprout up big and strong to protect her from his father, and that was just what he did when he outgrew his old man. Once his father could no longer use him and his mother as his favorite punching bags, the old man left the family to fend for themselves. Brennan became man of the house and from that day on had taken care of his mother and younger sisters.

He made his way through the hotel lobby and into Neiman's. All the girls working the makeup counters seemed frantic as they cleared their counters and packed away their displays. Most of the salesgirls were pretty, but he figured this Pamela had to be something else, if she had been Brunswick's main squeeze. He approached one girl and asked her where Pamela worked; the salesgirl pointed to the next counter over.

At first he didn't see Pamela because she was bending down behind the counter, but when she stood up he wasn't impressed. She wasn't the knockout he had expected.

"Hey, miss, I'm looking for Pamela O'Leary," Brennan said.

"I'm Pamela." She smiled, and right away Brennan saw how that smile changed her whole face. He looked her up and down, and in a strong, confident voice, he announced, "I'm Detective Brennan. I know you have been cooperating with Detective Noelle, but I've taken over his case now, and I need to ask you a few more questions."

Pamela smiled, and there was something in the way her eyes sparkled that made him think she had appreciated the way he had looked her over. "Detective, I'm sorry; we've been instructed to wrap up and secure our stations. There's the hurricane expected to hit Houston in a couple of hours, in case you haven't heard."

Brennan noted her sarcasm and didn't like it one bit. He said, "Sure, I understand. Can we talk while you're packing?"

"Well, Detective, I'll try to give you my undivided attention as best I can." She fluttered her lashes. Brennan knew she was trying to charm him, probably the same thing she'd done to Noelle, the poor sap. Brennan wasn't about to get himself in trouble over some girl, especially this one. He knew at a glance she wasn't worth it.

His mother and four younger sisters would never let him hear the end of it. He looked Pamela straight in the eye and held her gaze, keeping his face stony.

"I thought I'd find you in mourning." Brennan's voice was calm as he pushed to see if he could make her lose her cool. "With your boyfriend murdered on the heels of all your girlfriends, hacked and chopped to death, I would think you'd be real rattled."

He paused to see if his brutal words would make her flinch, but they didn't. Pamela kept silent and bent below her counter to put away the boxes of lipsticks she had been packing. Brennan kept hounding her. "Why have you never asked for police protection?"

She popped her head up over the counter. "Well, Detective, I've had some police protection, and as you know, it didn't work out so well." She winked as she stood up straight.

"Do you know that Noelle's gone missing? You wouldn't have any ideas where we might find him?"

"Have you checked Sam's? He does like the cards and booze as much as he likes the ladies."

"The department thinks he killed George Brunswick because of you."

Her eyes flashed. "I refuse to take the blame for that. If he went mad because of me and George, that's not my fault. Nick knew about us from the get-go. I never lied or cheated on either of them. It was all out in the open. I told George that I had a couple of dates with Nick just to keep him on his toes. And for your information, I had already broken up with George before he went and got himself killed. If I were the Houston police I'd be looking into that batshit wife of his. I'm sure she had plenty of motives to kill her old man."

"I was under the impression that George Brunswick dumped you."

Pamela shuddered a bit, and Brennan watched as she pulled it together and gave him a little-lost-girl look. "Yes, you're right. He did call it off, but not because he didn't love me. It was a complicated situation. He was trying to convince his wife that we were through so she'd loosen up the purse strings to the family fortune. I'm surprised Nick didn't write that down in that big black notebook he kept."

Brennan smirked. "I think Noelle hid some of his information from us before he left."

Pamela bent over her counter as she reached for another box, making sure that her breasts were in full view for Brennan. "Detective, after Julia's murder I needed a friend, and Detective Noelle and I became close. But he was more like a father figure to me. I didn't grow up with a dad to give me good advice, and that's the kind of thing Nick liked to do. He was very kind in the beginning, and of course he ruined it when he fell in love with me, then tried to take advantage of me. Now I don't have his protection, so yes, Detective, I am scared. And for your information, just because I don't show up to work looking like the Black Widow doesn't mean I'm not in mourning, especially now with George gone, I need this job more than ever. I don't get to go anywhere social anymore, just to work and home. I've lost my girlfriends and my lover, who was the man I trusted to take care of me. Now I hear rumors that Nick might have been the killer all along. My life was hard enough before all this killing business started. If only I had gotten that full scholarship to UT, I would have had a chance to make something of myself and not be stuck behind this makeup counter."

Brennan thought, *Yeah, and if my father hadn't been a rager I'd be president of the United States*. He felt no pity for her sob story and said coldly, "Sounds tough. But you've got some looks, enough to snag a Brunswick, and you're young still, young enough to hook another big fish. You could make something of yourself, assuming you're not next on the killer's hit list."

She had fire in her eyes and snapped, "That's a mean-spirited thing to say. What kind of a cop are you anyway?"

"I know it makes you real angry, doesn't it, life's little twists, turns, and disappointments?"

A tear trickled down her face. "I could really use a friend right now."

"Look. Do you know anything at all? We don't have much time; this killer's lack of control is escalating and you should be scared. If I were you, I'd go straight home and lock your doors."

Pamela grabbed her jacket and began to walk away, then turned back and said, "It's been charming."

CHAPTER 34

After Noelle left Lowden's place, he drove out to the neighborhood where Pamela lived and parked in a spot from which he'd see her car coming and going. He'd learned a long time ago to grab some shut-eye when he could, so he pulled the fishing hat he'd bought down low over his face and tried to get some sleep, but the battering winds kept him awake. He decided to drive to the Galleria to see if Pamela was still there. He was surprised that the Galleria and Neiman's were still open despite the approaching storm, but sure enough, Neiman's employee lot was still full when he got there. He spotted Pamela's Mustang, pulled in near it, and waited. He got impatient and decided to check the store inside, but before he did, he got back into his coveralls and grabbed his toolbox. Once inside, disguised as a workman, he busied himself at an electrical outlet where he could see Pamela still at her counter. He remained out of sight but was able to watch as Brennan approached her. He watched the whole scene between them but never heard a word. He just read their expressions and body language and could only imagine what was transpiring between them.

He watched Pamela preening in front of Brennan, the same way she had with him. Her behavior made him feel so stupid for falling for her. He objectively studied Pamela's manipulating expressions, and for the first time, his instinct told him something was very wrong with her. He allowed himself to ask the hard questions: How come she hadn't been attacked? She was a lot like the murdered girls except for the money. Did the killer have a thing about money and beauty? Could envy bring forth such rage? Brunswick was rich, and the killer had gotten him too. Brunswick had also let Pamela down.

Pamela, who didn't get that scholarship and who had to work at Neiman's instead of lunching at the country club, had a thing for sure about the rich, pretty, and powerful.

Even though he couldn't hear Brennan's questions, he was interpreting much of what was actually being said. He revisited the idea about there being more than one killer. A lady serial killer could manipulate a stronger man into becoming her accomplice. Pamela had learned how to keep a guy on the hook, for sure. Noelle had unfortunately learned that the hard way. If the truth was as horrible as he was thinking, she most likely had other suckers like him doing her bidding. If what his gut was telling him was true, he knew he'd have to stop her.

He waited until Brennan left, and then he followed Pamela out of the Galleria. She never once looked back, but her Mustang was faster and zippier than his cheap rental car, and he lost her in the prehurricane-frenzied rush-hour traffic.

———

Brennan drove back to the precinct, where all hell had broken loose. One of the uniforms stopped him; the young cop's face had a wild mix of excitement and worry.

"You're not going to believe this. We got a call from a neighbor who saw Noelle coming out of Lowden's house dressed like a workman. Donnelly put an APB out for Noelle."

Brennan silently questioned this witch hunt. It didn't make any sense; he knew Lowden had killed himself. He started for the stairs but then turned back to the young cop and jabbed a finger in his chest. "Nobody's a killer until he's proven guilty. You remember that, kid."

As soon as he entered the squad room, Donnelly jumped up to beckon him. Lopez was already there, and Cullen was sitting in the visitor's chair. He looked Brennan up and down. "Donnelly called your place an hour ago. How come it took you so long to get back here?"

Brennan's jaw clenched. He didn't want to tell Cullen about his talk with Pamela. That would just get Cullen all twisted around and maybe wondering if Brennan would blow things the same way Noelle had. "Traffic's a mess."

The chief's face flushed. "I don't give a damn about the weather. I want Noelle found, right now."

Brennan saw Lopez stiffen. Lopez spoke up. "Chief, Noelle didn't kill Brunswick or Lowden or anyone."

Donnelly frowned, leaning back in his chair and giving Lopez a hard stare. "Lopez, if I were you, I'd do some listening and keep my mouth shut."

Steam rose in Brennan. "Lopez has been at every crime scene and interviewed every suspect. He knows this case better than any of us do. My bet's on Lopez here."

Donnelly stood up, his face flushed. "I'd keep out of this, Brennan; that is, if you know what side your bread is buttered on."

Cullen gave Brennan a cold look and waltzed out of the office.

Donnelly sat back down and held his head in his hands, tugging at his bald head. Finally he straightened up. "Okay, look. Lowden confessed to killing Priscilla, and she was left in the bayou like the others, so he must have done those too. They just weren't worth confessing about in his note. We figured he didn't feel any remorse for them, but when he killed his wife, he couldn't live with himself anymore. That's the story. The coroner puts Lowden's time of death before Brunswick's, so we know Lowden didn't kill Brunswick. Now we have a witness saying she saw Noelle acting suspicious around Lowden's place this morning. As far as Cullen's concerned, the case is closed. I'm not nearly as happy about this as you think, but this is where we're at. Let's just do what we have to do. Lopez, do you have any idea where Noelle is? He's not at his apartment, and he's not at Sam's."

"No, sir."

"Is he still seeing Pamela?"

"I doubt it."

"She's the only one left from that circle of girls. She could be next. If Noelle killed Brunswick over her, and she's dumped Noelle, he would go after her too."

Lopez made a scoffing sound. Donnelly held up one hand. "I said *if*, Detective. *If* whoever killed Brunswick also killed those girls, and *if* that person is Noelle, then who knows what he'll do next."

Brennan groaned. "That's nuts, Lieutenant."

"If something happens to Pamela, we'll all be dead or wish we were. Find her and bring her in. Tell her we're putting her under protection. Maybe she'll feel safe enough to talk."

Lopez flashed Brennan a look; Brennan knew just what he was thinking. Pamela knew something all right, but neither Lopez nor Brennan thought she'd talk about it.

CHAPTER 35

Before they left the station again, Lopez made the obligatory call to Pamela's home but got no answer. Neither he nor Brennan was in such a hurry to pick her up. They knew it would keep till the storm passed. Lopez had had it with all the pressure heaped on him and finally took off in his own car to pick up the extra supplies for his family to prepare for the hurricane. Brennan went home spent and disgusted.

At home Brennan dropped a couple of ice cubes into a glass and poured a nice cool drink of Tab. Tab was the one thing he and Lopez had in common. He carried it into the living room, took off his jacket and necktie, and put the Creedence Clearwater Revival album on his new hi-fi. He plopped down on the couch, put his feet up, and started singing along to "Bad Moon Rising." It got Brennan thinking about the case again. The only possible suspect he hadn't thought of was Brunswick's wife. She probably wanted him dead, but there was no way she had the strength to kill like that unless she hired someone. He wondered what the going rate would be to commit a crime so gruesome. He thought of Pamela again and how she had managed to twist Noelle's head around,

all while she was sleeping with Brunswick. If Pamela wasn't into
Noelle for money, what was it? It couldn't be for Noelle's hot body.
What were her motives? Pamela was the kind of gal who always
wanted something, and he wondered if there was someone else
close to Pamela. She had to be a superwoman to hold down a full-
time job and be dating two different men; where would she find the
time to sleep with anyone else? He even thought of her having sex
with her girlfriends. Whoever that someone else was, could he or
she be the one who'd killed Brunswick? It was pretty obvious that
whoever had done in Brunswick sure hated men. All his thinking
just had him going in circles, so he kicked back and started singing
to his song again.

> *Don't go around tonight,*
> *Well it's bound to take your life,*
> *There's a bad moon on the rise.*
> *I hear hurricanes a blowing.*
> *I know the end is coming soon.*
> *I fear rivers overflowing.*
> *I hear the voice of rage and ruin.*
>
> *Don't go around tonight,*
> *Well it's bound to take your life,*
> *There's a bad moon on the rise.*
> *Hope you got your things together.*
> *Hope you are quite prepared to die.*
> *Looks like we're in for nasty weather . . .*

Just as he was about to doze off, a thought struck him like a
bolt of lightning and he jumped up. It was the most obvious thing.
If Pamela was the killer or in cahoots with the killer, she wouldn't
be scared because she knew she'd never be attacked!

He grabbed his jacket and was about to go back to work when he heard his front door open and close. He moved fast, but not fast enough. As he put his hands up to protect his head, something hard came down on it, again and again. Blood ran warm down the sides of his face and the back of his neck. He felt the knife pierce his side, just under his ribs, and white-hot pain shot through his body. He tried to turn and fight, but the knife slid in again and his chest was sliced wide open. As the air left his body, his eyes opened and he saw the face of his attacker.

———

Noelle waited outside Pamela's apartment building for a long time, but she never showed up. On his car radio he heard the news report of Cullen's statement to the press about the case being closed because of evidence pointing to Richard Lowden as the killer of all the girls and his wife. He listened for the rest of the news about Brunswick's murder, but it didn't come up. He assumed they were holding it back until they got more on him so they could close the books on that one too.

The thought Noelle had been trying hard not to think bubbled up like sour acid again. He knew the answer to his question before he even asked it. He knew who hated beautiful rich girls because they didn't have to work a crappy job and everything came easily to them. He knew who resented those same girls because they didn't have to suck up to anyone to get the good things in life. They could pick and choose whatever man they wanted and could get a guy they actually loved instead of having to sleep with a monster.

His gut burned and he wanted a drink, but he knew that was the last thing he needed. If Pamela was the answer to his questions, then suddenly he knew Sally wasn't safe. Sally wasn't rich, but she had become beautiful. Pamela had been enraged when Sally had told her about what Brunswick did to her.

His hands shook from lack of alcohol and because he hadn't eaten anything but a quick sandwich early that morning. He had to get something in his stomach. He was going to need all the strength he could muster to set things right. He pulled into the back parking lot of a U-tote-M and tugged his fisherman's hat down over his eyebrows, keeping his head low as he walked into the convenience store, careful not to look closely at the customers or the clerk behind the counter. He kept his head down and his fingers crossed. The place was crowded with people buying canned food, matches, masking tape, and other hurricane supplies. He walked down the few aisles, staring at the boxes of crackers and bags of chips, avoiding anyone's eyes. He picked out a prepackaged sub sandwich and a beer and grabbed a cheap yellow plastic slicker with a hood. He put his stuff and a ten-dollar bill on the counter in front of the skinny teen clerk, and the kid just rang him up, handing him the change with a grunt and never looking up at his face.

Inside his car, Noelle ate the sandwich in a couple of quick bites and slurped down the beer as fast as he could. He belched and pulled back out of the lot undetected by anyone. It was a risk, but he decided to drive over to Brennan's place. He knew Brennan had last seen Pamela, and he needed to learn what she told him. He hoped that by now Brennan was up to speed and maybe also suspected Pamela. When he observed them talking, Noelle could see their facial expressions and Pamela's attempts to twist Brennan around, but he also noticed how Brennan didn't fall for her crap. It gave him hope that Brennan might be a good cop after all.

He found Brennan's place in one of those solid middle-class apartment buildings where cops, teachers, and nurses lived. He made sure his fisherman's hat was squarely on his head and low over his eyebrows. Very slowly he got out of the car and entered the building. Brennan lived on the eighth floor. Noelle checked his watch before he pushed the button for the elevator. It was almost eleven p.m., and he hoped Brennan didn't go to bed early.

He rode the elevator up and made his way down the hallway to Brennan's apartment. The front door was cracked open. Immediately Noelle's warning signal flashed red. He knew a cop would never leave his front door open. Noelle pulled on his gloves and crept inside. There it was again, that same smell that met him at every crime scene: blood and death, his most familiar companions.

Brennan's body lay broken on the living room floor with pools of blood soaking into the beige shag carpet, turning it crimson.

"Goddammit!" Noelle said as tears came to his eyes. This victim was not a pretty girl, or a pathetic lonely wife like Priscilla, or a rich monster like Brunswick, or a useless flunky like Lowden. Brennan was a good cop, and now there he lay with his entire neck slit from ear to ear. When he stepped in closer, he saw what looked like Brennan's tongue cut out and left beside his body. Could Pamela have done this just because Brennan didn't give her the time of day? Could that same woman he had longed for and pined over only days ago be this insane? If she'd done this, she had to be on some kind of rampage now.

His blood iced over as he thought of Sally and charged out of Brennan's place. He jabbed the button for the elevator, peeled the gloves off, and fumbled for his keys while rushing out to his car.

———

Sally lay tossing and turning in her bed, listening to the wild storm outside her window. Large tree branches were scratching against her building and casting weird shadows on the walls of her apartment. The shadows brought to mind the chopped body parts of those poor dead girls. She tried to fluff up her pillows, to count sheep, but nothing worked. Agitated and frightened, she tried to rationalize why she shouldn't be afraid. She wasn't rich or powerful, and she didn't even think she was all that pretty. Why would anyone want to hurt her? And with Brunswick dead, she no longer had him to fear.

She sat up instantly when she heard a rattling sound coming from the living room. She reminded herself it was just the wind and rested her head on the pillow again. Suddenly she heard the sound of glass breaking in the other room.

She jumped out of bed and dashed to her bathroom, locking the door behind her. With her heart pounding like a sledgehammer, she searched around the blue-and-white tiled room for anything she could use as a weapon. All she saw scattered on the countertop was the makeup she'd bought from Pamela, a box of Kleenex, some hairpins, and a hairbrush. She picked up the brush and held it in her hands, watching the door and waiting. Footsteps on the wooden floor grew louder, coming toward the door, and slowly she watched the glass doorknob twist. Sally was shaking from head to toe, and tears began to run down her cheeks. Like a prayer she whispered the words, "Nick, I love you." It was a call to save her, and a good-bye to the man she loved, all in one word: "Nick."

A familiar voice roared through the door: "Come out, come out, wherever you are, whore," followed by mad laughter as the doorknob fell out on her side of the door onto the speckled linoleum floor.

The door flew open; the hairbrush was smacked from her hands and strong arms grabbed her. She fought with everything she had, kicking, biting, hitting, and shrieking until a cloth came down over her nose and mouth, and she started to float off, far away.

———

When Lopez got home late that night, he found that his wife and daughter had already secured all the windows with masking tape and rolled up the carpets. They'd filled the bathtub with water and set every breakable lamp and vase in a deep closet. He felt guilty that he hadn't been home with them to do the man's work but grateful that Maria and Dolores were strong, resourceful women who could survive in the world without a man if they had to.

In bed with Maria sound asleep next to him, Lopez glanced over at the clock. It was after midnight, and he couldn't sleep. The wind howled and battered the windows, rattled all the doors, and scraped across the rooftop of their little home. Wild as the wind, his thoughts had been scattered in all directions. He decided to give up on sleep and went into the kitchen to make a cup of coffee. The storm outside couldn't take away the storm going on in his mind.

He paced back and forth from the kitchen to the living room, sipping his coffee, thinking. He'd been sure George Brunswick was the killer, until they'd found him a victim too. Afterward, they'd discovered Richard Lowden with a bullet in his head and a suicide note. Lopez knew he wasn't the smartest man on the force, but he just couldn't believe Lowden had killed those girls, or Brunswick. Lowden was too weak, both his body and his character. He was also impulsive, and these killings had appeared to be planned except for the one of his wife, which he'd admitted to doing.

He drained his coffee cup, deciding he had to find Noelle, no matter how late it was. He practically flew to his closet, threw on some clothes, and found his badge and gun in the dark. He left Maria sleeping and ran out into the approaching hurricane, staggering to his car against the force of the wind. He drove through the storm, his car pelted by leaves, sticks, trash, and sheets of rain. His wipers were barely able to shove it off before the glass flooded again. His lips were moving the entire way as he only half-consciously recited the Hail Mary.

After nearly getting lost in Washington Heights, he rumbled up to Noelle's building, parked in the driveway, and noted that

Noelle's truck was gone. He dashed up the stairs to his apartment, where he found the door unlocked and went inside.

The place smelled of whiskey, and it looked like Noelle had left in a hurry. A glass was knocked over on the table beside his armchair, and instant coffee was spilled all over the kitchen counter. Lopez hurried back down the steps to his car and drove as fast as he could through the rain-slicked streets to Pamela's apartment. He banged and banged on the door, but no one answered. The place was pitch dark and not even a night-light glowed from inside. Lopez decided to take a page out of Noelle's book and break the rules. When he jimmied the lock and opened the door, he didn't need to find the light to see the horror inside. He was surprised he hadn't smelled it from outside. The bodies of a woman, who he supposed was Pamela's mother, and a man were decomposing and smelling rotten.

Lopez ran from the scene, shutting the door behind him. The carnage only confirmed his suspicions about Pamela. Those bodies had to have been there for days, and there was no way she didn't know about it. His entire body was tense with fear, but it drove him even harder to find Noelle before she or anyone else could. Lopez knew that if she could kill her own mother, she certainly could have killed the others. Lopez decided to make an anonymous call to the precinct from a pay phone to tip them off about the murders at Pamela's house. He prayed it would put the investigation back on course. In the meantime he would find his guidance from the Lord. After he placed the call and jumped back in his car, he prayed the deepest, most sincere prayer he'd ever prayed in his life, and he asked his God for help. He let Jesus take the wheel when a voice from within told him to head for the bayou. He followed the command and didn't even think to call Brennan for backup.

———

Noelle's only thought was of Sally and finding her before anyone else did. He parked his car outside her building and stepped into a wash of water, soaking his feet up to his knees. He ran up the rickety stairs to Sally's room, almost falling in his soggy pants. He promised himself that once he found her, he'd treat her like a princess. He'd stop drinking and gambling for good, and he would find a nice house where she could plant flowers in the flower beds again. He'd give every cent he had to make her safe and happy.

He knocked on her door with their special knock so as to not scare her in the middle of the night. His hands were shaking again, and they were even worse when she didn't answer. He pounded on her door. His stomach was flipping and flopping from the rush of anxiety that rose up in him. Then he saw the broken glass next to the door. His panic went into high gear when he saw that her place was in shambles. He discovered the knob to the bathroom door lying on the floor. He didn't know what to do or where to go. Any minute now he knew the hurricane winds were going to knock down telephone lines, shatter windows, and tear off rooftops, and the rain could flood half the city. How would he find Sally? In his panic he almost missed the note on her bed.

Dear Detective Noelle,

Surprise, surprise! Your ex-wife, or should I say, your ex-hooker is all tied up and helpless, but that's nothing new for her. For all I know, that might be one of her biggest turnons. And you might get a thrill too if you come on down to the bayou at our favorite place and watch the event we have planned for you lovebirds. I promise you a bloody good show.

Guess Who?

Noelle sank to his knees and uttered a prayer. "Please, God, take me instead." He sprang to his feet with adrenaline pumping through every vein in his body. Noelle ran against the wild wind to find his girl.

———

Darkness covered everything. The few streetlights that had not been affected by the power outage cast only an eerie dim light here and there. Noelle drove like the devil was on his tail through muddy flooding streets, with fifty-mile-an-hour gusts pounding his car. Suddenly the floodwaters rose up to the floorboards of his car, and the car was lifted in the rushing current for several feet until it crashed into a fallen tree on the road. Noelle jumped out of the car, knowing he'd have to trek on foot the remaining distance to the bayou.

Bracing against the rushing waters, he made his way around to the trunk, stabbing the key into the lock, and grabbed a flashlight out of the toolbox. He checked his gun, making sure there was a round in the chamber. If he didn't get to Sally in time, it didn't matter what happened to him. He should have called Lopez, filled him in about Brennan and Sally, and told him that he was going after Pamela, but it was too late now. Even if he had seen a phone booth on the road in the black of night, he knew most of the power lines were down already. With no backup, he was on his own. He put the yellow rain slicker over him and slogged forward to his final destination. He knew his jig with the devil was up.

With the wind lashing at his face, he tried his best to keep his eyes open and scan the area. Lightning pierced the black sky. It lit up a path littered with scrub brush and tangled trees. This was the very same path he and Lopez had struggled through to the bayou the first time, when they found Julia's body. It felt like a hundred years since then as Noelle pushed through the dark, fighting the wrathful elements from the sky. Without the occasional flash of lightning, he couldn't even see his own hand in front of his face. He fumbled with his flashlight, switching it on and shining it on each step in front of him on the muddy, treacherous ground. He couldn't afford to break an ankle or fall into the mud and slime.

Another flash of lightning lit up an old black sixties-model pickup truck that was parked in the brush not far off the path. Sally had told Noelle about a black truck she had seen parked outside Pamela's house. Noelle scurried off the path and moved through bushes and trees, down toward the bayou's edge. His eyes adjusted to the dark and he heard sounds not far off. He spotted three dark figures in a clearing up ahead. One of them wore a flowing cape and another appeared like a shadow of a man holding what could have been a chain saw. Noelle shuddered and hoped he was hallucinating this scene that looked like something out of a Halloween Satan worship movie.

———

Lopez had to find Noelle before Pamela did. If she could manage to kill Brennan, who was much younger and stronger than Noelle, she could take him down too.

He believed in divine guidance, and he knew he was being led. Lopez drove through the streets to Allen Parkway, dodging downed trees in the middle of the road going as fast as he could, skidding around corners, running red lights at flooded, empty intersections, and breaking every traffic rule in the book—praying all the while, switching between Hail Marys and Our Fathers.

There was only one place the killer would return to: the bayou.

———

Noelle threw all caution to the wind and hurried down the path, nearly slipping in mud. He grabbed hold of tree trunks to get steady. As he got closer he could see the figures in clear focus now. Yes, one was a man with a chain saw, and the hooded figure in black was Pamela. He froze when he saw her holding a long pair of scissors, smiling and laughing at Sally, who trembled with her hands tied behind her. It appeared as if Pamela had just chopped off all of Sally's hair, leaving her almost bald. Noelle could see Sally's long red locks swirling in the wind. He pointed his gun straight at Pamela, his finger tightening on the trigger, but his hands were still shaky. He couldn't trust his aim or his steadiness and couldn't risk hitting Sally. He edged closer, careful not to slip again.

The wind died down for a moment and he could hear Pamela speaking in harsh tones, but he could not make out her words. Whatever she was saying, Sally didn't seem to be hearing. Sally looked numb or in shock. Noelle realized that all the abuse Sally had endured from the time she was very young had been too much, and now there wasn't any fight left in her. In that moment, Noelle knew he had plenty of fight left in him for the both of them.

As lightning flashed, Pamela threw back her hood. Noelle saw that her face was ugly, with a smile that curled her lip. He had found it just charming at one time. Now it looked like a snarl from a wild beast. Her eyes were wild with rage, like those of a rabid animal, something that needed to be put down for the good of humanity. Noelle edged closer.

"Sally!" Pamela screamed in her face. "How do you like your makeover now, bitch? Once I'm through with you, we're going to feed you to the alligators!"

Hearing that, Noelle looked toward the man who was huddled in a dark raincoat holding the chain saw. Noelle couldn't see his face. Pamela shrieked at Sally's unmoving stance. It wasn't enough for her to kill and torture; she needed to be sure Sally was conscious of her pain. Pamela tormented her. "It was all over the news; the alligators are out and hungry. How do you think it's going to feel? Do you think the alligators will find your titties tasty? Or maybe you still hope your dear Nick will come to save your ugly ass?"

When he saw Sally lean over and vomit, he couldn't take it anymore. He stepped out from the trees into the clearing, with his gun pointed at Pamela's head. "I'm right here, Sally, and Pamela, it's all over for you."

Instantly Pamela locked her arm around Sally's neck, with the scissors pointed at her throat. Lightning lit up the skies and Sally saw Noelle's face. The fight in Sally came back. Noelle saw her naked trust in him restored.

Pamela shrieked, unhinged, "Nick, I don't know what you were thinking when you picked this little nothing over me. But I suppose she doesn't require anything but love, which is lucky for you since you don't have much else to give a girl. It was fun to watch you, so starry-eyed, chasing after me, all the while knowing that George was fucking me up, down, and sideways too. And just for the record, I never killed Julia Brunswick. I got that old pedophile George to admit it just before I chopped off his love tool. Poor little Julia never had a chance. She told me how Uncle George raped her the first time when she was only seven and didn't stop until she ran away to that junkie hell. Makes you feel for the rich and powerful, doesn't it?"

Pamela was so into her rant that she loosened her grip on Sally and spewed on.

"George may be the one who got the ball rolling, but you can credit me and my assistant for the rest of those snotty bitches. I hated all of them. They never gave me anything they hadn't already used or worn, and they never let me forget I was an outsider. They all deserved to die! I have to admit, though, I had the most fun cutting up ol' George. After all, Detective, don't you think he deserved what he got? I think I should get a Girl Scout medal for my brave act of justice. Don't you? I would have taken home my trophy, but my poor dead mama would have had a cow if she saw that limp dick of old George's on a scythe over our mantel in the living room."

From the corner of his eye, Noelle saw the man with the chain saw stand up, but he held his position as Pamela raged on.

"You are a useless cop. It was hell sleeping with you too, pretending I liked the sex. So go ahead, fire that gun, but I'll slice Sally's throat faster than you can squeeze the trigger. That way you can watch us both bleed. Two for the price of one—you ought to like that, you cheap son of a bitch! They'll think you did it too, because I will be dead and no one will believe that I could have done any of this."

He looked at Sally. She stared back at him as his finger tightened on the trigger. Pamela's head was too close to Sally's; he couldn't risk a miss. He shifted his aim to Pamela's shoulder, away from Sally's head. He looked at Sally again; she nodded slightly and went limp, dropping to the ground to give Nick a clean shot. He squeezed the trigger and the bullet hit Pamela square in the shoulder. She dropped the scissors, grabbed her wound, and screamed in hateful agony, "She's a goner, you bastard!"

Lightning flashed again, and the chain saw revved. Noelle saw Howard Wolvensky move toward Sally. Of course, Howard. He was the one with the muscles and the tools—just another boy who let Pamela take him for a ride. He aimed toward Howard, but Sally's body acted as a shield for him. For a split second he thought of Howard's poor, kind mother and how painful it would be for her to learn about her son.

Howard yelled, "Pamela, don't worry. I'll kill the cunt first and then the dick with his own gun. We can write a suicide note from him. We'll be free as birds and I'll take care of you. I'll get rich and I'll give you anything you want! Just give me the order."

At this point Pamela was so deranged that she ignored the fact that Howard was wielding a chain saw. She held one hand to her bleeding shoulder and sneered at Howard. "You must be kidding. You think I want a life with you when I can marry Jimmy Brunswick? Now that we've narrowed down his selection, he'll have to pick me. You're sweet, Howard, but really dumb for someone with such a high IQ. In the end the police will see that you're the killer, the only one who can handle a chain saw, not me."

Noelle watched Howard's rage as he fired up the chain saw while shouting back at Pamela, "After all I've done for you. I am the only one who ever loved you! You actually think you can cut me off?"

Pamela turned to Noelle for help. "Nick, shoot him. Remember that night in the hotel, how we were a perfect fit? It could be like that again. I'll do anything you want; just don't let Howard kill me."

Howard's chain saw slashed through Pamela's bleeding shoulder. Noelle didn't stop Howard but watched Pamela's arm fall into the slime beneath her before she could even cry out. Something in the water surged up and snatched her arm, sinking back into the sludge again. Pamela, yelling in pain, backed away from Howard as Sally moved slowly away from them toward Noelle. Pamela stepped closer and closer to the rising waters, and with the next flash of lightning, Noelle saw a large shape crawling up from the water; its flat marble eyes, teeth, and claws were illuminated as the gator tore at the fleshy meat of Pamela's severed arm. The next second, another alligator crawled up on its lizard feet and dragged Pamela down into the mud. Pamela saw the face of hell itself as she slid so easily into the slime of the earth. Pamela's deep blue eyes wildly pleaded for the very last time.

Suddenly Lopez was there, standing behind Howard with a shotgun in his hands. Noelle had no idea how he had gotten there but was just glad to see him. He and Lopez exchanged glances; while Noelle tried to pull Sally out of harm's way, Lopez kept his gun pointed at Howard.

Howard laughed hysterically as he watched the alligator clamp its jaws around Pamela's leg and drag her deeper down into the mud and water. It wasn't long before all that anyone could hear was the rushing wind and water sloshing through the tangled bushes while pieces of Pamela's filthy blond hair floated by on the water.

Nick threw his rain slicker over Sally's naked body to warm her. Howard aimed the chain saw in their direction and began to come toward them. Lopez, without hesitation or even a warning, squeezed the trigger and blew Howard's head into a million pieces. This time Lopez had no remorse about not doing things by the book.

Sally caved into Noelle's arms. He held her, whispering, "I've got you now. It's over. You're safe and it's all going to be okay."

Lopez rushed over to them both. "I knew you were right, boss. I knew you were right."

The three of them huddled there, all holding each other.

CHAPTER 36

Suddenly the winds died down and the rain lightened up. Police cars were everywhere up on the road above the bayou, their engines running and lights flashing, as Noelle, Sally, and Lopez made their way up and out of the woods. Lopez directed them down to the remains of Howard, filling them in on the details while Noelle tended to Sally.

Some of the cops on the scene took their hats off out of respect for Noelle, now that they realized he had been wrongly accused. Sally collapsed in Noelle's arms after the worst of it was over. He laid her on the backseat of one of the squad cars and found some blankets to cover her as they waited for an ambulance. Sally stared up into his eyes in shock. Knowing how badly the streets were cluttered from the storm, Noelle decided not to wait for the ambulance but got behind the wheel and gunned it as fast as he could to Ben Taub Hospital. He feared the emergency room might already be swamped with injured people, but he was relieved that the worst of the storm was now behind them.

As soon as he pulled up at the entrance to the ER, he ran inside, shouting for help. Nurses and orderlies followed him out with a gurney, scooped Sally up, and got her right into a room. A nurse started an IV and a doctor examined her. After a short wait, the doctor told Noelle that Sally had a ruptured spleen and needed immediate surgery. Noelle rode up in the elevator holding her limp hand. She was still and quiet—they'd already given her something for shock and pain. Noelle was weeping as he let her go with the surgical nurses behind closed doors.

Noelle went back to the squad car and called Donnelly to let him know where he was with the car. Donnelly assured him that Lopez was fine. He was already at the station giving the full report about what had happened in the bayou. Donnelly congratulated Noelle for solving the case.

For hours, Noelle paced, until the surgeon came out. He let Nick know that Sally was fine but she'd have to be careful of infections in the future since they had taken out her ruptured spleen. He assured Noelle that she would fully recover; now all she needed was rest. Noelle found Sally in the recovery room, still unconscious, with an IV in her arm. He lightly touched her forehead and patchy scalp. Sally's eyelashes fluttered and she opened her eyes to smile at him. As she drifted back to sleep, Noelle said, "Sally, honey, we're getting married again, the way you've always wanted, not at some registry or the courthouse. No, we're going to have a real wedding, a honeymoon, and a new house."

She opened her eyes again and uttered the word "Yes," then fell back to sleep.

Noelle laid his head next to hers and wept. Now that it was over, now that Sally was safe and Pamela was dead, he couldn't believe what they'd all lived through. A slideshow of gory images from all the victims flipped through his brain. He couldn't help it; he continued to sob. He recalled that first time he'd seen Pamela at Sam's, when she'd taken hold of a piece of his heart. She had done the most unspeakable things, yet he still felt some remorse for her. As he wept he realized he was not so much crying for Pamela or

Sally or Brennan or even himself; his tears were for every victim in the world who struggled with pain, lack, and abuse of one kind or another. His tears were plentiful; they were enough for the whole big sorrowful world.

When a nurse came in, he quickly wiped his eyes. She told him Sally would probably sleep through the night and suggested he go home, clean up, eat something, rest, and come back in the morning. He looked down at himself and for the first time in hours realized he was covered in dried mud and blood. He smiled his thanks to the nurse and headed for the elevator.

The last of the hurricane had passed over the city while he had waited for Sally in surgery, and the skies outside were clearing. Noelle was shocked to find a crowd of reporters and photographers waiting for him. "Detective Noelle! What's it feel like to be a hero?"

Noelle, stunned, shook his head, "You got the wrong guy. It was Detective Lopez who cracked the case and saved us all. I'm just here to make sure my future bride gets the special care she deserves."

The reporters weren't having any of that, and photographers snapped his picture as the reporters called out more questions. Some nurses, doctors, and orderlies closed in around him and started to applaud him, clasping his arm, shaking his hand, thanking him, no matter how many times he told them it was Lopez they should be thanking.

At last he was able to make his way to the squad car Donnelly gave him the courtesy of keeping for the time being. When he got to it, Donnelly had just arrived himself to check on Noelle. "Detective, I'm glad I caught you," he said.

Noelle still felt some resentment surge through him. "Yeah, you caught me all right. Still want to arrest me?"

Donnelly flushed red. "We're all sorry, Noelle! We owe you a big public apology, and you will be made a lieutenant."

"Does that come down from Cullen too?"

"Yes. He's putting you up for a special commendation."

Noelle paused before he got into the car and said, "Apology accepted. But you know I don't care about any commendation. I'm not even sure I want a promotion. I'm not sure I'll be back on the job at all. I'm pretty sick of rolling around in mud with scum. Once Sally heals up, I think we'll move somewhere where we won't be reminded of all this."

Donnelly sighed. "Nick. We need you."

Noelle smiled a crooked smile. "You've got Lopez now. I trained him right on how to break the rules. Thank God; otherwise, Sally and I would both be dead."

"You're still one son of a bitch, Noelle. Go get some rest. Don't decide anything right now. Hell, you want to get those medals Cullen will be handing out—they'll look good up on a wall. Something you can be proud of to show the grandkids one day. Think about it."

"Give them to Lopez." He got into the cop car and drove off.

Donnelly yelled, "Don't forget, we'll need the car back soon."

Back at his apartment, Noelle threw his clothes into the trash and took a long, hot shower. He knocked back two stiff drinks and climbed into the brass bed. He'd go on the wagon tomorrow, but for today he needed that booze to let him rest. As he closed his eyes, he saw images of Pamela, the alligators, and Sally. He knew nothing would be as easy as he hoped. He knew giving up the booze and the cards would be a bitch, but he was hoping that Sally could help him do it. Nothing would be the same for him or Sally, not ever again. He had one more good cry before he drifted off to sleep.

EPILOGUE

One short week later, on a beautiful August day, the press turned out in full force for Lopez's medal ceremony. There were no signs of the hurricane that had moved inland and died. The skies were clear and there was a slight breeze, uncommon for the hottest month in Houston. Donnelly and Cullen had planned to give Lopez the medal in Cullen's office, but so many reporters and photographers were demanding to be present that Cullen agreed to move the ceremony outside, in front of the precinct's main entrance.

Lopez took his place between Cullen and Donnelly, and cheers went off like firecrackers. "Lopez, Lopez, Lopez!"

Lopez glanced beyond the press to his wife and daughter, sitting in the front row all dressed up. Maria wiped away a tear of pride for her husband. Lopez was glad she was so happy and proud of him, but he still had to set things straight. When the press asked for a statement, Lopez spoke up loud and clear. "This medal belongs to the man who taught me everything I know, Detective Nick Noelle. Even though he'd laugh at this, I'm going to say it anyway. It is my faith in something greater that made it possible to fight evil, but we should also be thanking Nick Noelle. I'm ashamed that our department wanted to arrest him, but it was Noelle's training that gave me the courage to follow my instincts and to break the rules."

Donnelly coughed and Cullen stiffened. Lopez spoke the truth, and everyone knew it.

Media personality Marvin Zindler was there reporting the ceremony for his show. With his wacky white hair and Texan cowboy suit, he spoke to his TV audience. "Yes, folks, our own best and brightest actually accused their top detective of committing those serial murders. What do you say to that, Chief Cullen?"

Cullen ignored Zindler's question like he hadn't heard it and stepped up to Lopez. "Congratulations, Detective Lopez." He pinned the medal on Lopez's jacket and shook his hand.

Lopez felt like a million bucks, but not because of the medal. He was so grateful that Noelle and Sally had survived with his help, and Noelle seemed finally at peace. For Lopez that was the greater reward.

The press shouted out more questions, and the photographers snapped more pictures of Lopez and his family. By the end of the hoopla, Lopez was exhausted. He shook Cullen's hand, thanked Donnelly, and waved a good-bye to the press. He kissed Maria and Dolores, sending them on their way. He had one last thing to do before he'd be home for dinner. He just had to see Noelle. He wanted to give him the medal.

When he got to the hospital, a nurse told him that Sally had just been released and Noelle had taken her to a nice hotel downtown, but she didn't know which one. The nurse told him that Sally had said they were going off somewhere for a honeymoon. He had just missed them by minutes.

Lopez thought of tracking Noelle down but then just let it go. Tomorrow was another day. He started toward home but found himself driving out to Miss Ima Hogg's place instead. Now that the storms were gone, he felt a weird compulsion to see the woods, the clearing, and the bayou again, in the light of day.

It took a while to get there since Kirby Drive still had only one lane open because of storm damage reconstruction. He switched on the radio and heard his own voice making the speech he had made only an hour ago. He didn't think he'd ever get used to being in the limelight.

Finally he was at the gates, exactly where he'd parked the Plymouth that night. The path was still a little muddy and he had on his good shoes. He made his way cautiously down, holding on to tree trunks for balance.

He spotted the shed at the edge of the water, the place where just a few months ago he and Noelle had found Julia Brunswick's body. The hurricane had torn the roof right off it. The waters of the bayou were still high. He could almost feel Pamela's spirit lurking there. He said a prayer for her, and for Howard, who was dead by his own hand. Lopez knew he would never be the same again.

He turned back up the trail, breathing hard. It was an effort to hike up the muddy slope and not slip back. He used a tree trunk to pull himself up. He stopped at the log where the other two girls, Lauren and Jennifer, had been murdered. He suddenly spotted a bloody knife jutting out from the rotting wood. The blood was new, fresh, and bright red. He knew it had not been there when the police did a final check and cleared the scene, after the coroner carted away what was left of Howard Wolvensky's body.

Suddenly it was so hot, the breeze had died down, and now the air was thick and heavy like the blood on the knife. Lopez's heart hammered in his chest and he struggled to breathe. Was this another killing or some wise guy making a sick joke? He started to move up the trail to his car to call in for help, until he remembered how Noelle had told him to wait until the two of them had looked over everything at that first kill.

He breathed in a long, hard breath. Yes, he would never be the same. He pulled on his gloves and got to work.

ACKNOWLEDGMENTS

I am most grateful for the many friends and family members who have supported my work.

At the top of this list, I thank Larry Levitsky and Tess Klingenstein for believing in this work and encouraging me.

A special thanks to Dolores De Luce, my writer friend and editor, who helped me find the best in my writing and took this book to the home stretch.

To Karen Bjorneby, my first-draft editor, who pointed me in the right direction.

To my sister, Lillie Robertson, a wonderful inspiration and writer who shares my dreams.

To Kelly Amen, who has always gone out of his way to fuel the fire of my creativity.

I could not have survived birthing this baby without the constant support and coaching from my great friend, Dale Nieli, who has been there over the years cheering my every step.

Also a special shout out to my dear loving friends June Muller, Eliza Perez, Lois Ehrenfeld de Buren, Arlene Samen, Taylor Misal, and Doris La Frenais, and my assistant and friend Laurie Becker, who listened for hours as I agonized over this story.

Big thanks to everyone who donated so generously to my crowdfunding—without your support, this book would not have been possible—and to every friend in my programs.

And last but not least, thanks to the eye that watches over all of us.

Author Biography

Keith Bailey

Alison Baumann writes under the alias A. R. Baumann. She was born in Houston, Texas, and found her writing inspiration from the many tales of high society she grew up hearing. After several years working in theater, she wrote the screenplay to the short film *Lorean*. The film, which she also produced, won many accolades and awards, as did her second film, *What's Next*. Baumann has published two essays: "I Have to Be Bad," in the anthology *The Honeymoon Is Over*, and "A Sober Reflection," in the *Daily Telegraph*'s *Stella Magazine*. She is currently completing two more novels.

LIST OF PATRONS

This book was made possible in part by the following grand patrons who preordered the book on Inkshares.com. Thank you.

Ahmet M. Sumer

Angela Melamud

Anonymous

Ardis D. Jerome

Arlene Samen

Carroll Ray

Christina J. King

Dale Nieli

Dolores Deluce

Doris La Frenais

Edward Frenkel

Elissa Epel

Elizabeth Woodman

Emelia Baumann

Eric P. Harrison

Fran L. Moss

Garth David Murphy

Gayle Karen Kho Young

Geoffrey Rosenblatt

Gil Evans

Heather Marburgh

Hillary B. Levy

Inkshares

Irina Yashkova

James E. Pitkow

James S. Gordon

Janet L. Odom

Janice Rearden

Jeanne M. Gillen

Jeffrey L. King

Jennifer Schreiber

Joanna Mcquade

John R. Risley

John W. Rogers

Karen Lee Bjorneby

Keith Bailey

Kelly Amen

Laura Spanjian

Laurel Timms

Lauren L. Anderson

Laurie Becker

Les Greenberg

Lillie Robertson

Lois Ehrenfeld

M. K. Albert

Mark Sheldon

Mary L. Castellanos

Mary R. Taylor

Max Baumann

Meihong Xu

Melissa Bondy

Michael W. Taft

Nancy L. Lerner

Nandini Malaney

Naomi Lawrence

Peter Baumann

Pilar Azuero Penerez

Richard Miller

Robyn L. Lane

Rosalinde Block

Ross Roseman

Sandra K. Rabon

Sheri Roseman

Tami Simon

Taylor Milsal

Thad Woodman

Theresa Lee Hinton

Virginia Muller

Wilhelmina Robertson

Wisdom Labs LLC

Zachary L. Weinberger

Zaya and Maurizio Benazzo

INKSHARES

Inkshares is a crowdfunded book publisher. We democratize publishing by having readers select the books we publish—we edit, design, print, distribute, and market any book that meets a preorder threshold.

Interested in making a book idea come to life? Visit inkshares.com to find new book projects or to start your own.